John Muckle was born in the village of Cobham, Surrey, but has lived most of his life in Essex and London. In the 1980s he initiated the Paladin Poetry Series and was General Editor of its flagship anthology, *The New British Poetry* (Paladin, 1988). His previous books include *The Cresta Run* (short stories), *Cyclomotors* (a novella with photographic illustrations), *Firewriting and Other Poems* (Shearsman Books, 2005) and *London Brakes*, a novel (Shearsman, 2010).

Also by John Muckle

It Is Now As It Was Then (with Ian Davidson)
The Cresta Run
Bikers (with Bill Griffiths)
Cyclomotors
Firewriting and Other Poems
London Brakes

My Pale Tulip

a novel

JOHN MUCKLE

Shearsman Books

Published in the United Kingdom in 2012 by
Shearsman Books
50 Westons Hill Drive
Emersons Green
Bristol
BS16 7DF

Shearsman Books Ltd Registered Office
30–31 St. James Place, Mangotsfield, Bristol BS16 9JB
(this address not for correspondence)

ISBN 978-1-84861-216-7
First Edition

My Pale Tulip

ONE

It started in the queue at the Miral Foodmart on the sea-front about nine months ago. Mum had sent me out to buy a ginger cake and a small jar of Nescafé. I was stood there waiting for Slack Jackie to finish telling old Mr Ramesh how she was going to pay off her book at the end of the week and could she please have another packet of johnnies on tick—not really, it was a can of beans and a can of tomato soup—when all of a sudden I felt this sudden, sharp, jabbing pain in my jacksie.

"Alright, Fat Boy?" Warren Hopkins was trying out his new flick knife comb on my rear end. "Coming down the shed later?" he said, suddenly pretending to be all friendly.

"Might do, might do," I said. This shed was what we called the local youth club, a glorified beach hut with a burned out Cavalier outside it, a far more recent model than it looked too, because—trust me—in the three weeks since Warren dumped it all the spray from the North Sea reduced the most of it to a big pile of powdery red rust.

"You little cunt," he said. "Show your face up there and I'll carve my fucking name on it."

"You'd have to learn to write it first," I says.

Pretty good. I felt quite pleased with myself for about two seconds, until Warren buried his big right hand in my guts. I doubled up, gasping. My big mouth had walked me right into someone's fist again. But soon as I'd got my breath I saw redness around the rims of my eyes. I have feelings. I am a human being. I grabbed Warren round the neck and hugged him up against me hard, trying to crack his skull like a fucking walnut.

I brought my knee up between his legs. Did he howl or did he not? It was music, music to my ears. I let go, pushed him away. He went reeling right back into a stack of toilet rolls and landed on his conk. I'd never done nothing like it before in my life. The toilet rolls broke his fall. He weren't seriously hurt. But what he did do was smack up against the back of the display so he managed to dislodge the whole unit. Half a ton of wood and cans came crashing down and the partition buckled over on top of the egg display on the other side. It happened in a microsecond. You could see all these levers moving one after another. And that's how it started: suddenly.

Old Ramesh was standing stock still. Then he comes round the till like a streak of brown lightning, grabs myself and Warren by the scruff of our necks and he starts shouting and shaking us. We just let him do it. You can't really understand him at the best of times, but he now turned into a gabbling nutter. He was only a little fat bloke but he had hold of both of us by our collars and he started flinging us around like a pair of glove puppets. I couldn't help it. I burst out laughing.

"Alright, alright," I managed to say. "It weren't deliberate or nothing."

That seemed to calm him down. Slack Jackie helped herself to a packet of Shreddies, picked up her other items off the counter and escaped with a "See you next week."

Ramesh went ballistic. "Is not alright. Is very much not alright. You boys. No more I want to see you in my shop. No more, you hear me good, or I call the police."

"I only come out for these," I said to him. I pointed to the squashed ginger cake and the jar of coffee on the floor with the other stuff. I fished two pound coins out of my pocket. I held them on my palm. He slapped my hand away and they went flying across his poxy little shop.

"Here, you can't do that," I said. "That's my money." I looked around to Warren for support, but he was still groaning—one hand was pressed into his knackers and the other one was holding the top of his head on.

Ramesh opened the cash register and handed me a couple of quid. "Both of you," he said, "get out of my shop."

Warren hobbled off along the sea-front "You're dead, Fat Boy," he said to me from about twenty yards away. "You're fucking dog meat."

He carried on down towards where they lived, at the far end of Brooklands, one stop before the caravan site, in a bungalow that sort of sprawled out into twice its size, with a lean-to tacked on the side and a scrapyard of half-dismantled motors littered around it. The Hopkins family was big in Jaywick. Les Hopkins was a dangerous, nasty cunt. Warren was aiming to become a chip off the old block, his father's son. There weren't a lot of other people to want to be like in Jaywick, so fair enough.

I looked down at the coins in my hand. The next shop was the VG up by the arcade, half a mile away. I looked at my watch. It was ten past six. By the time I got there it'd definitely be closed. Oh well. I felt calm and shaky, clear and proud. I'd seen off Warren Hopkins. I couldn't believe it! I went back into the shop. Mr Ramesh was picking things up. He was on his own in there and I could see he was still shaking. He looked up at me. I didn't say nothing. I started helping him put his shop straight, restacking a fallen pyramid of beans, picking up some egg cartons. Ramesh let me help him. We kept at it till the shop looked as it did before we came in. He didn't say nothing to me—and when we'd finished he wouldn't let me buy no milk.

Back home again I listened to Mum moaning and moaning on at me for half an hour or more. She weren't going to get no calmer, she never did, and when that happened I could forget about getting no sense out of her. I went around to Will's instead. I knew better than to mention it to him because he had the same unmentionable problem, but I thought maybe I could get a pint of milk from his mother and maybe she would even fork out a few spoons of coffee and a jar of sugar to go with it.

Will always wore this old trenchcoat he found in the Sue Ryder shop in Clacton along with the rest of his fab gear. He doesn't choose his clothes by the way they look, not exactly. Anything will do fine so long as it's from the fifties or sixties, which means he's got quite a range of styles to mix and match from. It all looks about the same on him, or it does after a time. That day he was wearing a new pair of specs, wire-framed with flip-up bottle green shades, and a pair of scuffed brogues from the bottom of his Dad's wardrobe. His old boy passed on two years ago, which gave us one thing in common, I suppose. The main other thing being that nobody liked us.

"Not today, thank you," he said, pulling at the swollen door. Suddenly it popped out of its frame and hit him in the face, knocking his flop-ups down. Outside it was pitch black. He turned his head from side to side, blind as a fucking mole.

Streetlights are yet another new-fangled modern invention we prefer to do without around here.

"Don't be a cunt," I laughed at him. "Something's happened. I might be in big trouble."

"So why are you smiling?" Will held back the door. "Perhaps you'd like to park your language in the gutter, sir, and step inside." He sniggered at his own joke. Which annoyed me. He's a posy little twat when you come right down to it. All this bollocks about no sex before marriage was going straight out the window if ever he had an opportunity to dip his wick in anything more inflammable than a mug of Horlicks.

But to be honest, he always had more chances in that direction than I did. Aside from his dress sense girls would definitely go for Will. Inside his bedroom was a thief's cave of junk, his clothes chucked around everywhere; old records crackling there under your foot like the shells of black beetles, along with all his horror and science fiction books, some yellowy comics and a semi-gutted radiogram he'd retrieved from his favourite time zone. I trod on a live soldering iron and the sole of my boot melted in a groove of black smoke.

"Watch that!" he said.

"Jesus fucking Christ!" I stamped my foot to put it out.

"Mind the carpet," he said. "Has it gone right through?"

"No," I looked down at the burnt gouge in my sole, "lucky for you it ain't."

"Never mind." He pulled the plug out of the wall. "I could always find you another pair. No problemo, amigo."

The bottom of his wardrobe was crammed full of old shoes: plastic beach sandals, white surgical footwear, a pair of old Derry boots—they was his Dad's, his motorbike boots—some Chelsea boots with the elastic gone and a pair of plastic imitation leather shoes his mum got him on Clacton market, which looked okay but made his feet sweat so bad he got an instant case of athlete's foot on the first day he wore them. I didn't bother sifting through them.

We talked about more or less everything, Will and myself.

"Guess what, I just had a fight with Warren Hopkins. He started on me as usual, right? But I'm telling you, Will, I actually beat the cunt. I kneed him in the balls. He fell over and hit his fucking head." I was laughing and laughing at this.

"Where did this incident occur?"

"In the shop. Ramesh banned us from going in there ever again."

"Is Warren still alive?"

"Yeah, of course he is."

"Oh well, I only wish I could say it was nice knowing you."

"Warren started it. He gutted me."

"Warren's round the twist. All that lot all are. Next thing you'll be talking to his Dad. And when I say talking you know what I don't mean. I don't mean talking to him, I mean begging him to let you die."

"Hmm." I slumped down on his army surplus camp bed. He had a point, a good point, but as usual he was being over-dramatic about it. "I know." I smiled at him. "It didn't half feel good though, not half. Boff—right in the bread-basket. Fancy coming down the shed tonight? I reckon the best thing is just to face it out. I mean, look at me. If you'd lost a fight to Lee Hookaway how many people would you be telling about it?"

"Don't go anywhere near him, Lee. Warren's a muppet. He's not worth bothering with. No, your best bet's to leave the country right away." He was rasping through a stack of unsheathed 45s. "Want to hear my new record then? I found it in Jennie's. Come Outside by Mike Sarne. Pauline Fowler's on it too. Great. Great. Very Alfie, you know?"

"No, I don't fucking know."

But there was no reasoning with him. He turned on his old record player with about twenty five years worth of fluff wrapped around the volume control, ran his thumb under the stylus and clicked the auto-changer. The hiss sounded like a wave sucking away and then the record started up with a surge of crackle and muffled echoey twang.

This fellow with a cockney accent was talking to his girlfriend. He was asking her to come outside for a bit of you know what and she was saying no, it's too cold, it's too cold outside. Needless to say it was utter crap; but I knew I was going to have to hear about how it was a classic of something or another. I was seething mad.

It weren't that he didn't care. He just couldn't tell the difference between reality and this stuff. I couldn't listen anymore.

"Yeah, great," I said before it finished. "Thanks for your interest. When you're in trouble you'll know where to come." I stood up. "I'm off." He ignored me, nodding with enjoyment as the song ended. "By the way, I couldn't ponce a bit of sugar and a few spoons of coffee?"

He looked up. "I suppose so."

We went through into his Mum's tiny kitchen, much the same as ours, except they always done their shopping at the cash and carry in catering sizes. His uncle worked there, or something. He sorted me a couple of empty jars and filled them with coffee and powdered milk from giant containers. I slipped one into each pocket of my coat. "Pay you back," I said.

When I got home Neighbours was just about to start. I made Mum a nice cup of coffee and give her one of the Penguins I'd nicked out of the cupboard. Say what you like about Mum she does appreciate a nice cup of something warm with her feet up. She crumbled a little bit of dope into her key-ring pipe and we settled down happily side by side, her puffing away frantically a few more times before collapsing backwards to lose herself in the daily doings of Ramsey Street.

"Look at that," I said. "She's lovely. I love that little dark-haired one, Mum."

"Yeah. She's … caaaw, a bit of alright," she said. "So's the other one though." She was being fair to both of them. They was both twins.

"What one's that?"

"Her sister. Paul's wife. They're identical twins. Caroline and Christina."

"Yeah, they do look a bit similar."

Paul appeared in the scene, acting like a complete selfish arsehole as per normal.

"He should die, that bastard," I said.

"He does, apparently."

Mum thought it was definitely well worth seeing again. She put another pipe together, toked up and went out in the kitchen to make us our beans on toast. There was a film she wanted to see after that, a pirate adventure with Burt Lancaster in it. He had a sword clenched between his big grinning teeth as he sailed the bright blue seas and pranced about in a pair of tights in the rigging of a clipper ship. I started to moan about it but she instantly told me to shut up and I went through to my own room at the front of the bungalow.

I laid in the dark on my bed and smoked one last Silkie I'd been saving. I thought about the twins. I considered having a wank. Nah. I'd leave it till later when Mum had gone to bed. Will was right. I was going nowhere near the shed. Great. That's when I thought I might as well do my English homework.

I pulled out the folder and read through what we was meant to do. But it was a boring load of shit and I wasn't going to waste my time on it. Sorry. I lobbed it across the room and instead tried to write down about my fight with Warren. I couldn't get no words to come, no right ones, anyway. I laid there in the dark. A fire engine siren came close then fell away. My chest was tight. I took a couple of blasts of Ventolin and wondered if another chalet had gone up, if it was an accident, an insurance job, or another suicide. If it was anyone we knew. And that was about that. The end of another exciting Friday in Jaywick Sands. I picked up a pad and tried again to concentrate on English.

Really boring. I chucked the pad down beside my bed, turned the light off and tried to fall asleep. I was sure there was something wrong with what I'd wrote, but I couldn't bring myself to get up and look at it again. I was lying there thinking of other stories that could branch off from the main one. To me they was like branches of a tree. I could see it above myself, just out of reach. If I found the right foothold and trusted my weight to that thin branch near the trunk, maybe ... but the top branches of this story was where it touched the blue of the sky. That was where it ended and touched reality, feathery and far off, far up, impossible to touch, really, without crashing through the branches and falling back to the ground.

I dreamed I was doing my GCSE English exam for the third time. I was sitting in the exam hall trying to write a story, but every time I wrote a sentence it came out as a drawing. Not a good drawing either. It didn't look like nothing. Time ticked away in the exam. I thought I'd just have to make this drawing as good as I could get it and hand that in. Then you came up behind me and told me I'd have to start again. Which I did. I managed to get a few words down, but they looked really scruffy, not like words at all. More like another drawing. Bollocks. I scribbled over the paper and tried to make it into a stormy sea. Easy. Pass.

My eyes opened to this glaring stripe of quartz halogen lamp light splashing right across the far wall, where it lit up the big curving mouth of Kylie Minogue. Half a second later a brick came crashing through the window; but the curtains caught it and it clumped down onto the floor. I didn't move. I listened. Outside was it was dead empty quiet, a ticking motor, all of a sudden torn by screaming revs, a dropped clutch and some obligatory tyre-spin. Just Warren enjoying himself. I breathed out. I hopped out of bed, shaking, looked for the brick, and picked it out carefully from under some long wicked smashettes of broken glass. At least he hadn't come in after it. I felt a warm prickly slice, a wetness there under my foot. Fuck. I realised I'd cut my foot open. Ouchy smouchy. I hopped along to the bathroom. It weren't too bad, just a little nick in the sole.

TWO

I swept up the glass and tacked up a piece of hardboard over the hole. I made a nice neat job of it. Mum was starting to shout at me again. She wanted to know why it'd happened. I explained it was probably Warren, how he'd taken some sort of a dislike to me. Then I started to explain who Warren was, but she knew already of course. She knew his father, Les, like everyone did. Les Hopkins was a living legend around Brooklands estate.

"Oh my God," she said, "You're killing me, you are, Lee." She collapsed on her chair, clutching at her heart, but (surprise, surprise) it was only a little twinge. Then she fumbled her stash out and shaved a curl into her pipe off the tiny remaining lump. "Why do you do it? Why do you have to mix with those people? Can't you just leave them alone? You've got a nice friend. Listen to him."

"I don't mix with them," I shouted at her. "I spend my whole life walking away from them. It was him. I told you. He tried to knife me." That was a slight exaggeration of course, but I wasn't having no more of it.

I wouldn't mind if she knew what she was talking about, but she always gets hold of the wrong end of whatever it is. Blame is meat and drink to her. How she loved to dish it out. And it weren't as if she hadn't got plenty to complain about. She knows a lot of dead people, my mum. I was one of the few still living, to hear her talk, and I was slowly killing her. She burned her finger on a match, flicked it away, and pulled on the pipe. Her cheeks collapsed inwards as if she was trying to suck fire down, then she collapsed in the chair, hacking her guts out. Her eyes fluttered and she laid quite still, a bone skull on a heaving bundle of dry sticks.

"I don't care," she said. "Leave me alone. Don't worry yourself, I'll be out of it soon enough."

"It's me who's in trouble," I said. "You're being totally useless you are, mum."

"I can't think about it, Lee." She opened her puffy, red-rimmed eyes. "I just can't afford to right now."

I laid my palm on her forehead. Her skin was dry and coolish to the touch. She was only thirty-five, but lately she'd been getting a sort of very sharp look, which made her look like she was tough. She isn't though. She isn't tough at all. "Forget it, mum. It's all over. He's had his bit of fun, hasn't he. I'll stay out of his way, alright?"

I made her another cup of tea. Then I decided to walk up the parade and I asked her to make a list of what shopping she wanted today.

Will was hanging around outside what used to be the Las Vegas arcade. When it was actually open he never went near the place, but since it closed he'd become a regular. He liked peering in round the back. The place was empty inside and it had that fascinating look about it of gone dusty pleasures reaching back to the old days of Jaywick, the days of the Morocco Club when it was kicking long before we came and you could fall asleep to the sound of a summer dance band, donkeys on the sands, the old miniature railway, sky-writing planes circling into the airport and the voice of a bingo caller floating over from the caravan site. The machines was all gone and part of the roof was gone too, flexes hanging out of the walls like forked whips where the games used to be stood; and a smashed old pinball table was capsized on a carpet of glass, the rafters hanging with cables that once fed all the lights and all the machines. The party was definitely over.

Outside they'd left a scuffed Dalek and a pale blue Supercar— opposite the VG and the greedy little bloke in there ran them both. As every mum in Brooklands came in there he done quite well. He emptied the cash boxes each Sunday. He'd bought off Les Hopkins by hiring him as a bodyguard, at least that's how it looked to us. Will was playing on Supercar, his hands between his knees held onto the flaking chrome handlebars, trench-coat trailing like a pair of wings in the mud. Quiet intense rocket noises issued from his head. He didn't even see me. What a pillock. I stood there in front of him and stared hard. He didn't see me.

"Oi, pillock!" I shouted.

"What?" he said, coming to life, casual like.

"It's me."

"Still alive. I take it you didn't go down the shed after all?"

"No," I admitted. "I thought I'd give that one a miss."

He got down off Supercar and I told him about Warren's little visit last night. It seemed to shake him. Anyway, it certainly shook me. I took a fag off him and he tried to light it with his storm-proof lighter, but it obviously weren't designed to deal with wind conditions in Jaywick. The tip was trembling in my mouth. We went over into the VG and done Mum's shopping. It was only a few bits and pieces. I knew she was bound to think of something else later.

"I'm going round Jennie's," he said when I came out. "Fancy wandering down there?"

She was more a friend of Mum's, about the same age, and both with the same don't give a fuck sort of attitude. Probably that's why it took so long for them to get to know each other. They both liked a puff though, so it had to happen eventually in a place this size.

"How's Angie?" she asked right off. "Haven't seen her in a long time. Is she okay?"

"Yup."

"Tell her I've got something for her if she's interested."

"Will do," I said. "She'll be pleased to hear about that."

Jennie's shop was a larger version of Will's bedroom. In other words it was a waste of time if you was looking for anything of use. She sat there in her spindly red winged armchair in front of the paraffin heater. Her legs was folded underneath her. She stood up with an easy uncoiling action, bounced out the back on the balls of her feet and put the kettle on. She was wearing a pair of grubby ballet pumps with frayed out toes. I'd never seen her in nothing else, not even in two foot of snow.

One of the Alsatians stood up on his front feet and growled softly. Will didn't notice, his fingers laboriously walking along the tube of ancient vinyl that ringed the walls of the shop, threading behind wardrobes only to emerge beyond another chest of drawers. Thousands of old 45s. Pieces of cardboard pushed in as markers every couple of yards, but they didn't have nothing reliable written on them. You just had to look through the whole lot. I perched on the edge of a creaking bamboo table, hoped the dog would ignore me.

"Off that," Jennie shouted. "Move the box over and sit on the sofa."

I put the mug on the table and done as she said. The box was full of reclaimed light fittings. Suddenly I remembered the siren. "Did you hear the fire engine last night?"

Will looked up from the records. "I did."

"That was atrocious," Jennie said. "It were that old girl Mrs Forbes in Standard Road."

"What, dead?"

"No—going out with a fireman."

"It weren't never deliberate."

Jennie nodded at her ancient heater. "They found the paraffin can on its side in the bedroom. Apparently she was lying there on the bed. They say she took something before she did it."

"Like what?"

"Sleeping pills or something."

"I don't see how anyone could be so selfish as to take their own life," Will said. "It disgusts me."

"Let's hope you never have to find out, boy." Jennie stood up, walked over to a waist-high stack of old knitting patterns and roughly started squaring them up.

Will carried on looking at the records, oblivious to the fact he'd made her annoyed. They made a pattering noise as he rapidly flicked through. I sat back against the sofa. I didn't have nothing else to say.

Some of them was done out with home-made turrets and gnomes on plastic grass up Golf Green Road, all those places surrounded by breeze-block walls covered in painted seashells. Most of ours was leaky rotten shacks. When the floods come over the wall, it come in so hard and fast you couldn't run away from it. Quite a few people died in that, like I says, but plenty lived to tell the tale, and they never stopped telling it. What was left of the bungalows soon dried out. A lot of them was still there, rotten shacks, and in the summer months they went up one after another—whoosh—like bundles of driftwood on a beach fire.

I could easily see the place going up around the old woman, but however hard I looked at the mental pictures she was always banging around and trying to break her way out of it. Falling rafters blocked her. She lit the heater, it fell over and her skirt went up in a sheet of flames. No way could I see her lying on the bed as Jennie described her, folding her arms and coughing weakly as smoke swam up in her head.

My own eyes felt warm, heavy. I let them shut and I hoped she wouldn't disturb me. I breathed in the heavy, sweetish smell, an occasional creak of warming metal, a guttering paraffin mantle, the insect tick of a travelling clock propped on a kitchen stool by her chair. And then I was looking at it from another angle. The Brooklands roofs was spread out below me in a broken fan. I peered down at the edge of a boiling sea. On the landside a bungalow puffed instantly into flame, another went up to the left, more of them flared up like a row of barbeque torches in separate bowls of fire, and an arm of flame reached down an alley to join up two dots. Burning lines sprang up and similar paths raced across them till the night was criss-crossed with orange fire and whole streets collapsed in glowing embers. Fire delivered itself to each letterbox, turning on in the centre of each home like a telly. Flames jumped into the sky above the grey breakers, but no one even screamed, no one was trying to get out. Just pale, silent shadow people banging around in them.

Will was tapping my foot. I opened my eyes.

"Drink up," he said.

I reached mechanically, picked up my mug and gulped. It was bitter, lukewarm, no sugar. I made a sour face, put it down.

"You look shattered, Lee." Jennie was playing with Prince's ears. His giant head lolled on one side, his eyes narrowing in dopey bliss. "Don't forget to tell Angie," she said. "Or shall I give her a bell?"

"She'll be pleased to hear from you." I stood up, blinked. "You know, she needs a slight prod now and again."

"Don't we all." She started laughing. I didn't know why.

Will led me through the door. He was carrying a couple of ex-jukebox singles, pale blue labels without centres, hurrying away with them in the general direction of Alvis Road. My legs was sleepy and cramped. I tried to catch him, but I couldn't move as fast as I'd done in the dream. I called out for him to slow down, which he done, and I caught up a few seconds later, completely puffed out. He's about six inches taller than myself but the exact same weight as me, which we found out one day on the big old red machine on Clacton pier, where it printed out two identical tickets that both said 12st 3lbs.

Will's Mum was banging around in the kitchen and talking to herself in Spanish.

"Weel-yam!" she shouted soon as he'd closed the door. "Where is jars from cupboard? In bedroom? They are mine. I get them for something. You will look, please. Me, I cannot go in there."

She appeared in the doorway rubbing her fingers on a starched drying-up cloth. "Oh. Is Lee Hookaway." She tried to smile but I could see it was killing her.

"Hello, Mrs Woody," I said. "How are you?"

That always seemed a peculiar name to call her, as though you was taking the piss. Will Woody sounded really stupid. Woodentop as they'd called him at school. Come to think of it, I don't know why she didn't take Will and go back to Spain. She'd never learned to speak English properly in twenty years over here.

"Is run off my feet." she said. "And your Mum?"

"Mum's alright," I said.

"And," she smiled maliciously, "is still no work for her? Is sitting round the house all day? Oh dear! Is must be so boring! Like a prison, no?" he's a right bitch, Mrs Woody. "Oh well," she breathed out. "Is no peace for wicked. And you will find those jars, please?"

The jars was at home, of course, still half full of milk powder and undrinkable coffee from the cash and carry.

"What jars?" Will said.

Anyway, there was a bit more of that sort of crap, then we went through to his room. I moved a bin liner out of the armchair and sank down into it. It was always freezing in their place.

"Here. Put the fire on," I said. "Mind if I get a bit of shut-eye?"

He turned on a one-bar electric fire by my feet. "I don't care," he said, "I want to listen to these records."

"Great." I settled into my coat. "What you got?"

He didn't answer. I'd never been interested before, so why pretend now. Anyway, it was more of the same. He was obviously following a particular line, but I didn't think he knew what it was all about. He was digging a hole where a hole don't belong.

I tried to get comfortable and drift off to sleep. Could I? He'd left the arm of the auto-changer off, so it would repeat and repeat.

"Give it a rest, mate," I said after it'd gone round for the fourth time. "What's that other one you've got?"

I wished I'd kept my mouth shut. It was another one, a similar one, more or less exactly the same. I couldn't see the appeal of it myself. But we listened to it more than once. Every time you thought it was finished there was an extra annoying little bit on the end. When the record rejected again he carefully took it off, found a couple of spare sleeves and filed them both in his singles box. No wonder Jennie put up with him. He must have been her best customer. "Ain't you got no modern music?" I knew he didn't. "You know, like the Stones, Jimi Hendrix or David Bowie or something."

Will's got this habit of when he thinks you're not interested he doesn't answer you. He turned away with a bored look and flicked through the LPs. That'd been getting on my nerves just lately. Who did he think he was, after all, when you was only trying to pass the time of day? I was going to give him a mouthful about it. He pulled out that Stones album with Sympathy for the Devil on it and put that on, which I must say I found a bit of a relief. He had Bowie's Station to Station, which I thought was a pretty good album, and we listened to that one right through, the Thin White Duke throwing darts in our eyes.

The wind was blowing up a right gale off the North Sea. In case you don't know it's because the land heats up during the day, hot air rises and the cool sea air rushes in to take its place. I hurried along the sea wall, swinging my carrier bag. I leaned against the wind into a sheer drop off the edge and I started wondering what would happen if the wind suddenly died. I'd lose my balance and plummet onto the road, that's what. I saw it all so clearly and I stumbled a bit. But luckily I recovered just in time, just in time and jumped down on the road surface.

I don't know why I mention that, except then I felt that the sea road weren't safe enough. What if Warren came hammering round the corner in a stolen motor? What if they was waiting for me somewhere up ahead with cricket bats? I was walking a line between the land and the sea. I had nowhere to go really but over the edge or back home to face the music. When I let myself really think about it, I knew you didn't go around making an enemy of anybody called Hopkins, not if you valued your peace of mind, not in Brooklands. But when I walked in the door I got a surprise. Jennie was there. Mum and her was all talking and joking. Stoned out of their minds, of course, and the fact I hadn't come back with the shopping seemed to represent some kind of giant cosmic joke to them.

"Here he is," Jennie called. "Here comes trouble. You're for it now."

"I got the stuff," I said, holding up the carrier bag.

They burst into hysterical laughter. I laughed along with them and sidled out to the kitchen. I'd got one of those family size frozen steak and kidneys. I put it in the cooker along with a tray of oven chips, enough for three of us, although I was sure we'd manage if Jennie weren't staying. I sat down at the table and flipped through the Yellow Advertiser.

"I'd better get back and feed the dogs," Jennie said. "They'll tear the place apart if I keep them waiting."

"Yep," I heard Mum say, "I'll have to feed mine too. Anyway, it was really good to see you, Jennie. Thanks."

I wondered how much puff she'd scored. Should be worth a few days peace and quiet. Next door I heard Jennie gathering up her stuff and struggling into her moth-eaten fur coat. She appeared at the door. Mum, blurred and haggard, came along behind her.

"Oooh, that's nice," she said. "I wish I had someone at home to put my dinner on for me." She smiled and gave her tinkly little wave on the step, her silver earrings of dolphins jumping through half-moons flashed in the kitchen light. "How would you like to come round and cook something up with me, Lee?"

I buried my head in the freebie paper.

After we'd had dinner we settled down to watch a bit of telly. I can't remember what was on that night. Mum was glazed out anyway. Occasionally she would spring to life as though she'd been gathering force for some explosion of activity, which turned out to be no more than putting another pipe together. I wondered where she went to when her eyes dulled and sunk back into her head like that. Nowhere, I thought. But she obviously went somewhere.

"Darling," she cooed, "you don't feel like making me a nice cup of tea, do you?"

"Okay," I sing-songed back. She's lost it, I thought, she's totally lost it. But I made us a cup then watched her breathe in the tea-vapour from her mug.

"How's your back?" she said.

I'd been waiting for this. "It's alright, mum."

"Shall I have a look at it?"

"It's too cold, mum."

"Oh go on," she said. "Just a little one."

"Okay." I pulled the cushions off the sofa and I laid them in front of the fire and stretched out on my stomach. I pulled my jumper up and laid there feeling like a great mound of white beached sea lion. Partly it was the cold, but I hated exposing parts of myself to the air.

She took a last long toke on the pipe.

"Come on then," I said, "if you're going to do it, do it."

Then she was kneeling beside me. I cradled my head on my arms and tried to relax. It's something she likes to do when she's really stoned. It's not as if I can reach around. I like the feeling of being probed and examined and giving myself over to it. After a bit of that she found a juicy one. I heard the disgusting small feeding noise she makes with her mouth when she gets really excited.

"Got it!" she said, and rubbed the white stuff away with the edge of her hand.

I started to lever myself upright.

"No." She pushed me down. "I've found a couple of lovely ones. Let me just do them and we'll be finished for tonight."

Her nails dug in my back. I flinched. Then I give in, and relaxed, and I let her finish me off.

23

On Monday morning we always waited up by The Three Jays for the college bus to come through and pick us up. Will kicked a drift of soggy leaves around in the corner of the car park and I just stamped about, puffing on the sharp air. Nobody else was waiting and a light milky mist hung over the stubble of the empty fields. I watched as a few crows landed and took off again clumsily, flappily, unfolding one after another like big black umbrellas.

"We must've missed it," he said. "Come on, let's go. We can stay round my place. Go up the tower later."

I pretended not to know him ready for when the bus came around the bend in West Road. I can't say I weren't sorely tempted, but at that point a faded orange double-decker ground into view, lit up with warm yellow light, and the blurred faces that peered half-interested out of the smoky top deck give me a familiar jolt. There was a world outside, after all, and people going on about their business. We mounted up into the chariot of light and carried on upstairs. The front seats was taken so we lurched down to the back, swinging between chrome uprights, trampling crisp packets through a fog of smoke and abuse. I knew half the people on board. I nodded a couple of times. No one said hello or nothing, probably because of Will.

Last year I asked a girl in BTEC Finance why she found him so creepy. "He's so fucking wonky," she said, and she shuddered. That was the best she could do. Charley Price, a silly little cow with a narrow, pretty little head, like a swivelling hatchet attached to her neck, a triangular shaped girl with the point at the top and a flipped up collar and an absorbing interest in XRBi owners. But at least she knew what it meant. Because, whatever they might say about Will, he did have more twists and turns to him than a wormcast.

Warren Hopkins never even came in to use his dinner tickets, so that was okay. The college left him alone, because they didn't want no bother with him. The Hopkins' are a special case, but you'll find it's true in general. If you mention Jaywick they'll all say: "Of course, they wasn't meant to live there. It's illegal." Ignorant people take the piss, you can expect that—if they're willing to listen you can correct it. But when they just blank you, you know you're wasting your time. They don't want the hassle of listening to what you've got to say. Because they already know they'd like to see you bulldozed out.

No-one ever talked to us on the bus. They was too busy munching through their bags of crisps and tossing back cans of coke and talking about going down the Hippodrome at the weekend and they didn't want to have to ask what we done. Fuck the lot of 'em, I say. We're alright. Leave us alone and we'll sort it out. I've gradually picked that up, even though I'm not born and bred. But it's true of a lot of Jaywick people. We chose to come here, it appealed to us. And ever since people started living in the chalets they've said they wasn't built to live in, called it a shanty town and treated us like a load of pikeys they could move on.

In those Essex floods of 1953 thirty-five people drowned in their beds, but the survivors rebuilt the place. In the seventies when the sea got through again they got straight back up on their roofs. Between floods the council bought up chalets as they fell empty and flattened them. Next they tried to site a big rubbish dump here. Jaywick citizens of those times held a demonstration in Clacton. They dressed up in Sunday suits, unfurled a banner they'd made, and marched solemnly from the station along the sea-front and on to the Town Hall, led by Union Jacks on poles and a stiff-backed old soldier from the first world war, an old contemptible, and for a time the tide of public opinion turned in our favour.

Tendring council was full of hotel owners. They'd never liked Jaywick, which is why they never let Frank Stedman, the founder, plumb his original chalets into the water mains. We badgered them, fought them in the courts, until eventually they was forced to give way. The painted seashell brigade and the old dears all prattled on about how they're the real Jaywick, but when they sold up, Golf Green Road and the Tudor Estate magically turned into West Clacton. They was behind the Beautiful Jaywick campaign. Not a campaign exactly but a committee that gets the dosh out of the JRA to put up these white painted boats planted full of red geraniums on every corner, trying to get a placing in the best kept Essex village competition and beat the Brightlingsea snobs at their favourite game. Brooklands stays Brooklands. Golf Green turned its nose up at Tudor, Tudor looked down on Grasslands, and we was considered to be the lowest of the low: at best a useful early flood warning system.

English was first on Mondays, which as you know ain't a bad excuse for sleeping in. Not really. You know we all loved you, mate. I seem to recall you'd let us out early that day, because the student common room was half-empty. I bought a cup of tea and a Kit-Kat with my last two beverage vouchers.

Carolyn Bristow stood next to me. I offered to buy her a coffee with my last voucher. She looked at me as if I was mad, shaking her curly ginger head. I don't think she understood what I was saying to her. I took my coffee over to the window to wait. We'd probably sit around having a laugh with the others for half-an-hour then piss off down Magic City. Pathetic, you might think. But that's what we was going to do with ourselves. Carolyn sat down at the same table for some reason, there was plenty free, and that funny little bloke from Harwich, Justin Dorset, his greasy hair tied back and parted in the middle, crooked teeth, a weird jokey way of talking as if he's unsure whether he's taking the piss or not.

These types of people always make a beeline for me.

"Good weekend?" He sipped and turned on his gappy smile. He was wearing a faded Mighty Mouse T-shirt under an untucked denim tent, big gashes at knee height across his sister's jeans.

"Not bad." I grunted and looked out the window at Marine Parade, Clacton. A couple of catering students in kitchen whites was sitting on the wall sharing a fag in a minute of breezy winter sunshine. I watched their moving mouths. The boy standing held up his hands, shook his head and laughed. The girl made some small comment to a bloke next to her. I weren't curious about what they was saying. No one else was about, the kerbs was laced with Maestros and Cavaliers, rich boy wedges from Manningtree and assorted clapped-out Marinas of local origin.

"I woke up at 7 a.m. this morning," Justin started droning, "the radio came on and I knew it was going to be a really great day."

"Why was that?" Carolyn asked.

"Because when you wake up at 7 a.m. and Abba's on the radio it starts you off on the right foot in the morning."

"Yeah, it does," she agreed. "I've noticed that."

I caught her reflection in the glass. She was making a face. "You're quiet this morning, Lee. Been out raving all weekend?"

"Right." I tried a hollow laugh. It sounded hollow.

"I went to a party in Jaywick once. They burned the house down at the end of the night."

"Good was it?" Justin asked.

"Okay."

"How did you know you was in Jaywick?" I blurted out. "You probably didn't know where you was after a few diamond blushes with your skirt over your head."

"Are you calling me a slag?"

"Well—you said it."

"You know all about it, don't you." She spoke calmly. "Anyway, you don't call me a slag." She stood up and threw her plastic cup at me, stomped away. Unfortunately it weren't empty.

"I didn't mean nothing," I called after her, dabbing my coat with a soggy napkin. When I was speaking I'd thought it was a joke. "We like you really."

Justin was laughing. "I knew today was going to be special."

"Yeah, and you can piss off." I looked outside. Will's class was coming down the stairwell in the teaching block across the road. I wanted to get up and go after Carolyn, but she'd sat down with a table of girls. If I went over there they'd slaughter me. I looked again. Will and the others was coming down the path.

There was a massive handful of throttle at the end of the road followed by squealing tyre meltdown. Someone was pulling a hand-brake turn, laying rubber as he spun the wheel and put his foot on the floor down Marine Parade. Several students had already stepped off the kerb, amongst them Will and Charley. She pulled him back and everyone else scattered. A lime-green Golf GTi streaked past and slewed away into Rosemary Ave, braking again in front of St Joseph's Church. St Joseph the Worker. The car was driven by Warren Hopkins. Truscott looked up from the door of the teaching block. He was trying to coax a few words from a pair of identical Chinese sisters who sat silently each week through all his classes.

I could tell from their big laughs and their movements they was talking much louder as they hurried across the road in a pack and piled into the common room. The volume shot up into party-time. Will had a smile on his face on the way over from the counter. Charley was getting credited with saving his life and she was developing a sudden morbid interest in him. She was a weird girl, Charley. Charley the Flid. No one called her that anymore, but it was because of her left hand and, to an extent, her arm, which was shorter and ended in a sad little broken paw with stunted fingers, like a cat's paw.

Will sat down with his tea, shaking. I put my hand on his shoulder. It was the first time I'd deliberately touched him. I let go. He was still there. Fine. I relaxed and started talking, right at the minute when I shouldn't have relaxed. When I should've been thinking straight and getting out of there. Jesus. I could've just gone up the library.

Warren had left the motor in a cul-de-sac somewhere and come back to gloat on us. Nobody turned round or went quiet. Nobody knew him. He'd been driving too fast to be recognised. Except by myself. Will maybe. "Look who it is," I said stupidly. "Warren—our hero."

I watched him getting served at the hatch. He weren't physically large or even powerful looking, just an average-to-skinny teenager in an oversized cheap rally jacket. But there was a slight woodenness about the way he moved, as though he was being jerked around on wires. People at the counter automatically gave him room. His hand was cocked around a plastic cup; his whole arm and shoulder came forward to protect it. When he tilted it towards his mouth he elbowed a space in front of him. The victim spun around to glare and quickly turned back to his mates.

Probably if I'd just kept looking out the window he wouldn't have seen me. I should've sat tight. Justin was still perched there, having not taken me too seriously. Will and Charley was at two and ten o' clock on the low plastic face of the table. To some extent they would have masked me. Instead I stood up and said,

"I'm going up the library." I leaned down in passing. "Warren's over there, dickbrain."

Will looked round in surprise just in time to see him coming towards me in a straight line, fast, leaving a trail of slightly annoyed people, who turned aside as he got hold of me and slammed me over the edge of a chair onto the floor of the student common room.

I knew I was about to get a kicking. In a way I sort of accepted it. I didn't try to get up, just huddled into myself and spun around thrashing at him with my heels. When his boot went into my shoulder I looked out at the blur of watching faces. Girls screamed at blokes who shrugged helplessly with cups in their hands; others who'd only then heard the commotion turned around, still laughing.

Everyone at this table got up and backed away. They stood holding their chairs as if somebody important had just come in. Will was the only one who hadn't moved. He was almost as close to me as Warren, hands casually held together, waiting for it to finish. I appreciated the company. Then I twisted again and Warren caught me in the chest between my elbows and hands. I lashed out at him, which must've made him angry, because the next time he booted me straight in the side of my bonce.

Mr Truscott was stood over me when I woke up. He said something I didn't hear then vanished. Will told me he'd gone to phone an ambulance. I tried to sit up then. I felt fine, aching but with a definite buzz. The back of my head was numb. I couldn't see very far, just a patch of whatever was in front of me. Will's hand was on my shoulder, pushing me down. I let myself go back. An inch from the floor I realised a coat was folded under my head. I turned and saw blood on it. My eyes opened again sometime later. A hand in a uniformed sleeve was moving calmly away. I tried to roll my head to follow it, but something soft was stopping me and underneath was a dull pain.

"Can't you hear me?" He leaned into my line of sight, raising his eyebrows.

I could hear him fine and said so, but we had to go through a ridiculous procedure of remembering my name and address and counting to ten.

"You've got a nasty gash on that face," he said, satisfied my brain was still working. "We've put a temporary dressing on. There's a lump on your head and you've got a bruised ribcage. You're going to be X-rayed. Just lie perfectly still, son. We'll soon be there."

"Where?"

"Clacton General Hospital."

I started feeling better.

"Your friend's come along to look after you," he added on in slow-talk.

Great. I managed to lift my head. Will was sitting at the back of the ambulance. He was braced on a narrow bench against the doors. His mouth straightened in what looked like a straight line of embarrassment and he looked away. I followed his eyes around. Charley Price was perched in the opposite corner, at the foot of my trolley. She glanced up soulfully. That I could've done without. I collapsed, jarring my head against the backrest through a thin pillow.

"Idiot," the ambulance bloke said to me. "Lay still for five minutes, can't you?"

But I must say they fixed me up pretty quick in the hospital. They bound my ribs and sewed up a two inch gash in my left cheek. I said I'd tripped and hit the edge of a table. So far I'd seen no sign of the law. I hoped Truscott hadn't phoned them. All the various pokings and X-rays took a bit longer. The bump on my head weren't throbbing so hard by the time they'd finished, but it was very tender there. They said to take it easy for a week and come back to get the stitches out, sooner if I had any blackouts.

"Is anyone with you?" The nurse asked me.

Will was outside in the waiting room on his own. Charley had evidently got bored and returned to college. He'd found an ancient copy of Weekend in which the true life drama that week was one woman's personal account of her kidnap by flying saucers, and he told me about it all the way back into town.

"You can watch that sort of crap any day on telly." My stitches ached as a draft whipped right through the fresh gauze and cotton wool.

"But those are made up stories," he said. "This one really really happened. Wyoming, 1966."

"It's all made up, Will, you fucking tosser."

"You can say everything's made up if you want to."

"Okay, so what makes this be more real; because it's from the sixties?"

"That's not what I'm saying. Look, this is a real woman. You can tell if you read it." He pulled the magazine out of his coat. Its cover was long gone. He pushed it at me. "I suppose she could be making it all up. Or maybe what really happened to her was even stranger, so weird in fact she could only describe it as something she'd already heard of, like a flying saucer. When in fact, it was …"

I knew whatever he said it was would eventually turn up on telly as a mini-series, but I didn't want to know. "Put it away, Will. Leave it, alright?"

"I don't blame you for being pissed off."

"Of course I'm fucking pissed off. But there's nothing I can do about it. That's what makes it all such a —"

"Pissed off with me, I mean."

"What?"

"I just stood there, didn't I, while he booted you in the face. There was two of us and I just stood there like a wanker."

"You couldn't have done nothing. You know you couldn't of. Not unless you wanted to get the same treatment."

"But you're supposed to just do it. Charley had the bottle to pull me out of the road. I was pathetic. I didn't even try. "

"You came down the hospital, didn't you?"

"Yeah, but—"

"Look, I'm the one who got hit. Forget it."

Mum was a bit surprised when I walked back in early. I'd fully expected her to start kicking off at me but she didn't. She went quiet instead. I told her I was okay. I give her the same story as the hospital. Well, it does happen. Only they hadn't thought it was suspect. I suppose they saw a lot of messy accidents and they just didn't care that much. After she'd prodded all my wounds she heated up a can of tomato soup and we shared it in front of the fire. She was toking heavily again that night. We watched Emmerdale, Neighbours, Eldorado, Coronation Street, Brookside, all on the trot. At the end of it all I felt wrung out.

She turned the telly off and laid back in her chair. You know, I wish I could think of something else to describe the way my Mum is, some gesture of hers or a turn of phrase she has. It's all there, but somehow the only thing I can ever see her doing is stirring up the cinders in her little pipe, refilling it, and sucking on it hard.

"It was that Hopkins boy, wasn't it?" She didn't look away from the screen.

"No, like I said. I tripped up in the canteen."

"Don't lie to me."

"No, really. I tripped."

"I'm not stupid, Lee. You didn't get that by tripping over."

"What if I didn't?"

"I knew it. I told you. I told you what'd happen." Her voice broke, shrilled. "I told you to stay away from them."

"Why do I bother telling you nothing. You don't listen." I looked across at her, about to say something else, but tears was streaming out from her eyes. "He just attacked me, mum."

"This is killing me, you do realise that?"

"I know what's killing you," I said. "Smoking that bloody stuff night and day." It was my Dad's voice I heard as I was saying it.

"It's good for me. It helps me think."

"So that's what you call it."

She fired herself up out of her chair and took a swipe at me with the flat of her hand. I hadn't seen her move so fast for a long time. I tried to pull my head back but there were nowhere for it to go. I put my forearm up to protect my cheek and she swung with her other hand and caught the unmarked side of my face. When she tried to slap me again I ducked my head into my arms. She beat at my head with her closed fists. I didn't feel much—till she started kicking out at me.

"You don't talk to your mother like that," she said. "Alright? Alright?"

"You could've torn my bloody face open."

"And what do you think you've done to me, you and your father?"

"What?"

"I told him the same. Stay away from them, Lee."

32

"I didn't know he knew them."

"Your father lived in a dream world." All the fight went out of her and she sat down. She held her arms out. "Come here," she said. "Come and talk to your Mum."

But I weren't going nowhere near her, not this time. "Never mind," I said. "I'm totally shagged out. I'll see you in the morning." I walked out and slammed the partition door behind me.

I put the fan heater on, crawled into my sleeping bag and pulled the duvet over it. I warmed up, then I started to sneeze. That's the problem with those heaters: they blow dust around and dry out the air, and before you know it your windpipe's closing up and you're spraying snot everywhere. I leaned over and turned it off and laid there in the quiet, listening to the muffled crash and roar of the sea. The covers weighed on me, the bandages was tight around my chest. Each new breath was harder. I coughed and made it worse, dragging barely enough air in afterwards to keep from suffocating. I pulled the inhaler out from under my pillow and shook it. Not much left. I took a couple of puffs, snuffled down.

There was a lot I still remembered about my Dad, but only in short flashes. I couldn't recall as much of what he said as of what Mum said to him. Because she talked more than him, and as soon as he'd gone she was saying the same things to me. Before I was five year old he'd taught me the names of every car on the road. That was when granddad was alive, before we moved out here. Sundays passed by sitting on the cracked red leather seats of his 3.5 Rover, gazing into the whirls of the walnut dash while the pair of them patched door sills with a pair of snips and a pop rivet gun, respraying with a borrowed compressor in granddad's lock up. When it turned itself off you could hear the peck and clatter of a dozen sewing machines on the next floor. The first time granddad sent me out to the shop I thought he'd said, "Go and get us a couple of Bibles."

"Bibles?"

"Yeah," he said, "from the bible shop on the corner."

"Bibles."

"Right," he said. "Couple of cups of tea and all. Get us a cheese Bible—and a ham and tomato Bible." He handed me a fiver. "And whatever you want."

Bagels. That's how he talked, my Dad.

I'd help him pick up all the tools I'd passed him, like granddad's old hammers with their splinted handles bound up with tape, trying to lift axle-stands with almighty two-handed concentration, stopping to look at the grown-up grease on my palms: a deep print on my thumb and finger from turning the knobbly adjustment wheel of a crescent wrench. In the garage I had to keep back from the arcs of stars at the bench. I remembered trying not to look at the white pill of heat at the heart of a blue acetylene flame as it splashed over a dull red hot wing like water from a tap. I couldn't help it. I could never help myself to stop from looking right into the hottest part of the flame.

FOUR

Mum would never say she was sorry or wrong about nothing, but it was obvious she knew she'd overstepped the mark. Well, it does happen. But I think you have to forgive people for being what they are, and hope they'll forgive you back. Besides, I didn't feel so bad by the second afternoon. I weren't in no hurry to get back to college. I spent the next few days in bed. I took the tablets they'd given me and tried to sleep as much as possible.

Will came round to see how I was and that, but he didn't hang about for very long. The dressing had fallen off my cheek and his eye kept flicking over the scar on my face. He was slightly subdued. He'd got this ridiculous idea in his head that he should've done something. In his shoes I'd probably have done the same thing though. What the fuck: it was my fight. I thought he seemed to have an exaggerated idea of what you was supposed to do for your mates.

"When you coming back to college?" He shuffled awkwardly at the end of the bed.

"Maybe Friday. I'll see how I feel by then."

"Do you want me to say anything?"

"My old girl's already phoned them. She really give Truscott a load of grief."

"What about?"

"Anything that came into her head." I tried a shrug and pain shot through my shoulder. "It usually works."

"Did she tell him who it was?"

"He knew. Somebody must've told him. They've only chucked him out."

"He was never there, anyway."

"You've got to do a lot more than that to get chucked out of there. Something to do with the money they get for us. They have to keep the numbers up."

"Warren's not going to be too bothered."

"They've also told the pigs."

"Oh."

"Exactly."

"Have they been round?"

"Not yet," I said. "Maybe they won't bother."

"They'd have to, if the college got onto them."

"Yeah, maybe."

When he'd gone I thought about what he'd said. But I truly weren't worried about Warren, not much, nor none of it really. Nothing could happen to me so long as I stayed in bed. If the pigs did come I'd be tempted to press charges. But I wouldn't really. What particularly struck me was the funny way Will had been talking. Not so much talking, but looking. Looking at the scar, yeah? It was a handsome one. But looking straight at me. Not sideways over his glasses. He didn't talk sideways neither, all convoluted and sarcastic, it was weird, like he was becoming a different person.

Maybe it was the codeine. Swallow a couple of them and you felt your fingertips tingle and go numb. I started to go all muzzy about our friendship. Will must really think something of me. I wondered why though. I'd never even thought about it much—you don't with people you've known forever. But when I did, it weren't me he was worried about, it was himself. He saw himself a certain way and he didn't like it one iota, that's what was really bugging him.

Or maybe I was being too hard, or just reading too much into his coming round, which was nice. That's the main trouble with lying around in bed. Plenty of time to think, but it does all tend to get a bit morbid. Another visitor was Jennie. She turned up on the Tuesday afternoon and I weren't delighted to wake up to her chainsaw laugh coming in short excited bursts from the other side of my partition. Goodbye Mum. She'd been human for a couple of days. I stretched out, laid back with my hands behind my head, resigned to days of chaos.

Their voices dropped down to a murmur. I listened to them toke and giggle like a pair of schoolgirls, and the long spiralling silences between words. I drifted in and out of a sleep, half-dreaming of driving around these lanes with Dad with the heater full on, drowsing and wandering into a bright foggy whiteness.

But then I heard my own name.

"...doesn't realise all that, Angie. Well, you know as well as I do..."

"Yeah."

"Did you ever—?"

"No," a sharp breath, "no."

They went very quiet.

"What do you reckon to the mirror press?" Jennie asked her. "I thought it was quite nice myself."

"Fine, fine," a toke, "I don't want to wake him, otherwise I'd put a tape on."

"You know how they got here, don't you? The Hopkins?"

"I thought they'd always been around."

"Yeah, well. No, it was in the early seventies. Kevin, it was, was chucked out of the army and tried to sign on in Colchester. They told him they wouldn't pay out without an address. He was desperate, half out of his mind. Then this social security woman suggests he breaks into an empty chalet and signs on from there."

"Actually suggests it?"

"Yeah. Before long he's got them paying his rent."

"I never knew that."

"Les and Yvonne was next, and Warren. Half of them up there was derelict then. They went and broke into the slightly bigger one next door."

"ERZANIZ?"

"That's the one," Jennie said. "Where their old boy lives now."

"I've never really kept track of them to be honest with you. The less I hear the better."

"So you wouldn't remember Yvonne?"

"No," she said. "Warren's Mum had gone by the time —"

She broke off—because I'd sneezed, I couldn't help it. I scrabbled around on the floor for a wad of toilet paper that'd been there earlier. "That's alright," I called, "I'm awake. You can stop talking about me now. Ain't you got nothing better to do?"

Steely Dan came blasting out at high volume. That was my answer. Silly bitches. I could hear the both of them cackling away under the bass line of *Countdown to Ecstasy*. What didn't I realise? I replayed the conversation. Something Mum hadn't told me. All that. How they got here. But what did that have to do with anything? I eased myself upright and swivelled on the bed. No, I thought. It must be something else entirely.

I unwound the dirty bandage from around my chest. The yellow bruise covered one side of my upper torso like a big birthmark faded at the edges. Another one, from the side kick I'd twisted into, sat there over my left shoulder like an army cap. The dressing on my face had fallen off a couple of days earlier. Mum thought it better to let the air in. On my cheek a deep scar was scabbed with dried blood, laced unevenly with black stitches of a kind I'd seen before when she tried to repair my school blazer. The swelling around my eye had gone down, but the back of my head was a twinge of bad memory.

I pulled my gut in and flexed, leaned forward and peered at my face. The wound had closed up nicely. I glanced down at a pair of nail scissors lying beside her disgusting hair brush. I could just snip them off and save another trip to the hospital. I was edging the point under the first stitch when I heard a brisk knock at the back door.

I struggled into my sweatshirt and answered it.

"You've been in the wars, young man." Mrs Lambert, the JRA collector, looked up from a notebook she was scribbling in and smiled briefly. I'd never liked the woman, one of those dried out, wiry old biddies that could've been anything between sixty-five and eighty. "Is your Mum in?" she said.

"She's out, but she won't be long."

"You'll do. I'm selling tickets for the Christmas hamper. Can I put you down for five?"

"How much is that?"

"Well, they're thirty pence each."

"Okay." I rummaged in my pockets and came up with one pound fifty. "So what's in it?"

"Oh, you know, the usual," she said flatly. I counted change into the palm of her hand. "By the way, you're not displaying your membership card properly."

"Aren't we?" I remembered the yellow JRA membership card had been fixed to the window Warren's brick come through. "It must've fallen down."

Mrs Lambert simpered in an unamused, official sort of way. A light drizzle was falling on her unfolded plastic rain hat but she didn't seem in no hurry to put it on, depart, be gone. "Well, perhaps you could stick it up again." She twinkled with laughter. "Otherwise you'll have George Spires knocking on your door. Unless your Mum's unhappy with us?"

George Spires was chairman of the BRU, which was the breakaway Brooklands resident's union. Nearly all our neighbours had switched to them, but Mum showed no interest. We carried on paying subs to the JRA as we'd done when Dad was alive and most of Jaywick people done, right back into the days when the JRA's Bisto Kids ("Mmm ... ahhh!") still came round and emptied the Elsans twice a week and Mother Kelly was a force to be reckoned with in the steamy Nissen hut meetings of olden times when the people's wars with Clacton council were being well and truly fought to a standstill on the matchwood barricades of our homes.

"I don't think so." I shrugged, trying to get rid of the woman with her endless raffle tickets and her woolly Tibetan hat.

"Have you got one of these?" She pulled a leaflet out of her bag. "It's for the joint emergency meeting tonight."

"Oh." I reluctantly took it, peering as if I couldn't read.

"It's about the road through the back."

"What road?"

"The bloody road we've been trying to get built here for the past five years." My ignorance disgusted her. "Oh well," she made to leave, "Come along if you want to find out." She felt the rain and shivered a bit. When I closed the door she walked away, hunched up, discouraged in her mission to stir up trouble in the name of politics.

I felt a bit sorry for the old girl. But she should've explained if she really expected me to be interested. I looked at the leaflet crumpled in my hand. I smoothed it out and left it on the kitchen table for Mum. I realised she probably wouldn't lose no sleep if we did join up with Spires and his crowd. It would save her the trek down here from Broadway. Well, unlucky. We was freeholders. We owned our own property and therefore was entitled to the JRA's representation.

That's what Mum used to say, until she stopped pretending to care. I weren't too flustered one way or the other. I had heard about the road though. It was to be paid for out of the sale of some derelict land for a development of weekend flats. That was the price of our agreement to the council's deal. One way of looking at it was that we was getting a road. Another was a load of yuppies was going to move in and take over, that's what the voice of the people said.

I weren't sure which side the JRA was on, but my guess was they'd be in favour of anything that might increase the value of their properties. But who was these yuppies? Probably just some people who couldn't afford to buy nothing nowhere else. Everyone was going to benefit from this road. I couldn't work out the BRU's objection. Surely, if a thing was going to happen it would just go and happen: it would happen anyway.

A few steps down to the sea was a sheltered place tucked into the corner of the beach, slightly out of the wind, where we always went, sat and looked out at the lights on the water and the stars up in the sky and listened together to the lap lap lapping of the sea till it came right in. We didn't do nothing there. Just sat and talked a load of bollocks. One night we went out there, I forget when it was. It was warm and the stars was brilliant in the sky. As usual there weren't that much to say, so we just sat there looking out in different directions for half an hour. Will said:

"Look. Look out there. There are moving lights in the sky."

I followed the point of his arm, strained a bit, and there they was, plainly visible, different than stars, brighter, three of them, dancing, or wobbling up in the beyond, high up, way over Mersea island way.

"They're not moving. They're just stars, or satellites or something."

"No," he said. "Satellites move across the sky in a more or less straight line. They don't hover like that."

He was right. They weren't stars. They wasn't planes. I'd heard most flying saucers were weather balloons. "They're weather balloons," I said.

"Too high. Anyway, weather balloons don't give off a light like that, why would they?"

"Well, they're silvery, metallic material. It's probably a reflection of the moon on their plastic skin."

Will didn't say nothing. We kept straining to see if we could bring them closer and actually see what they was made out of. But we couldn't of course. We stared and stared at them, it was hard to believe they was only balloons. More distanter, too bright. They didn't twinkle, or wink, or blink off and on. They just shone. And they definitely was moving. Not changing places or nothing. Nothing spectacular, just hanging in the sky, hovering, moving around a bit. For a minute you'd think they was perfectly still, then one of them could jump up a little, and another sank down; but they stayed in the same pattern, hanging like bright midges under a tree. Except there was only three of them. Three bright high up moving stars.

FIVE

I dropped the weights on the floor behind my head and laid there panting and gasping in the narrow space I'd cleared beside my bed. This must be what they called going for the burn. My heart gradually slowed and I looked down over my sweat-stained T-shirt. My stomach made a shallow ski-slope away from the cliff of my ribcage, but that was always deceptive. Everyone looks thin lying on their back. I lifted my arms in the air and tested my biceps. Much better now. Hard little walnuts of muscle where only a few weeks before I was all flab.

I felt brilliant: lighter, stronger, springier. More confident, that was the main thing. If anybody ever attacked me or a friend of mine again they'd get a bit of what they wasn't expecting. There was no point going through this world meek and mild. First you had to realise what you wanted, then you set about getting it. Nobody was going to help you, that was for sure. From now on I was in control. And what I wanted most was Carolyn Bristow. I thought she was a definite possibility. She had a sort of a well-scrubbed look, red hair, freckles. Nobody was going to touch her with a barge pole, not for a few years, which meant it was a definite possibility she'd go out with me.

That was the first stage. After she'd got me into the swing of going out with the opposite sex, I'd move on and up to the heights. I looked at my cheek-scar in the mirror and I was fucking impressed.

The trouble with you and people like you, is you don't think we're capable of nothing. But we are, we are. I think we are, anyway. It's just that we've heard so much about what we can't do—nothing in your opinion—that we believe it ourselves after a time. That's Will's opinion by the way. But when I said why don't we nick a car and drive it over to Holland and just see how far we can get before anyone stops us, he said he thought I was being stupid.

"We could do it," I said. "Just nick some motor—and then we drive it on the ferry at Harwich—and then off at the other end."

"They'd stop us," he said. "Straight away. We couldn't even get on the ferry."

"Why would they stop us?"

"Well, we'd look a bit suspicious wouldn't we. We look like kids. They wouldn't believe it was our car."

"Warren Hopkins has got a car—so have a lot of other people. What about all these girls from Brightlingsea. Every other one of them's got their own new car."

"I'm not being funny, Lee. But it's the way you look. No one could ever believe you owned anything. You look weird and that's that. Besides, they ask you for your passport before you get on."

"I ain't got one."

"There you are then," Will sounded pleased with himself. "I've got a passport."

"What are you doing with that?" As far as I remembered Will and his Mum had never been nowhere as long as I knew them.

"It's a Spanish passport," he said. "It proves I'm a Spaniard. A Spaniard in the Works, like John Lennon."

"Who?"

Will didn't reply.

"Don't you have to have an English passport like everyone else?"

"No, because my Dad's English. So I can have any one I want. So I thought I'd have a proper Spanish one like my Mum's."

"Let's have a look at it."

He was eager to show me. He pulled it out a small brown suitcase—a cardboard sixties one, of course—from under his bed and showed me this little red booklet, quite new looking, which was his Spanish passport. "It came a few months ago," he said. "Mum sent off for it for me, she thought I should have one."

I flipped it open and pointed. "Is that your real name?"

"Yeah. It's my Mum's name and mine."

"How do you say that then?"

"Fuck off. How do you think you say it?"

"Gomez."

"That's right," he said. "William Woody-Gomez."

I wondered for a minute, but I knew why he had it. It was for a school trip at our old school, Colbayns in Clacton, but then, at the last minute he couldn't afford to go. I remembered because the same thing had happened to me, except in my case we hadn't got so far. We was always broke. We gave up at the first hurdle on that one.

"Okay," I said, "I tell you what we do—we nick a Spaniard car and you drive it on the ferry. You just flash this passport and pretend you don't speaka no English."

"That might work."

"Course it'll fucking work, it's bound to work."

We decided to give it a try. Being as it was tourist season there was loads of Spanish cars around Clacton, more than you imagine, not necessarily Spanish cars but cars with Spanish number plates, because it's a fact that the very minute the Costa del Sol starts to fill up with English tourists is the same minute they all head off elsewhere, it seems, and believe it or not some of them come over here, to Clacton, to fill up on fish and chips and good old English beer.

The first one we found was a Fiat. We knew it was a Spanish one from the ES sticker on the back, obviously, and from a tan bag on the back seat, which had a Spanish newspaper sticking out of it. Will and myself had about a thousand keys between us. Mostly they was from Jennie's shop—she had jars and jars of them waiting to be useful one day—but this time none of them worked and we had to give up, not before I'd kicked the arsehole's door panel in, and went and ate some chips down on the front and thought again.

"You shouldn't have done that," Will said. "It wasn't his fault it didn't work." "Wanker. He should've left it open."

Then we went and had another go—and found a weird car that looked something like a replica of a Vauxhall Victor, Spanish plates, the same, and this time we got straight into it and drove it straight away on a rusty key. Fuuck. But we didn't have no stuff on us, so we drove straight back to Jaywick to pick up a few clothes and what have you for the journey and for Will to get his passport out of the case. At the last minute he decided to take the case itself, stuffing loads of stuff into it in a sort of whirlwind, putting on an old trench coat I'd seen him wear last winter, but I just put a few bits into an old shoulder bag of Mum's and walked out. Mum was round Jennie's, lucky enough, but there weren't no loose change around the house.

It was a Peugeot, the classic old motor, a blue metallic finish, clean but not a restoration job. Column change. Will drove it out for a practice and we headed down into Clacton town again. He stopped outside Woolworths, surprisingly enough.

"What you gonna do?" I asked

Will put his hand in his coat pocket and pulled out an old brown briar pipe. When he put it back in he made it stick out like a gun. "This is a stick up," he said.

Before I could stop him he rushed out of the car and I just sat there like a dummy waiting for the police to come along. But he was soon back and he had someone with him, a girl in a Woolworth's uniform. It was Charley Price and she had a canvas cashing up sack cradled in her arms like a little baby. She'd cashed up early alright. Will opened the door for her and she dived in the back seat. I was driving. He slipped in beside me and I got the fuck out of there. The funny thing about it was nobody seemed to notice, or care.

Charley was just the sort of a girl who started shaving her minge when she was fourteen and she'd never stopped talking about it ever since, her minge that is, and how she'd tried Nair on it, and that other one, Immac, before settling down with the safety razor every other night for a lady shave. She leaned over the back between us and she opened up the top of her Woolworth's uniform to give her tits a slight airing. Small white things. I liked them.

"I've been thinking, right," she said. "I own you two. You're mine. I saved your lives, right. That means you belong to me—to do whatever I like with you, whatever I want."

"You didn't save our lives," I said

"I saved his," she said, narked at me.

"Yeah, that's true," Will said. "She saved my life."

"She did."

"I saved yours too. If I hadn't been there…"

"I don't remember you being there."

"She was there."

"Anyway," she said. "I own both of you. And that's that." She laughed as though she'd proved something.

"So you're coming to Holland with us?"

"Yeah," she said. "I ain't coming back here to this dump neither."

"Nor me."

Will didn't say nothing. He was looking out at the hedges. We was away now, away at last, over towards Weeley, and trimming along out towards the bypass.

"I want to go to Colchester," Charley said. "I ain't got nothing with me. I need to pick up a few things."

"What things," I said. "Can't you get them on the boat?"

"When's the boat?"

I didn't know.

"It's about half past one every day," Charley remembered.

Will consulted his chronometer. "That's no good, it's half three now."

"Jesus. What a bunch of dipsticks."

"Come on, let's go to Colchester and spend some dosh. We can get the boat later. Tomorrow. Or we can get the night boat over."

"When's that?"

"We'll find out," Charley said. "I'll go in the tourist shop and ask."

"We'll be saying hello to the Old Bill if we're not careful."

"Pull off here, pull off. I need to pee."

I pulled off. The place was well spotted. A few trees to pull up among, a shady spot at the edge of a cornfield. I nosed in and turned off the motor. Charley hopped out.

"Come with me," she said. "I'm frightened to go on my own."

Will and myself got out the car and followed her towards the woods. Before we'd taken a few steps we came across her, squatting down in front of us with her Woolworth's uniform hiked up and her knickers in her hand and smiling up at us like a pleased cat as a yellow river flowed over the roots of a twisted old oak and wended its way across the path towards a carpet of cool ferns. She's a dirty little cow, Charley Price, and what happened next was even dirtier. When she'd finished she wiped herself with a tissue she found under her sleeve and tucked her knickers in her top pocket. "What's the matter," she said. "You never seen a girl pissing before? You ain't seen nothing."

She didn't have to tell us to follow her. One thing I had noticed was her minge wasn't shaven at all. It was a minge with a fringe, a minge with a view, a minge of her own. She had quite a bit of bush down there and that's where she was taking us—through the bushes, over the ditch and over a strand of rusty wire into the cornfield. We slipped in after her. She was giving us a good eyeful of everything she had and when she saw the corn she ran into it and dropped down out of sight, and it was like she'd dropped through a hole in the ground or something, off the face of the earth; as if myself and Will had only dreamed her and now here we was, on our own and feeling foolish. But that was just a moment. We followed her out there and there she was, rolling out a bed of flattened stalks.

"Come on you lucky boys," she said, just like that. "Come on down here and keep me company." She held her arms out and myself and Will didn't need no further encouraging. We threw ourselves down on either side of her and started feeling her all over. She'd pulled off the Woolworth's thing and was laying on it, just in her bra and shoes. She was moaning and squirming and kissing us. "Come on," she said. "This ain't no fucking good. I'm starkers and you've still got all your clothes on."

We took our trousers and pants off and the sight of a pair of stiff cocks sent her into overdrive. Mine's about pork sausage size, about as big as I'd ever seen it; Will's was more like a fat python, it was lolling back against his stomach ready to strike, and it certainly seemed to get her going. She'd pulled her bra off and I was rubbing her tits all over, hard like she said, feeling as if I'd come if she touched me even once. "I'll make you come," she said, "you can come all over my tits if you like." Will was playing with himself. He also had some fingers up her fanny and was really giving it some. "Don't let that go to waste," she gasped out, "stick it up my minge. It's alright, I'm on the pill."

Will was trying to get up on top of her but she was half twisted round. "I'll show you how I like it," she said, "so I can come really hard and fast—like a man." She laughed. "Bet you didn't know that. I'm Charley Price, the girl who can come like a man."

She turned over and stuck her arse up in the air. "Go on my son," she said, and as soon as Will got his todger in her she went fucking mental, wanking herself off furiously while he stuck it up her fanny. "Jesus Christ," she said, "that's fucking brilliant. Just do it hard like that till you come." It was only a few seconds before she started shuddering all over and she was making a hell of a racket, like a cow giving birth, and then I saw Will let loose up her and she went off straight away and collapsed on her front, weak as a kitten. "Fuuuuck," she moaned. "Fuuuck." Will collapsed beside her and she rolled over and put her fist around my prick, then her mouth, cupping my bollocks while she worked at it. It didn't take long, I tell you that, and before long Charley was lying between us with spunk running out both ends of her and we squashed up against her, hugging her, and the three of us was joined together. We was in it together as one. Anyway, whatever happened next I knew there'd never be nothing else to compare with this moment of pure bliss.

As soon as we was ready, soon, it started again. This time she got on top of me, guided it in for me and bounced up and down onto it. She started bouncing and I felt like a human Space Hopper. Eventually she flopped down on my chest, grabbing hold of as much of me as she could get hold of. Which was a considerable amount. Then she relaxed completely. Will got his second helping, and after we'd all had a second helping we laid there for a while. Charley liked feeling my fat. She started getting me to roll over her, and then she'd roll back over me.

"Urggh," she went as I crushed the breath out of her.

"Do you like that?" I asked her.

"I like it," she said, "it's like rolling over in the sea."

Then we got dressed again and went back to the car holding hands all the way, not wanting to let go. We stood by the doors hugged up together, pushing as close as we could, because we all knew it was a special thing between us, and it'd never be the same again. Really, we wanted to go back in the cornfield and stay there But we couldn't stay no longer, not if we was going to catch the shops. Will drove and I sat beside him. Charley sprawled on the back seat, giving her fanny a good airing in the breeze from the open windows as we carried on up to the first bypass.

I parked the Peugeot on the edge of New Town up to the left of the Gulliver's Fist and we sat there in the car and made a few quick plans for the future.

"How much money you got, Charley?" I asked her.

"I'm not telling you," she said. "That money's mine. I nicked it and it's fucking mine."

"She doesn't know," Will said. "She just grabbed it all out of the till and stuffed it in her bag."

"And there was Chantel's money as well," she said, starting to boast about it already.

"That's the truth." Will said. "She just opened up her till and Charley stuffed that in as well. So that's more or less a whole days takings on the fags counter, the fags and sweets bit."

Charley was bouncing up and down in her seat. She couldn't hold herself back. She grabbed the corners of the bag, bounced to one side and emptied it all out on the seat beside her. A fuck of a lot of money, a few hundred quid at least, I thought. She was trinkling it through her fingers, digging in to a mound of quids and two quids, fifties and other silver and loose change with drifts of notes stuck in it—fivers, tens, twenties, even a few big red fifty pound notes. Fucking hell. She upended the bag and shook it out—another folded clip of notes that was stuck in the bottom fell out on top.

"There's a couple of thousand quid there," Will said. "At least that."

"Well I nicked it, so it's mine." Charley was stuffing it all back in the bag as quick as she could. "But you two can have twenty quid each for now."

She handed us a note each, which we accepted as a down payment.

"Stuff it under the front seat," I said. "It'll be alright there. We ain't had a chance to open up the boot yet."

"We ain't got no time for that now." Charley looked at her silvery little watch, shaking her wrist as if that would make it come clear. "It's five o'clock. We've go to get down into town before everything shuts up. I'm serious. I ain't going nowhere like this."

She'd already started running ahead of us before she finished talking, Will and myself walked after her, playing it cool. Why make it obvious, that's what I thought. Why make it obvious we was up to no good. We followed her on down the subway and out by the dole office to the top of Jack Street. "Where do you think she's going then?" I asked.

"Methinks to Debenham's emporium," says Will. "Where all manner of female accoutrements may be had for ready money."

"She could go up to the High Street."

"No, she'll go to the precinct, it's quicker."

Charley darted down Long Horn Wyre. He was obviously right. I couldn't think of much to do except go on up to Macdonalds, but we didn't have a lot of choice, we had to stick with her. As it happened she stuck to the little shops along there and by the time she'd been in the first one for a few minutes we'd caught up with her. We hung back on the other side of the road till she came out Carrying a couple of carrier bags. I'd expected her to be wearing a new pair of jeans but she'd had the sense not to change in the shop. She looked at us, clocking us, then marched on ahead, swinging her bags, tossing back her short blonde hair.

Next time she stopped at a rack of coats, cheap being it was July, and selected this anorak thing, which this time she slipped on over her Woolworths thing when she came out. It weren't cooling down either, so if anything she looked even more stuck out in that. We came up beside her.

"We're not going to the North Pole," Will said, "only over to the Hook."

"We won't be staying there long," I said. "Soon as we get there we're going to be driving like fuck."

"Where to?" Will asked.

I didn't have no answer on the tip of my tongue right that minute.

"You don't know where we might end up," Charley said. "Anyway, leave me alone. I'll meet you down Macdonalds in ten minutes." And with that she ducked into the open door of the Doc Martens shop.

Will and myself cut through the precinct out to the High Street and we was both halfway through a Big Mac and fries when she turned up again. She was wearing the new-looking jeans and a loose Indian-type top that made her look older. She'd combed her hair down straight and carried the anorak thing over one arm and had a new pair of green Doc Martens on. To tell the truth I wouldn't have recognised her as Charley Price. She looked different, more like a college type of girl, more like how she wanted to look. She dumped her bags and went straight up to the counter and before long we was all eating something.

Not saying much, just eating, taking ages over it as well, eating with this super-concentration as though this particular Big Mac was the best one we'd ever tasted in our lives, which it definitely was, but also because none of us had much to say, and none of us had no idea what we was going to do next.

"Where did you change?" I asked her.

"In the bogs in the precinct," she said. "They didn't half give me some funny looks in there. Frustrated cows."

"Have you got different make up on than before?" Will asked.

"I ain't got no make up on, " she said. "I cleansed myself with cleanser."

When we'd eaten up we just sat there. Will remembered about the tourist office but it was gone half-five. They'd be shut now.

"Phone from a phone box," Charley said. "I'll do it."

"What're we going to do now?"

"Get some stuff from Sainsburys."

"We can get stuff on the boat."

"Not on the night boat," Will said. "It'll all be shut."

"You been on it before?"

"Years ago. With my father."

"Lets go over the park," I said. "We can go to Sainsburys on the way back."

"What we gonna do over there?"

What we done was get a bit pissed. I bought a big plastic bottle of cider on the way over there, just past the Town Hall. We walked down and got in the bottom end by the boat pond, sat down on one of the benches and started to get hammered. We passed the bottle between us and watched a bloke roping up all the boats to the island.

"I hate it here," Charley said. "This place is full of creeps and perverts. All sorts of scum come in here."

"It's alright," I said. "What's wrong with it?"

"I told you what's wrong with it, dipstick."

"She's right," Will chipped in. "We don't want to get too inebriated."

I wanted to argue with them, but I could see Will was just trying to get on the right side of her. It was him who was keen to come over the park at first, for the same reason as myself. Hoping we'd get a bit more of what we'd got out of her earlier. But no luck. They stood up. I did too and we walked up through the park, one on each side of her. "Come here," she said, and she took our hands, and we walked hand in hand up past where the Roman wall cuts across the bottom of Castle Park, then up to the open pavilion.

"Let's go in here," she said, and we sat in there for a while, the three of us cuddled up on the bench, each feeling each other up and tugging back on the cider.

We was all a bit down in the mouth somehow. But it was just too funny. We couldn't stop laughing. Will got up and broke ahead of me and we was walking in a line up past the empty playground and we carried on up to the gates, joined hands for a moment and then let go for the walk up through town. I felt like I never wanted to set foot in this place again. We went to Sainsburys and got a few giant packets of crisps but we couldn't think of nothing else to get with them. We still had a fair bit of the cider left so what with the duty frees on the boat there didn't seem much point in getting drink. Charley got a big bar of chocolate and a thing of shampoo. I could see she wanted to buy up half the shop but she didn't. There was a can't be bothered feeling which had crept into the whole business and we was glad to pay and carry on up to the car without too much bags to carry. But when we got to there and the Peugeot was where we'd left it, a slightly scruffy motor that fitted in well to its surroundings. We was pleased to see it and we hopped straight in.

"They'll be looking for us by now," Will said. "The pigs will have our descriptions. Do you realise that? This is a marked car."

"Yeah," Charley said. "We should dump it and get another one."

"It's got to have Spanish plates," I explained.

"Er, excuse me—why?"

"Because Will's a Spaniard and he's got to drive it through onto the boat."

"Will's Spanish."

"Half Spaniard, actually."

"You two are mad," she said. "What have I got mixed up with? You're totally fucking mental."

She slumped in the seat, sort of seemingly in resignation to whatever was going to happen next, and I drove off, circled once around town for luck then turned straight up the Harwich Road.

We was shitting ourselves by now, but there weren't nothing we could do about it. We didn't talk very much. Will turned the radio on and fiddled around with it till he got Radio Two—wall to wall sixties stuff. Groan. Groan.

"Put on Radio One," Charley moaned. "Let's hear some modern music."

"What about Radio Essex?" I said. "We might be on the news."

"Good idea," Charley said. "Go on. Put that on."

Will fiddled and got it more or less straight away, but there weren't no news, only traffic news. Music for people driving home from work. That'd do us.

After some time on the road to Harwich a police car did go by, in the opposite direction, very fast, but they didn't seem to see us. I took heart from that. Somehow I knew we'd be perfectly safe so long as we didn't do nothing to draw no attention to ourselves. I told myself this and it seemed to work alright. At least, no more police cars went by us. We sat tight and listened to the car radio and had a good clear run all the way out to Parkeston Quay. I followed the signs round to where the ferries docked, round to where the loading cranes pecked at the sea like giant birds. And all of our hearts was pounding away, like anything.

SIX

We sat at a table tucked in at the side by the window. I got her a White Mule in and myself stuck down a double scotch. I hate whisky but there you are, there wasn't nothing for it but to get slaughtered and sit there in a little bubble of warmth until it opened up. I kept my eye on the Peugeot to see if anyone was sniffing around it. Outside it had turned cold. Rain was gusting in right off the sea. We snuggled up together. No need for it really because it was warm in the bar, everyone was lurching around, sweat pouring off them as they poured the beers down for the journey. We became a pair and we tried to get lost in each other— not getting cheeky or nothing but it was just nice to smell her hair and feel her softness next to me. I could have done with an age of it. Will turned up with a smile on his face. He slapped his coat pocket and said something that ended with *por favor*. He got a drink at the bar, a double brandy and coke, then he sat down with us and tried to nuzzle in close to Charley. I knew he would do that.

"None of that," she pushed him away, laughing at him, "from now on you're like our Dad."

"We don't want to know about your bloody Dad," Will said, then he cut off and went deadly quiet.

Charley said nothing but I could see straight away it was one of those things where you say something and wish you'd never spoke. It didn't seem to matter though because it was getting on for eight and the boat was starting to load. We went out to the car and got ourselves ready.

Will got in the driver's seat and we decided Charley should get in beside him. It was strictly because they looked older than myself. Will in his old fashioned clothes and Charley in her new disguise. I huddled down in the back. We drove through a sort of windswept empty maze, the customs, taking the nothing to declare lane. Nobody was about. Nobody wanted to stand out in the rain. We went straight through and into the queue in front of the yawning mouth of the ferry like a portal into another world where you drove out the other end into a land of acres of green grass and tulips. Will cracked his open and held up the boarding passes and his Spanish passport, but the officials hung back in their cubicles and their green peaked caps. A solitary motorcycle pig sipping a takeaway cup of tea from the machine looked in the opposite direction from anything that might make him have to put it down.

We clanked up the ramp into the line of few cars, a couple of big trucks—the boat weren't even half-full—and then the flap was winched up behind us, and fixed, and there we was. Somehow or another we'd got away with it. It clicked with me. For some reason no one had reported the car missing, or us. I was sure Woolworth's hadn't written off Charley as having gone home with a headache. Yeah, what about that, I thought.

It was as if some sort of trick was being prepared for us. There was a catch to it all which was going to catch up with us later. We locked up the motor and went up to the passenger decks, past the locked up duty free shop into a bar-lounge area where the lot from the bar at the terminal was already piling into their first round, and in the corner a battery of swirling coloured lights lit up a little deserted dance floor area. "Go on, Charley," I said. "Give us a show."

"You first," she said. "Blimey, I've seen better than that in Clacton Hippodrome."

"Yeah," I said, "but they chucked you out for it."

This story about Charley was well-known. "Fuck off," she said. "That was fucking ages ago."

First thing we done was we went back upstairs and had a look at the sea before it got totally dark. We went up top and stood there watching England disappear at a fair rate of knots, winking towers on the dockside, the lights of Harwich itself, and beyond that the misty flatness of where we lived, what we was leaving behind. We went round and stood up front, as far forward as we could get, watching the grey sea splash up at the prow, hanging over the railings. "I wouldn't want to fall off here," I said.

"You'd go straight under the hull," Will said, "and if you survived that you'd get chewed up by the propeller on the way out the back."

"Yeah," Charley said, "and if you survived that you'd drown before they could turn round and go back."

"If they bothered," I said.

"Which they wouldn't," she snorted.

"Of course they would," Will said. "They'd have to—by law."

We pulled ourselves away from that strange hypnotic blasting effect of the droning engines, the buffeting wind and we went back indoors. At the back of the lounge was a cinema, if you could call it that, and a notice saying a film was starting in fifteen minutes. "Let's go and see it," Will said, which we all automatically decided was something that had to be done.

The film was called The Shadow. I didn't really know what it was about. There was a sign saying no smoking or drinking in the cinema. Charley was the only one of us who smoked, so she puffed away while I went to the bar and got us a round of doubles, which we all duly bolted down before taking our seats in the darkened room, which started to fill up with a few people. It was shuddering like the rest of the boat with the sound and vibration of the motors it ground through the North Sea like a power tool through a sheet of metal, cutting it in half for us, cutting out a shape which you couldn't see what it was going to be.

"This is going to be good," Charley said. "Well worth coming out for, yeah?"

She was sitting between the two of us again, which was how I liked it better, and the film started, hard to concentrate till a few seconds had passed and then we forgot the noise and the crappy washed out big video screen and got right into it. I did anyway. The film started in the desert. I looked across at them. Charley's face was still, colours passed across it. Will leaned forward—this was right up his street—and I saw the sands reflected in the glint of his specs before looking back at what was happening on the screen, in far away Tibet.

It weren't a desert at all but a snowy waste with big blue mountains around it. The camels in the camel train going down the harsh road wasn't camels but llamas, and I started watching properly. A bloke in the back of one of the wagons, wrapped up in thick furs, was actually a white man who the little Chinese-looking people was taking towards a big temple made out of wood and bricks and with a metal roof on it. He was led into the building where the head priest or leader of this place, a little bloke, sat perched up on his gold throne.

"Ah," he said. "So you are the American, Lamont Cranston."

I think there was some magic after that. This Tibetan priest could put pictures into his mind. They was pictures of something evil like a poisonous snake about to bite him or someone getting their head chopped off. And for some reason he gives Lamont Cranson the secret of how to do this, the secret of knowing the evil in men's minds—which having knocked about in Tibet a bit, he knew already—on condition that he used what was left of his worthless life to combat that evil wherever it might show itself and become a hero a bit like Indiana Jones, saving people from the evil that was all around them, and inside them waiting to get out.

Then the scene switched to New York. Lamont Cranston was just another rich man, like a film star going in all the best places with amazing-looking girls, but as well as this he was secretly the Shadow, the crimebuster who knew everything that was going to happen before it ever did and could stop it, because he alone knew what evil lurked in the hearts of men. After a while of it, when it settled down and we knew too what would be happening, I pulled out the rest of the bottle of cider we'd been drinking in the park—I'd kept it in reserve—and we passed it back and forth between us till it was all gone. I looked across at Charley. Her head had gone back on the seat and she was spark out, asleep like that. She didn't half look sweet. She was dribbling like a baby. I reached across and wiped her mouth with a tissue she had on her lap.

She opened her eyes and looked up for a moment, frightened. "What? What?" she said.

Then she was gone again, and myself and Will—who was looking across as I done this—turned our attention back to the film. It weren't bad as they go, the effects was quite good, but the main trouble with it was that Lamont Cranston didn't really have to find nothing out. He just knew somehow. So these enemies and crooks didn't have much of a chance. There was no way you could keep nothing a secret from Lamont Cranston, and if he didn't find out what you was up to by looking into your mind— or his own—there was always these other people who owed him their lives because he'd once saved them. They told him a lot.

Owing your life to Lamont Cranston weren't that good, because he was always calling in the favour; he didn't just let you get on with your life, you had to help him save others—and quite a few of these helpers whose worthless skins he'd saved got sacrificed to kill the new crooks, and so it went on: you just knew they'd keep popping up for the rest of his life. His work was never done. It was a full time job being him and not a very good one either, although he fully deserved it having been such a bastard in the past.

Yeah, I thought, Lamont Cranston weren't that good himself, not really. How could he be? He was another part of the shadow world. Sooner or later he was going to break into some room where they was torturing somebody, or printing money, or brewing poisoned whisky, and find it was himself in there making all the bad stuff happen for everybody. He was his own worst enemy. He didn't seem to realise it or something. Anyway, it wasn't that great a film but we watched it right to the end.

Charley woke up on cue when the lights came on.

"You missed a good film," Will said. "It was... good."

"Yeah, yeah," she said. "I only dropped off for a minute."

Charley got to her feet groggily and we headed outside to the bar looking forward to a night cap. I could see by the way he was holding himself, looking cool with his coat collar up, that Will had turned into Lamont Cranston. He was walking slightly ahead of us as if he was clearing a path, looking out for any evil to protect us from. It's funny, but although I didn't like the film that much, I felt the same way. It had given us the idea, maybe we had it already, that we was there to protect her from danger. Will went overboard on it, making big shoulder gestures and sighting everywhere long range.

But the bar was closed, the cage pulled down and behind it was empty, just a lot of piled up glasses left for the morning. The lounge was full of circular benches with a fixed table in the middle, and every one of them had a person in a sleeping bag curled around it. The lights was dimmer than before and there we was. We didn't have no sleeping bags, only our coats.

This was just as well, because it was getting fucking freezing in there. All those doors had gaps underneath, they seemed designed to let the North Sea wind blow under them, to keep the passengers half-awake, not too comfortable, in case of emergency. In case you hadn't paid for a cabin. We looked around for somewhere to kip. There was plenty of room, some places only had a few people nodding off in them, but we didn't fancy them. In the end we ended up back in the cinema. It was warmer in there for some reason. We went back to our old seats and nestled down with our coats over us. The trouble was you couldn't lay down, the seats didn't go back, so you could only curl up as best you could. We both tried to curl up against Charley.

"I'm not having you two on top of me all night, I'll feel like I'm suffocating."

Fair enough. So we done what we could to get some shut-eye. The others soon went off bye-byes, but I got up and wandered outside to walk around the boat a bit before bedtime. I wasn't tired. There weren't nothing to do. Everything was shut up, every lounge had a few crumpled forms of sleeping people. Only at the side of the boat, I thought, there might be a bit of a view, if you strained for it. I wandered down there. A bloke was sitting on his own by a window, smoking a lot of fags and looking at a book. He looked harmless. I sat down opposite him. The outside was black except for the odd glint on it and the smack, smack, of the sea passing by. No view. Just your own ugly face in the glass: the very thing you was trying to get away from.

In the morning Charley managed to find some showers and came out looking as fresh and great. Her hair was still damp, but she said she'd dried herself off the best she could with her Woolworths uniform, which she still had in her bag, and then chucked it away in one of the waste bins.

"Pity you couldn't dry your hair off," I said. "You'll catch your death of cold if you're got careful."

"It's not too bad," she said. "I put my head down by the hot air dryer. I could feel it burning my scalp. That's when you know it's done."

She looked alright, a whole lot better than us. It's funny how girls can always find a way to look after themselves in that way. I mean, we could've done the same, we just didn't bother. It was still about an hour till we got to Holland.

Bacon was frying somewhere down below, so we followed our noses down to it and had the full English breakfast. They wanted an arm and a leg for it but we paid up and took it over to a table beside a port hole.

"Do you know," Charley tucked into hers, "everything that's happening to us is totally impossible."

"It can't be impossible," Will said. "It's happening—therefore it is possible."

"Right," I said. "But it seems impossible to me too."

"I mean, let's face it, we're all pretty thick. I mean, look at that," she pointed at something that was going past, "I don't even know what that is, do you."

"No," I admitted, "what was it?"

"What was what?" Will said. "I don't even remember seeing it."

"What's this?" I held up a bit of bacon dipped in egg on the end of my fork, put it in my mouth. "I dunno."

"You must be the thickest then," Charley said, "because even I know what that is."

"That's right," Will agreed. "He's the thickest and I'm the most intelligent."

"How do you work that out?"

"I've read more books than him."

"I've never read no books," Charley said. "Only ones we had to do at school—I don't remember much about them either." She frowned, putting it to the test.

"I think I'm the most intelligent one," I said. "Because I'm the best one at English."

"You're crap at English—why are you in the resit class if you're good at English?"

"I weren't trying the first time."

"Yeah yeah. I've read more books than you by miles."

"So what? That don't prove nothing. If you can't spell or write you're just as thick as someone who ain't read no books."

"What you talking about books for?" Charley said. "What's that got to do with anything? I'm the most intelligent of any of you."

"Yeah? Why's that then?"

"Do you want to know?"

"I asked didn't I?"

"Because I've got this, that's why." She opened her legs under the table and patted herself right there. "Which you want, right? You have to do whatever I say to get into it. Therefore—I've got your brains as well, haven't I. I can make you two do whatever I want."

We had no argument. We just ate our breakfast after that. As soon as we was finished, as if it was waiting for us to lay down our knifes and forks, an announcement came on the tannoy system for us to go down to our cars and prepare to land as we was docking in ten minutes.

"This is where we find out how intelligent we are," Will said.

"Wrong," Charley said. "This is where we find out how lucky we are."

But thinking about it I knew we'd probably be alright. If anyone knew we was on the boat they'd have stopped us before now. Nicking an old Peugeot with Spanish number plates weren't exactly brilliant: it was an unusual motor you'd spot a mile off even if you wasn't looking. Will was the only one with a passport, that was why we'd had to have it, that was why. I know I'm making myself sound thick, but you do think these stupid things and you do forget other things sometimes. I realised I hadn't thought about my Mum even once since we left home, and then as soon as I thought that I forgot all about her.

They opened the doors and light flooded in from the other side of the sea. It was an amazing light unlike no other I had ever tasted. And I knew I would taste a lot more of it before this time was over.

We clunked off the boat. Will blipped the throttle, crashed the column change, and then the fucking Dutch customs went and pulled us over. Bastards. He wound down the window and held up his passport. The bloke looked at it, passed it back, said something in English I didn't catch. Will answered him in Spanish and the bloke ordered him out of the car.

I was really shitting it, so was Charley, but she kept a stupid looking smile on her face. Will pulled the rusty old key he'd got from Jennie's out of the ignition and went round to try and open the boot with it. I turned round to watch. Charley kept staring straight ahead. Fuck me. I was amazed when it swung up. One size fits all on some of these motors. The bloke's head disappeared under it and rooted around in it. A couple of minutes later he slammed it down. Will got back in the car and they waved us through. We couldn't resist it. We waved back.

"Was there anything in the boot?" I asked him.

"Loads of stuff," he said. "*Millares de cosas. Abundancia.* Plenty."

SEVEN

Holland is a country like Essex. Go over there and the first thing you notice is extreme flatness. The second thing you notice is that everything really is flat—except for the beer, it's foamy—but otherwise this original flatness continues forever, it is totally flat and without no noticeable bumps, except for the first part where you bump off the ferry onto a wide road leading past well-spaced silos, warehouses thrown up by the side of the road, a few bars with big signs up you can see coming for miles, and further on the windmills and fields of tulips, or turnips. It is FLAT. It's as flat as a platter of pancakes. I started wondering if they'd ever been joined, and if they had anything in common due to this fact.

We hadn't gone more than a hundred yards before Will pulled over and stopped dead at the side of the road. He slumped forwards over the wheel, shaking like a leaf. I thought he was having a fit or something.

"Will!" Charley shouted, losing it straight away. "Get up! Get up, you cunt!"

I got up and grabbed his shoulder, trying to pull him straight. We was stopped right beside the main path and all the people from the boat was walking along it, down towards a big supermarket up ahead. They was looking over at us. Something was obviously wrong. I don't know why they noticed us, maybe because of the way we'd stopped so sudden.

"Get off me." Will sat up. Tears streaming down his face. He was still shaking, weak as a fucking kitten. "I can't go any further, I just can't," he said.

Whatever he had was catching, because then Charley kicked off. She started shouting and screaming. I couldn't make out what she was saying—nothing, really—but she started banging on the seat with her fist, hitting the dashboard, crashing it over against her window. She was crying too. She put her head down and slumped over against her door. "Oh God," she was saying. "Oh my God! This is the end of my life! This is the end of my whole life, do you realise that?"

I wasn't much better. I felt weak all of a sudden, totally helpless. Trapped there in the back of the car while they both went mental in the front. Totally pathetic and incapable and stupid. More people off the boat was looking over, then walking on towards the giant off-licence. I got out of the car and went round the front and opened the driver's door.

"Get in the back," I said. "I'll take over. Look, everyone's looking. They'll be calling the law in a minute."

Charley started shouting again.

Then I managed to get Will out and into the back. I slammed the door after him and got in behind the wheel. I turned the ignition and the Peugeot jumped forward. He'd stopped it in gear. I managed to get her going and pulled out into traffic. Fortunately there weren't much about because I'd got it as well, bad, the kangaroo shakes.

My feet was jumping around on the pedals, I forgot everything about driving, everything I'd learned as a nipper by driving around a field with my Dad shouting at me in an old Fiesta, and we hopped out into the road. I remembered the bloke I'd talked to in the night. This is what it's like in the zone, I thought. But I changed gear and clamped my hands on the wheel and we pulled straight. I was going much too quick: the back of one of these stupid little cars rushed towards us.

"We've got to think," I said, "we've got to try and think what to do next. We've got to get away from here." Neither of them said nothing back. "Try thinking of something," I shouted. "If any of you two have got a brain, now is the right time to use it. Because I'm driving. I'm not thinking about nothing except staying on the fucking road."

We was on the wrong side of it too, which didn't help none. I mean, the right side to them, but it was wrong to us. We was on a dual carriageway. I eased off and we cruised in the slow lane out of immediate danger. Out of the corner of my eye in one of the shady streets of houses a car was nosing out, a police car in any language just as the houses was houses, places people lived in the same as houses anywhere. I tried to use that to calm myself down. We wasn't in some zone where up might be down, inside might turn into outside, or your arm disappear forever into some another place. It was a country the same as ours. Just twisted to one side a bit by that separation of the sea, so people spoke a different language. Why though? Why didn't everyone talk the same?

The Dutch piggie wagon cruised along behind us. I looked at the road and drove. They pulled out suddenly and passed us, not too fast, just going on ahead, gradually pacing us out until they was nothing more to worry about. The others had still not said nothing. They'd gone dumb with fright.

I saw a Jet sign coming up straight ahead.

"I'm pulling in for some juice," I said, "so we better decide what we want to do. I can turn round and go back if you want. We can just get back on the next ferry home."

"Where are we going to, that's what I want to know," Charley said.

"Let's get a map. They're bound to sell them."

"We've only got English money," Will said. "They probably won't even take it."

"Yeah, they will. Then we'll have to change it over."

"A bank," Charley said. "Ask them where there's a bank."

"See?" I said. "Just keep thinking and thinking and everything'll come out alright. No one's going to take no notice of us. We can go for miles and miles. We can go just as far as we like."

"Listen to him," Charley said. "I'm knackered. I can't think."

I pulled up at the petrol pumps. This place weren't self service like ours are and a short-haired Dutch fucker in a short-sleeved Jet shirt came over to serve us in his own time.

"English money? I held up a twenty pound note. "English?"

He nodded, shrugged.

"Fill," I said, "fill up."

"It's okay," he said, "I understand perfectly."

Charley went over to the shop and came back with a map of Holland, a Mars bar each and a carton of two hundred Dutch Marlboros. "I thought I'd try these," she said, as though they was going to be different. She tossed Will his bar over and then passed me mine and we all tore them open and pulled off again, eating. "We'll have to go to the bank in town," she said. "We get the best rate there." Charley was full of knowledge. She unfolded the map and pastel coloured countries swarming with black dots spilled open on her lap. She beat it flat and they scattered away from where we was, which she spotted straight away, right by the blue sea, right there in the claw of the Hook of Holland.

Now we could drive out of it. The town came up pretty quick—I think it was a place called Healdwijk—and we cruised in there down a wide main street with trams on it and done a left down a quiet side turning. I parked and pulled on the hand-brake perfectly. One thing, I was definitely going to enjoy driving. I think it's in your blood to be a good driver and being as how I'm the son of a mechanic, I am one. Will spotted the bank over the road on the corner of the main drag. We sorted out the money and decided how much to change over into Guilders.

"Not too much," I said. "We want to do it a bit at a time, a bit at a time, gently. Because otherwise they'll get suspicious and call a pig. What are you doing with all that money sonny? he'll say. Perhaps you'd like to accompany me to the station."

They agreed I was making perfect sense.

"Yeah, but won't they get suspicious if we keep changing bits and pieces of money everywhere we go?"

"No," Charley said. "People on holiday do that sort of thing all the time. To keep a check on how much they're spending. You know, as a way on holding some back."

"Tight bastards."

"How much should we get?" Will asked her.

"Couple of hundred?"

"Five hundred, I reckon that'll be alright." Charley reached into the bag and pulled out a wad of notes, counting out five hundred quid on the seat in tens, twenties and fifties."

"Much left?"

"Quite a bit," she said. "Shame so much of it is change, I don't think they take that."

The bank was a big, impressive building, much more than something you'd get in a High Street in England, and inside it was fairly plush. Once again Will was going to do the honours. We just thought he looked older somehow. Me and Charley waited for him as he queued at a red rope. There wasn't many people about at that time of the morning. He didn't take long. He came back with a serious expression on his face. She held out her hand for the money.

66

"Outside," he said.

"What's wrong with in here?"

She didn't half push it sometimes. Will handed over the envelope of notes, which she folded in half and tucked inside her blouse in plain view of everyone. We got out of there pronto.

"What shall we do now?"

"I fancy a piece of cake or something. A cup of coffee or something. We can look at the map a bit more."

We passed a posh-looking baker's, a sort of café place with well-dressed people having a late breakfast.

"I think we should keep moving," I said. "Try and get somewhere good by lunch time."

"Where's good?"

We walked past the place and went back to the car. I got behind the wheel again. Charley studied the map on her lap. No way couldn't she understand it, obviously.

"Let's go to Amsterdam," Will said, "we'll have a really good time there."

"I don't want to go to Amsterdam." Charley stated this matter-of-factly. There weren't going to be no argument about it.

"Why not?"

"Perhaps we could go back there later," she said. "I want to go to Delft. It's closer anyway, it's the next place on."

"What's so good about Delft when it's at home?"

"They make porcelain there, that's all I know. I've seen it in the shops in Clacton. I think we should go there. I think it'll be a good town, not too big."

"Yeah, yeah." Will said. "Sounds interesting. Why not?"

Delft it was. We got out on the road again. It weren't a motorway, just a single lane road running along, flat like all of them, and Delft was only about eight miles along it according to the signs. We hit the outskirts in about ten minutes. It was as though we just wasn't thinking big enough in our plans, because once we'd decided to go there we didn't think no further. We could only hop along, I thought, like grasshoppers, except we planned it hop by hop instead of just going off anywhere. That was something anyway, an important advantage we had over grasshoppers.

"So, you want to look around this place?"

"Not really," Charley said. "Not now. I'm tired. Can't we stop somewhere? In a hotel or something?"

And there they was at the side of the road, little hotels, cafes, what have you, very inviting, but all of them seemed to have boards up saying NO VACANCIES in the English language.

"Keep an eye out can't you, Will?" I said. "I'm trying to look at the road here."

"Slow down, slow down," Charley was fiddling with the radio, getting a station with a load of hits I remembered from a couple of years back and lively talk in roydee-doydee Double Dutch. I was only going about twenty-five mile an hour, I couldn't really go much slower if I tried, not unless I wanted one of their fucking little Dutchmobiles stuck up my backside.

"Over there on the right," Will said, "Just back there. I thought I saw a place that'd do us."

"Let's hope so," I said.

This place was tucked away, if it was possible to tuck anything anywhere in Holland; like everything there you could see it coming a mile off. It was hard to say how we'd missed it: things just held themselves up for you as you passed by, saying here I am in my little Dutch roof, and this one was a tallish, odd-shaped building with a bar underneath and no board saying full up, piss off and carry on to the next one. Therefore we decided it would do us fine.

We went in the place, which was open, and asked the bloke in there for a room. He was a slim, bearded type, his hair a bit askew but very serious-looking. "One room?"

"Two rooms," Charley said. "A single and a double."

"No double," he said. "But we have a single—and another with two single beds. Okay?

"Yeah, even better," I said.

"Okay," he said. "For how many nights is it?"

"One," Will said. "Maybe two."

"Okay, okay, I'll show you," he said. "They are upstairs, at the side." He plucked a pair of keys off a board behind him and came out into the street with us, to where an outside staircase led up to the top of the building. "You have luggage?"

"Yes," I said, "in the car."

"Quite a haul up to the stars I am afraid." He smiled a thin smile. "But you are young, you can manage, I am sure."

And as soon as he left us alone I locked the door behind us.

"What you doing that for?" Charley said. "Gimme my keys. You're not locking me in here."

"Don't you want to look through the cases with us?"

"Course I do," she said. "But first I want to lie down for a bit."

"Okay," I give her a key.

Will went over to one of the cases.

"Leave it till I get back," she said. "I want to look too—I'm not having you two bar stewards nicking all the best stuff."

Will immediately left the case where it was and flopped on his bed. I picked up the other case and placed it more neatly next to the rest of the Spanish people's luggage. Charley smiled, went on out. "Good boys," she said. "I'll seize you later."

"Don't be too long," Will called at the door.

"She's a pain in the arse," I said.

"She's brilliant," he said. "There's nothing much wrong with Charley."

"I suppose not." I hadn't had all that much experience with women, none really, except with Mum. Charley reminded me of her in a way, especially the way how she always had to get her own way and always had to be the centre of attention. Both of them thought the world should stop when they wasn't looking at it, when they'd had enough of something, and if you let them they'd try and make that happen. Ping.

I was thinking I wouldn't mind having a bath, and before I could stop it happening my eyes was closed and I felt the dark covering myself up and although I weren't asleep the main people I knew was all there talking to me, I was talking to them, if not telling them what to say then what they was saying was a bit more reasonable than nothing they usually said. Mum for instance. We was standing in the back door. She was there against the starry sky, behind her the sea crashing and crashing as she took one last drag on her fag, which she then dropped and stubbed out. I was coming out with the can of paraffin and a rag stuffed in the pocket of my coat. She was in her leather jacket, skinny, small, wiry. I looked nothing like her. But we definitely made a good team together.

She put her hand on my shoulder. "We'll show them, Lee. We'll show them who not to take the piss out of, won't we?"

"Yes, Mum."

"This way," she said, "out through the back."

There was a hard-faced sliver of moon up in the black sky. I followed her out under it in the darkness and we went down the middle of the track. Something that looked like small candles was alight behind all the closed curtains—and I started whistling off to work we go. She laughed, shushed me with her finger and we was weaving along to somewhere—the track kept changing but we knew exactly where we was going—and then we was in front of a place like ours and she stood her guard in the road whilst I sloshed pink paraffin through the letter box and down the front of the door. I stuffed the rag in, the fuse. Mum came up with her zippo and set light to it—and it caught straight away, and we melted away into the shadows and we was back indoors before it went right up—wooof—and she was putting the kettle on for a cup of tea.

"Lee. Lee." I opened my eyes to see Charley stood beside the bed. "Wake up, sleepyhead. We're going to open up the cases."

I rolled upright. Will was already at the catches of the first big one and it suddenly cracked open like a safe in front of me and everything bulged out of it before my eyes like what you'd expect, like a treasure chest full of all mysterious things, of someone else's clothes and stuff, a bit of themselves spilled out in front of you, like guts, and it made you go all tight and airless to see it, almost choking with the excitement of doing something so wrong. Charley was right in there, picking things up and smelling them—it was a woman's case and she held these odd looking things against her, such as she wouldn't be seen dead in, I thought, bunched them up and chucked them anywhere.

Under the clothes she found a pair of high heels wrapped in a plastic bag—and she couldn't resist kicking her shoes off and trying them on. They was a light blue colour with little bows on the front, but Charley trying to squeeze her big clod-hopping feet into them was like one of the ugly sisters trying on Cinderella's slipper.

"Try that shirt on," I suggested. "I think that might suit you."

"What, this?" She held up a brightly coloured silk top, and then she couldn't resist it she pulled off what she was wearing— her jumper I think—and we got a glimpse of her in her bra for a few seconds before she got her shoulders into the Spanish woman's blouse and closed it around her. It fitted better than the shoes, looked great on her, grown up, and that cheered her up again. Charley started cramming stuff back in the case. "This is mine," she said. "You shouldn't be looking at it. I'm taking it next door to try on properly." Before we could look at nothing she was snapping the locks shut and sitting on the closed case in her new shirt.

"You look like a real señorita," Will said to her.

"Do I?"

"Yeah," I said. "You look really good, Charley."

She looked pleased with herself. "Go on then," she said. "Open up the other ones—let's see what's in them."

Will opened up the other big case and I looked through it with him. It was the man's case, the Dad's one—and it had his equivalent of his wife's holiday clothes. A few pairs of trousers with a sharp crease in, loads of shirts, short-sleeved coloured ones, white ones, a pale linen jacket folded neatly in the top, a pair of shiny black pointed shoes that seemed elegant and typical Spaniard. Will liked the look of these and he done the same as Charley, tried them on, except in his case they fitted him perfectly. He was getting excited, I could see he wanted to put it all on and become this Spanish bloke. In his case he'd become another him. The smaller case was their kiddie's stuff and it was disappointing. He was a kid, that's why. There was nothing in there that would fit anyone, especially not a fat boy like myself, not much else neither: a couple of story books in Spanish, which Will hooked straight out, and a toy cap gun, a silver six shooter.

"That might come in useful," I picked it up, pulled the trigger. It went off with a crack and a wisp of smoke curled up from behind the hammer. It was new, silver—and loaded. I fired again at the two of them—crack, crack—and they laughed at me. I put it down on the bed, the sharp smell of caps still hanging in the room: a struck matchbox. I thought of what I'd been thinking about when I was dozing on the bed, and what I was getting away from and what I would have to go back to sometime soon. I picked it up again and stuffed it down the side of the boy's suitcase.

Will had found the bloke's spare wallet, with all his extra cash. Pesetas. Spanish money. He was trying to count it up, but it ran into millions. "I don't think we should touch it." he said. "Then, if we get caught, we can say we was only borrowing his car for a while, we didn't mean any harm."

That put a damper on things—because it seemed pretty likely that we would get caught fairly soon—and dead sure nobody would ever believe that we was only borrowing his car. But I thought he had a point about the Spanish money. We shouldn't touch it unless we thought we needed it for something important. It was obvious though that seeing it reminded Will of being Spanish, and he didn't like the idea of ripping off Spanish people like himself. None of us really liked the idea of this being reality.

There was a big white towel in the bloke's case.

"Right," I said, "I'm going to have a bath now."

"Okay," Charley said. "I'm going to take this next door and see what I can put on—then we can go down and check out the town, yeah?"

"Yeah, right."

There was a bag of soap and shampoos and a flannel in the bloke's suitcase. I took it out and went through to the bathroom. It was a nice shiny new one, which I was surprised to see in an old dump as this one was. I ran myself a bath, hopped in, washed my hair with Spaniard shampoo and soaped myself over. I had a nice long soak there—sort of like enjoying it, floating. I kept trying to think about what was going to happen next and all that, but I'm not very good at that, for some reason, which is one thing I've found out, although I am good at getting things done, at actually doing it, and I tend to think that if you do a thing right then what comes next isn't going to come as such bad news.

I thought we was a good team, myself, Will and Charley. Different, and yet, I thought, between the three of us we was probably going to come up with the right answer to whatever questions happened to come up along the way, which I did see as going way on ahead, even though I didn't know what was round the bend, but I thought, if you're going to nick a car and drive it to Holland and God knows where else—you might as well be prepared to take it as it comes: that's if you have no choice, which we most probably didn't have—no choice except to carry on.

I got out and dried myself off. I wondered what to put on—because it was obvious none of the stuff in the cases was going to fit me, and I wondered if maybe they'd let me spend some of the money in different clothes, holiday clothes, so I could give the ones I'd got—my jeans and T-shirt and coat—a bit of a rest. I hoped that would be alright, even though I didn't think of them as being in charge of myself, not like my Mum—and my Dad, when he was still alive. I got dressed in my old clothes and went back through to the bedroom.

Will and Charley was in bed together, giggling under the covers, which she pulled up over her when I came in. For a minute I thought my luck was in too, but in a split second's time I realised it weren't. This was how it was going to be from now on—myself on the outside looking at them two having it off. I went over to my bed, laid down on it, and looked up at the ceiling. Bastards, I thought to myself. Let's see them get out of that one. They did, awkwardly. They got up, pulled their clothes together—they'd been into the dressing up box—and went through to Charley's room.

Charley looked back at me. Sort of saying sorry. Will didn't even do that much. I laid there feeling sick as a dog. She looked really great in the Spanish woman's clothes. She looked completely different to anyone I'd ever seen before.

EIGHT

I was on my own again, on my tod, my own-i-o, and to be honest I was really starting to miss my Mum bad. I wondered what she was doing—nothing much, I suspected, but—I counted them up—we'd been away three days? two days? It seemed a lot longer than that, and I supposed she must be worried sick about me. I wondered if she'd called the pigs. No, they'd probably been round to see her, that's if anyone had seen us nicking the car, driving off in it. Charley was a liability. Woolworth's was going to be straight onto the law on this one. Will's Mum would be straight on the blower. She was more likely to report him missing than mine, and so drop him, and all of us, straight in the shit.

I decided to have another look through the cases. That would take my mind off things. There was definitely some clean socks and pants in there. I got off the bed and rummaged through the man's case—and soon found what I was looking for. It was obvious none of his other clothes wouldn't fit me, but the pants and socks would do fine—they was fresh and folded and new-looking. Then I started poking around in the bottom of the case to see what else there was—anything Will hadn't spotted. There was something in there alright, something hard wrapped up in a plastic bag inside a hand towel.

A gun. A small black flat gun, a bit like a little .22 pellet gun, but sort of heavier and better. I knew it weren't a pellet gun. A real gun. I held it in my right hand, weighed it, pointed it at a few things around the room—the lampshade, the mirrors, a vase on the dressing table. I didn't really fire it of course. But what I done was wrap it up again in the plastic bag and put it somewhere else. In my coat pocket. And I decided then and there I weren't going to tell the others nothing about it, because it was mine—I'd found it and I was going to keep it for a rainy day.

I changed my socks and pants, put my jeans on again and laid back on the bed. I felt a lot better with my head back on a nice fresh pillow—and I fell asleep again, this time without no stupid dreaming or thinking about stupid stuff to do with my Mum and Dad, or the other two next door. They woke me up again soon enough and when they done that they was both dressed up to go out. They looked like Spaniards, whatever a Spaniard looks like—and I still looked like what I always would be: an Essex scruff-bag from Jaywick Sands.

We decided to leave the car where it was and walk into town, which didn't look too far, and have a good butchers at it—maybe get something to eat. But it was a long old walk though, further than it looked, and just our luck we'd come across the only place in Holland where it's slightly hilly, rounding a long bend on a dual carriageway. People was looking out of their cars at us, mainly because of the way they was dressed. Will had to put the bloke's best dark suit on, his off-duty matador number. Charley was done up to the nines in a plain dark yellow dress. They looked like they was ready for an evening out somewhere decent instead of an afternoon looking around the shops in Delft. They was holding hands now. I was well gutted, trailing along behind, feeling nothing except the clunk clunk of the little hand gun against my leg.

I wanted to tell them about it. I'd decided not to though and that was that for now. I wanted to tell them because I wondered if they would have any better answers than me to the question I was asking myself, which was why this Spanish bloke had a gun in the first place. I mean, he'd smuggled in through customs, taking one hell of a big risk there alone, and he was going to have to take it back if we hadn't done it for him. That was one part of the question. The other one was, like I said, why he had it on him at all. What for? To do what—shoot somebody? He was probably a gangster or something. For protection? Maybe some people was allowed to bring guns into the country.

It was a hot day. I was too hot. I wished I'd left my coat behind in the room. Having the gun weren't much of a secret, unless I told someone, not till the exact moment when you told someone about it, the moment when it stopped being one, then it would all be over, be not a secret at all, and then there would be something else—I didn't know what—to worry about, like what you was going to do with it. Like fire it. Point it at somebody and make them do what you wanted them to do.

We walked down the road, just walking, me behind, and then we came into the town of Delft. Delft—it was the home of bone china tea sets, coffee pots, dinner plates, and little figures made out of it—shepherds, for instance, little boys and girls in bonnets—as we found out when we started to look round the shops. I must get something for Mum, I thought, so as we was going to be looking around for quite a while I thought I'd keep a look out for something I thought she'd like as a souvenir. Not that Mum really likes that sort of stuff, but I knew if I looked hard enough I'd see something that fitted her perfectly. It was all the same colour—white and blue.

There was load of people about in town, even though it was a weekday. Tourist season, and all of them was thronging up and down these streets filled with shops selling this gear. Which weren't cheap, you could tell, even though I had no idea how many Guilders to the pound or nothing like that. They could look after the money, I thought, since they seemed to think so much about it, and I'd look after the gun. Charley soon got bored. She bored easily that girl—even before we'd looked in the shops she said they reminded her of Woolies. Everything reminded her of something bad.

"Let's get something to eat," she said. "I'm starving hungry. Then we should go in a bar somewhere and get really pissed—and that's final."

Will and myself didn't take much persuading. We looked round for a Macdonalds so we wouldn't have to talk much. We searched high and low, but even though Delft was a reasonable sized place—about the same as Colchester—there didn't seem to be one in sight. We popped into a place doing all different kind of pancakes instead and had one of them each to take away, and ate them on a bench in a little square we found by a canal. There was lots of little canals lacing the place together. Will told us this story about a boy, I can't remember his name. Will reckoned he put his arm in the sea wall at one time to stop the whole country being flooded out like Jaywick in the fifties. I wondered if he was born in Delft.

It was an old place, well-preserved, a lot of history to it, you could tell, running down to a river about the same width as the Colne where big sailing ships must have come in long ago carrying all sorts of things from all over the world. There was an old painting of it—by Vermeer of Delft—in some of the shop windows. Another painting I liked was of a little bird, a goldfinch, sitting on top of a bird box, so lifelike. Another one was of a bloke stretched out on the pavement asleep, blind drunk it looked like. His little black dog was trying to wake him up. The title under it was in English. The Watchman. A bit of writing underneath explained he was the guard of the armoury, where they kept the gunpowder, and it blew up a few years later, flattening most of the town: the biggest explosion in history.

Another one showed a man sitting by a couple of musical instruments, one of them a lute, which loomed towards you, and he was looking out at the street as though he was expecting someone to come round the corner. In front of him the road climbed up steeply over a small bridge across one of the canals. That one summed the place up, I thought, after we'd looked round it for a bit longer, all piled up and turning over right on top of you. Not the sort of place you wanted to hang around in for long. Nice though.

Charley's favourite was of a girl sleeping at a table, leaning on her elbow and having forty winks.

"Why don't you buy it?" I said to her. "You could do, easy."

But she didn't want to. Will didn't want to buy nothing either. Copying her. I thought they was pathetic. All of a sudden they was into acting cool, as if nothing was interesting enough for them, and it was all a load of crap. Which it weren't, not by any means. They both wanted to get pissed. Fair enough. I still wanted to get something for Mum, so I got some dosh from Charley and went in the biggest china shop by myself and left them to wait outside or do whatever they wanted. I was going to find something not too expensive in the shops to take home to Mum.

There was a lot of stuff on the tables in there, which is why I chose it, and I was quite relieved in a way to be on my own again, poking around. Will should've loved this place, I thought. Charley as well. It was the sort of place girls usually like, so long as they're not complete dipsticks. Anyway, it was her idea in the first place. The blue and white porcelain was clever, you could tell when you looked at it up close. They'd obviously had plenty of practice at it over the years, but they did tend to do the same patterns and figures over and over again.

I looked around for one of this boy putting his finger in the dyke—that would have been perfect for Mum—it would remind her of me forever. They didn't have one though, not that I could see. It was all a bit of a high price. I counted up the notes I had on me, looking round for things in my price range. That narrowed it down. Only a few little plates, saucers where you couldn't find the cup, things like that—I knew they would soon get broke. Mum has never been too keen on ornaments, I thought, so if I didn't break it getting it home, ten to one she would manage it herself.

I was about to give up when I did see something right. Tiles. Square tiles with different patterns on them, old traditional blue ones that looked like everything that reminds you of Holland— spokes, stars, canals, curves and reflections, windmills with big sails, and some with little birds on, the lot—and all a bit flat—at least, that's what struck me about the ones I was looking at. They wasn't too dear. You was supposed to buy a whole box or two and do out your bathroom in them, but I soon worked out I could buy a few anyway. Mum could stand them over the fireplace if she liked, or put her ashtray on one and her cup on another. I could have one in my room to remind me of this trip. I picked out a few good ones and took them up to the counter, paid an arm and a leg, and the woman smiled at me and wrapped them up in tissue paper and put them in a carrier. I was well pleased with myself. The bag was quite heavy, which made me think I'd got value for my money, and I knew I'd also got hold of something special.

Will and Charley wasn't there when I got outside. I sort of knew they wouldn't be—and now they wasn't. Gone off to get pissed in one of the little bar-café type places, or maybe they'd gone back to the hotel for another shag. Leaving myself with next to no money. I spotted a bar under an arch almost next door to the shop. Ah, I thought, that's where they've gone. They're waiting for me in there. We can all have a few of those foamy beers, get totally slaughtered and remember who we are. I went inside. It was dark, a bit gloomy but cool. They wasn't in there either. I thought of having a beer on my own but I didn't like the way this barman was looking at me, like he wanted to refuse to serve me, so I went outside again into the sun.

I decided not to bother no more looking for them. They could be anywhere, anywhere at all. I weren't too bothered about it. I decided to go off for a walk on my own, down to the river, and have a look at that for a while instead. I toyed with the idea of getting something else to eat, but I didn't really feel like it somehow. It was true I was losing weight. I felt my clothes loose on me, only hot and thirsty for a drink, which I did get, a can of Orangina from a corner shop, and walked on feeling better with my tiles in the carrier bag.

The town was an oblong shape, bulging out at the sides like a shoebox with the wrong size shoes crammed into it, and I puffed up and over a couple of bridges, stood still for a minute in the middle of each one to look along its narrow glittering canal at a little boat tour gliding along it—a flattened single-decker water bus with a clear roof for the people inside to look up at the old buildings, bowed over like trees, looking like they might fall in on top of you, propped up there forever defying gravity and time, roofs curved, flipped up like a Dutch milkmaid's cap, and the twin needle towers of an old church or something, and at the same time it was a low flat place with plenty of clear blue sky up above. I was carrying a piece of the town along with me to the river front.

People at the little cafés was drawn down to the edge by the coolness of the river, which was wide, and a bit of town continued on at the far shore. I decided to walk along the river itself for a stretch of my legs. They was already well stretched. As soon as I got past the cafes I sat down on the wall by the water and let the breeze blow through me, imagining what it must have looked like when there was ships there and low wooden barges with dark red sails bellying in it, lumbering along full of coal and golden wheat and dark and pale cloth to make the olden clothes out of, and little boats piled high with pairs of fresh carved clogs for the fat little women to wear as they staggered along under oxen yokes with a full milk bucket slung on each end. A speed boat arced out across it all leaving its cotton-wool wake on the brown churning river, and a few gulls flapped up and veered and squawked across a whitish yellow streaky closing down sky—a sky that was nearly the same colour as the sea.

I got up and carried on walking around the bend, away from people, till you couldn't hear their laughing or tinkling, far enough away, and after a bit I came to an old shipyard with a broken down fence and slipped through into a bit where it was just flat broken up concrete and rubble, a few dark iron claws of cut off blocks of cradles where they used to make all these big boats, and behind it, further back, some big empty open sheds. I made a beeline for them, walking back over the abandoned yard and right into the end of the furthest one. I took the tiles out of the bag and propped them up against the far wall in a line on the lip of the bottom crumbling concrete sill. Then I walked back a few paces and took the gun out of my pocket.

I unwrapped the plastic bag and took it out. At first it had seemed heavy but I'd soon got used to carrying it. There was a full magazine clip in the bottom, and a safety catch, which I clicked off. I knew this was going to make a lot of noise, but held it out at arms length and aimed at the first tile. I pulled the trigger. A jumping shock went up my arm, fire came out and the sound went off a second later, echoing and building around the high empty shed so it must have been heard miles away and no one would mistake what it was they was hearing. A gun going off somewhere. I didn't see where the bullet went. I thought I saw a chunk jump out of the wall, but when I walked up there the first one of the tiles was not. It was smashed to a thousand pieces.

I looked around the shed, turning in a wide circle. I thought someone hidden must have done it for me, taken the shot. But there was no one about for miles. I was on my own in this shed. Fluke. I'd got incredibly lucky. I stepped back to where I'd been before, where the bag was on the floor, and I took aim at the second tile. I fired. This time it stayed where it had been put. I fired again and clipped the corner of it and saw it fly up into the air spinning like a wobbly Frisbee. Bang. It fell on the ground and shattered. This was brilliant. I waited for the echoes to die away and thought I heard it come back faintly across the water, the first original crack. I took careful aim at the third tile.

But there was only five. I went over to the last three and picked them up carefully and wrapped them again in tissue paper and put them in the bag. I stood there looking at the gun. It felt hot on top, still warm where I'd fired it and it seemed heavier. It seemed to belong to me now, to just fit nicely and snugly into my hand. Three shots. I put the safety catch on and pulled the clip out of the handle. Seven left. Seven shiny bullets that could rip you open, kill any living thing. That's what it was for, and although it seems obvious, it does bring something home to you, especially when you realise you're a good shot. I wrapped the gun up and put it back in my coat pocket, picked up the tiles and walked back out to the river. It still weren't dark, but it was going to be soon, and the spectacular sunset was catching my eye as it closed like a red helmet over the sky.

Amazingly there was no one else about, or didn't seem to be. Nobody had heard me, nobody knew I was there with this gun in my pocket. What I done then I done by instinct, I didn't know why except that I thought someone had probably heard the shots. I turned and ran away from that spot as the dusk fell fast, as hard as I could. I went through the fence and back the way I'd come, then veered off to the left as soon as I saw an opening and kept running like fuck by another route back into Delft.

My chest was heaving. I plumped down on a bench at the edge of a little square beside a still canal. I was off the main streets, there was nobody else about. I sat there in the dark listening to my breathing slow down to normal. I was alone. I was far away from what happened down at the river, but miles away from the room on the other edge of town. I wondered if Will and Charley had got back yet or if they was still out getting hammered somewhere. I sat for a few minutes on my own. I was tingling from head to foot. I was feeling good about what I'd done out there, partly because no one would ever know about it. I had the gun in my pocket and I knew how to use it. I got up again and started on my long trudge back to the hotel room.

I went back through the centre of town, which was lit up now and happy people thronging on the cobbled pedestrian streets around the old churches and the town hall and the cafes were lit up, people dressed up good in holiday clothes and smiling at each other. I couldn't help smiling myself. I had this great big grin plastered on my face, because somehow I'd saved these people from the gun in the Spanish bloke's suitcase, and the reason I'd been able to do it was, in a way, because I was such a good shot. Pow pow pow. Two out of a possible three weren't bad. There was plenty of birds in the holiday crowds and one or two of them smiled back at me, maybe because I was smiling to myself, or because they thought I looked out of place.

Floodlights on, lighting up all the buildings; there was a big blue glittering egg standing on the pavement by a church, a sculpture-thing, and one or two people looking at it, wondering what it was, and the whole place bathed in a whitish light, and the evening air was mild. I'd say it was quite pleasant. I imagined it was a celebration, of being saved, by myself, from the floods. I was the boy who put his finger in the hole in a dyke to stop the water coming in, who put his finger over the hole in a balloon to stop the air getting out. This was their way of saying thank you, thank you, Lee Hookaway, you saved us from ourselves—now we're going to enjoy life for a night or two, if you don't mind—which I didn't.

NINE

The pair of them was having a little party in the double bedroom when I got back. Charley was perched on the edge on my bed with a paper cup in her hand. Will laid back on his own bed with another cup the same. On the bedside table between them was an open bottle of champagne. A radio was playing some pop tunes in double Dutch.

"Lee!" she put her cup down and got up and came across to me and started kissing me on the face with these big sloppy kisses. "We looked for you everywhere, didn't we Will?"

"Yes," Will said. "We searched high and low."

"You could have waited for me," I said. "I was only in there a couple of minutes."

"Champagne?" She pulled off another paper cup from the roll of them and poured it full for me.

I took it off her and drank it down too quick.

"We went to a little café," Will said. "A brilliant place, really old. Everything in it was brown."

"Yeah," Charley said. "Everything in it was brown—there was brown tables, brown chairs, brown walls, brown everything."

They both thought this was hilarious.

"I got some tiles for my Mum."

"Let's see," Charley said.

I pulled them out of the bag and laid them on the bed in a row.

"They're nice," she said. "But there's only three—what's she going to be able to do with them?"

"They're just for decorations. I was going to get five of them—but they was quite dear."

"Nice colours."

"Didn't they have any brown ones?" Will said.

They both laughed at me.

"Not that I noticed."

"Yeah," he said, "they're good."

"I'm going to do some shopping tomorrow myself." Charley said. "I just didn't feel like it today."

"This is weird," I said. "It's like we've gone into another dimension."

"Yeah," Will said, "you're telling me."

"I wonder why we done it?" Charley said. "We was talking about it earlier on."

"We just felt like it, I suppose," I said. "I wanted to get away from that bastard Warren Hopkins."

"Do you think we're being stupid?" Charley asked. "I mean, I know I am. We're never going to get away with this."

I didn't know what to say. I held out my glass and she refilled it with the bubbly. I'd never tasted it before—it had a harsh, sharp taste, bubbles went up your nose and it burst in the back of your mouth and went straight to your head. It was obvious why rich people like it so much. I liked it too.

"I got really pissed on this once," she said, "at my cousin's wedding." She was laying back on my bed in the Spanish woman's skirt, which I could see right up. "I made a right fool of myself."

"I think they'll put us inside for this," Will said. "Youth detention centre. The short sharp shock."

"How long?" I said.

"I don't know—about six months. Except Charley—she could just say we led her on, we made her do it."

"Never would I say that," she said. "Never would I say that in a million years."

"I don't mind," I said. "You can say it if you want."

"You're nice," she said. "A nice bloke, and there's not many of them about"

She should know, I thought. "Anyway," I said. "I think we could definitely get away with it."

"How's that?" Will asked. He poured the last of the bottle of champagne into his paper cup.

"We have so far."

"Six months isn't long," he said, "as far as I'm concerned, it's well worth it. For the experience, you know. I mean, it's the sort of thing that's only going to happen once in your life."

"Like being abducted by aliens," I said.

He didn't answer.

"Aliens?" Charley said. "Don't they take all your clothes off in their space ship and interfere with you? Like that woman in Wyoming you was telling me about?"

"Don't get too excited," I said. "They don't fucking exist."

Will couldn't resist coming back on that one. "How do you know they don't exist?" he said. "There was an ancient civilisation on Mars—it's been proved—or it will be as soon as they get up there. They're probably driving around in their beach buggies on the great plains—herding reindeer, pitching their tents on the red sand beside a parched dormant canal, waiting for it to spring up with yellow water in a million years or two. Sulphur. They live on sulphur up there."

We both started laughing.

"Right. They're a sulphur-based life form. They live in hell and they're waiting to get off it, kill us, jump in our ships and head down here to take over our planet. And that's why we should stay where we are."

I felt dizzy. A champagne bubble had burst in my head. I dropped back on the bed and landed against Charley's right foot. She didn't move it. She stroked my ear with her toe.

Will was laying back with his cup on his middle. "My Mum might as well have come from Mars. She's still there in her head. She's spent her whole life trying to get her feet on the ground, only to find it doesn't really exist."

"Why didn't she want to go back to Spain?"

Will sighed. He had an old look about him. He always seemed tired, as if he'd seen and done it all before and he knew it came out badly.

"My Mum just floats above it all," I said.

"My Mum is a selfish cow," Charley said. "She's totally selfish. Self self self, that's all she ever thinks about. Her-fucking-self."

"In what way?"

"Oh, you know." She sat up suddenly. "You've still got your coat on, Lee. Why don't you take it off?"

I put my hand in my pocket and felt the gun. "Okay, I will." I got up and took off my coat and hung it carefully on a hook on the back of the door. Then I came back and sat down exactly where I was before, close to her feet. Will was sitting on the edge of his bed. He was leaning towards us, poking his nose into the situation.

Charley sat up and leaned towards him, put her arm round his neck and kissed him. At the same time she opened up her legs wider and give myself an eyeful of her minge. She weren't wearing no knickers. She held up her other hand and beckoned me to come up towards her, which I done, and soon we was all over her.

When it came time to get dressed I just put my old things on again, but them two wanted to pick out a whole different outfit from the suitcases. Charley went next door to find something to put on.

"That's it now," Will said as soon as she left the room. "That was the last time, okay. You're not going to do that again. She's my girlfriend now." He was talking to me patiently, like to a moron. I didn't answer him.

Charley came back in her jeans and top she'd bought in Colchester. She'd had enough of dressing up for now.

Will selected something more casual from the bloke's suitcase. It was weird to myself how all of this middle-aged Spanish bloke's clothes seemed to fit in so well to what he normally wore. Anyway, we all had a bit of a headache. It weren't too late though, so we decided to go downstairs to the bar and maybe have some chicken and chips or something like that.

A few people down there was still supping beer, but it was getting late. Charley asked the bloke about food but he said the kitchen was closed for the night. We made do with a round of drinks and a couple of bags of Dutch peanuts, which I had to admit was quite similar to the real thing. We went on talking, talking more and more crap and laughing about it, laughing about nothing except here we was somehow, we could do anything we liked it seemed, and life was just the opposite of what you might think it was set up to be, for us anyway, and for the time being we wasn't going to do nothing to spoil our run of luck.

I was going to do whatever I liked, whatever she liked. Because nothing like this had ever happened to me before and I knew it was never going to happen again—not like this—and as far as I was concerned he was just getting greedy. I weren't though. I was just taking it all as it came along, but if I was honest I'd of much rather it had just been myself and Charley on our own, say driving around on holiday, and I knew that if it was like that we would get on really well and be able to talk about all sorts of things. I knew Will probably felt the same way but touch luck.

And another thing I knew was that, good though it was, there was something not really right about it—and not right about her.

Next morning we took it in turns for the bathroom then sat around wondering what to do next. Breakfast. We decided to go downtown for it, first pack up all the stuff, pay the bloke and then head off to the next place, wherever that turned out to be. We'd slept in the same room. Charley kipped down in Will's bed worse luck, but it was still a nice thing that we was all there together and I didn't mind much waking up in the fresh sheets and looking across to see her curled up against his side. The sheet had come off her back and the long curve of it down to the top of her bum made me want to reach over and softly stroke it and see if it made her shiver.

Charley tidied up the rooms and we dragged the cases back down to the car and paid up. That was Will's job. He had the Spaniard passport and the mysterious charm. To tell the truth we was all worried about it a bit, because sooner or later somebody was going to get suspicious of us and call the law. Not this bloke though. I warmed the motor up. Charley was in the back. Will came out of the place and hopped in beside me. We drove off like we had done before, like the first time we got away—and as soon as we got out on the road again, she said:

"Let's not bother going into town, let's just get something to eat at the next garage and carry on from there."

Okay by me. I turned the motor around in someone's drive and we speeded off back out onto the main drag and on to the next town. Will pulled the map out of the glove compartment and passed it back to her. She unfolded in the back seat and she tracked the long yellow line we had to run down to get to Utrecht. We pulled up at the first garage. We still had plenty of juice left from yesterday, left over from our first spurt, so I pulled in past the pumps and we went back and a few sandwiches with chewy cheese in them and coffees from the machine and wolfed the lot down quick at the side of the road there, looking out at the blank flatness of the fields, turning to look along the wide empty road we'd be driving along. The sun hung low in the sky, pale under a sky low enough to make you bend low under it. We stood there for a minute around the car breathing in the smell of earth, then we chucked our coffee cups away over a fence and we got inside again and headed on towards Utrecht.

It was just a name on a map to us, the next place along by about 120 kms, and we didn't know nothing about it except it looked fairly big, and we was quite happy to find out when we got there what it was like. Charley wound her window down in the back and laid back and stuck her foot out of it and let the wind cool her down for a while and then went quiet, spark out again after a restless night in the room where it had been too close.

Will wound his window down to nose height, looking out at the slow procession of spaced out similar things. I hung on to the wheel, concentrating on distances, arrowing along in our own summer holiday bus between the other cars, the campers, the BMWs towing German caravans, local traffic and big Dutch lorries blasting past on the outside lane like American trucks. It felt like we should be heading for the sea but we wasn't—that was where we'd come from. We was heading further inland, into the heart of this long low country of thousands of names we didn't know but full of things we always seemed to recognise straight away, more or less: one thing I did know, or thought I knew, was that this something which everyone at home would of said was going to be the end of my life was actually going to turn out to be the beginning.

Charley had the little red radio they'd bought with her in the back. She turned it on and tuned in to a station of Garage, which ticked on and on for a couple of miles, till Will turned on the car radio, still on its Dutch pop station playing English sixties hits, which I must say I preferred, and then it was time for the battle of the radios. The battle of radios went on for miles and miles and miles, with both of them turning up their radios, edging them up to drown the other one out, till they was both hammering away at full belt.

"Can't you turn them fucking things down?" I yelled. "I'm trying to concentrate on the road here."

And then they both edged them down a little bit, just enough so they could hear each other shouting back and forth.

"I like this, it's good stuff."

"It's crap, absolute crap."

"I don't care, it's what I fucking like."

 "There's no tune to it, there's no nothing."

"Well, I like it. It's better than your boring old crap."

"Look, turn it off for a minute, just so I can hear this one."

"What is it?"

"It's good."

Charley turned hers off and sat back on the seat in a huff

The car radio was playing Herman's Hermits doing Something Tells Me I'm Into Something Good. It was booming loud, rattling the speakers. Will turned it down so you could still hear it, but better. Nice happy music ringing out loud and clear. But her in the back seat weren't having none of it and after a couple of the verses her rick-a-ticky dance beats faded up once again.

"This is the remix version, right," she said. "The super rub-a-dub twin turntable rave on mix." She cackled away back there, turning it up and down, and loving it. "This is the modern version," she says, as if we wasn't as modern as her.

Will turned up Herman's Hermits, then it was over and some Dutch talk came on, which was drowned out by the dance beats. Then another song I remembered from his bedroom. Will started clicking his fingers and singing along to it, which Charley done too from the back, her radio turned down for a bit, and even I tapped along on the steering wheel and sang with it as it shuffled along like a mile stone inspector at the side of the road, hoping the next one along would be somewhere he could take the weight off his feet. It was a song all about arriving somewhere and sitting down there, tired

But as soon as the song ended Charley turned up the techno beats louder. Will give up and turned the car radio off and we had to listen to that crap for a few kilometres. There was nothing in it to concentrate on, nothing to catch you interest -- it just pounded on and on like miles and there was nothing to do but count them as they dropped off the signs in a long countdown till the music finally stopped.

"Let's play I-Spy," she said. "Ready or not?"

"Okay."

"I-Spy with my little eye, something beginning with ... T."

Will looked around, couldn't see nothing.

"Is this inside the car or outside the car?" I asked her.

"Both," she said. "But especially inside the car."

"Hmm. When you say outside as well as inside, do you mean just outside here, or outside everywhere?" Will asked.

"Everywhere in the world," she said. "And in the car."

"Trousers," I said.

"No."

"Teeth," Will said.

"Go on," she said. "You'll never get it."

"Give up," I said.

"Give up," Will said.

"Go on," she said, "you're pathetic. You've got two more guesses each."

"Towels," I said.

"Wrong."

"Trowels," Will said.

"Don't be stupid—there aren't no trowels in the car."

"Or everywhere in the world."

"Tunes," Will said.

"That's true, that is," she said, "but it's not tunes."

"Tiles," I said.

"No," she said. "I won—it's tits." She pulled up her top and jiggled them around for us. "A nice juicy pair of tits."

I glanced in the mirror. Will turned right round but she'd put them away again.

"Okay, my turn," he said.

"No it ain't," she said. "You didn't get it, so it's my turn again."

"Let's have T again," I said.

"No," she said. "It's... I-Spy with my little eye. Something beginning with... R."

"Radios," Will said.

He was right. Charley went into a right huff.

"Okay," he said. "I-Spy with my little eye, something beginning with..."

"It better not be filthy," she said.

"Why not?" he said. "Something beginning with... F."

I can't remember what something beginning with F was. It weren't fuck and it weren't friend. It weren't fog and it weren't forgotten. I do know they kept playing it for ages and I didn't join in. I couldn't afford to be looking around and thinking of words. I kept my eyes on the road. But I do remember thinking there was a lot more words than there was words for things, and a lot more things than Will or Charley could see in the car, or passing by, more than none of us could imagine being out there somewhere, once we decided that was allowed.

If I thought about anything when I was driving it was where everything was relative to myself; that's all there was to think about really, in a fast way, because two seconds and bang, you won't be forgiven, you won't be able to reel it back and take it again, and the I-Spy thing that was on your mind wouldn't be there no longer, and you'd have nothing to think about except how stupid you was to be thinking about that instead of where you was going. I was miles away, still at home in my mind, remembering holidays with my Dad at the wheel, the few times we'd gone off somewhere with a tent for a couple of weeks, down to Devon was one of those times, another was all the way up to the Lake District.

I remembered being parked in a campsite at the side of one of those great big bottomless pools of darkness, too deep and cold to swim in without drowning, because they sheered off so sudden, and with nothing to do except throw a few stones and look away across at white houses perched up on the hillside for as long as you liked, and seeing a small man or woman picking their way down a path to the side of the lake, to a jetty where their long, thirties-looking speedboat was tied up.

Dad pulled everything out of the boot of the old green Rover: tent, water bottle, camping stove, sleeping bags, ground sheet, mallet, pegs. I remembered trying to bang some of them into the ground, stretching the guy ropes around them, Mum sitting in the front of the car as we done most or all of the work, finally getting out to help stretch the fly-sheet over the top, till it was finished: a little home with a tartan rug on the floor and a light inside it, a torch flaring against the walls and lighting it up like a monument to those times when we was all together and on the way to Eddie and Audrey's in Kendal. Eddie was a fishmonger who knew how to catch dabs off a bridge at night if only everyone would stop laughing and talking and spilling the flask of tea. And I felt good then and I felt good now.

Because my Dad had one of every car on the road and because I had a gun in my pocket.

Will and Charley kept on talking. The car radio went up again. I homed in on each of them, just idly thinking about what I thought about them. Will was my friend, somebody I'd known for a long time, or thought I did, but I was starting to see him in a different way since we got away on this trip. Not sure if there was more to him or less—more, I suppose, definitely more; but some of the things that summed him up for me was dropping away. He was much quieter with her around, quieter towards me than I'd ever known him to be. I thought something was going to come out of him on this trip that nobody—not even himself—had seen before.

Charley was going on about her waitressing days before she got the job in Woolies, when they used to do food over at the King's Head in Clacton and she used to do a couple of nights a week and Sunday lunch. How she wore a little black skirt and a white top, not too much make-up. How she had to carry two red hot plates, one in her good hand, the other balanced on her arm, steadying it with her thumb. How it really fucking hurt. How she used to get good tips, smiling and bowing low over the bloke, showing the lady her paw. She hated sharing her tips and the chef used to try and get her to help with the prepping when they was slow.

"I told him," she said. "Say what you like, I ain't canalaying no fucking carrot."

"What's that?" Will asked her. "Canalaying, I never heard of that."

"That's when they use a special tool to put the little grooves in the hard veg."

"What's it called?"

"I dunno. A canalaying thingy, I suppose, like a potato peeler except it cuts grooves. Anyway, that job came to an end, like they always do." She shrugged. "I ain't going back to waitressing, no way."

"Did you drop a load of plates or something?"

"No," she said. "I got really pissed in there one Sunday afternoon. We was all pissed up, I was passed out on the floor. When I woke up some old perv was cutting my tights off with a big pair of scissors they'd handed over from behind the bar."

"Bet you loved that," Will said, sarcastic.

"Yeah!" she laughed. "I did love it. But the landlord's wife blamed me for it. She said I was going to lose them their licence, the way I was carrying on. She should have seen the way my mate was carrying on with her husband in the spare bedrooms, even down in the cellar. I walked in there once right and he was giving her one up against one of the barrels. She had her legs wrapped around him, and she winked at me over her shoulder. She's a dirty little cow, Loret."

"I thought you was best mates," I said over my shoulder.

"Yeah, yeah. I loved her like a sister. Then she went and took my boyfriend off me, my boyfriend who I really liked, yeah." She fished around in her purse and pulled out an old single photo booth picture, which she passed to Will first, then me. I glanced down at It was of a Scandinavian-looking bloke, a blond super-stud type with long eyelashes. Next to him was a smaller, younger-looking Charley with different, longer hair.

"When was this?" I asked her.

"Three months ago."

All the stories I'd heard was true, all of them. Her mate. Herself. It was the same for both of them. She was up for it any time day or night and here we was driving across Holland with her. Charley was like something weird that had fallen out of a Christmas cracker. You couldn't play with it, you couldn't read it, and you couldn't put it on your head. But we tried alright. And I thought I was the one person who understood her, I thought I really understood what she wanted in the exact same way I understood myself.

TEN

As soon as we saw the sign come up Utrecht 5 kilometres I kept a look out for a garage and pulled into one on the outskirts and we filled up the Peugeot and Charley went into the toilets. Will and myself went in the gents for a slash and when we got back in the car we was all ready for a new place and whatever might happen. I said we should try to find a bed and breakfast like the last one but we agreed to drive around first and see what there was to see. We hadn't eaten much and I thought we should look out for somewhere fairly decent and have a nosh up there on whatever they ate in these parts, which was what we'd come on holiday for, after all, to enjoy ourselves. There we was, bolt upright in the car, spruced up and expecting something special was going to happen to us.

"This is brilliant," she said. "Totally fucking sick."

It was a bigger place than Delft. We kept our eyes peeled for pigs, passed a couple of police wagons but none of them give us the eye, fortunately, and so we slid into the main line of traffic and around the one-way system of a town of high blockish buildings and narrow lanes, old most of it, and unlike any place we'd seen before, including Delft. It was a proper city almost, but not quite how you expected a city to be. It was a foreign place, it definitely looked foreign in a way that not much of what we'd seen so far really did. In the centre was a big red shopping bit, which stretched out down four wider streets like the legs of a spider. There seemed to be a lot of cinemas, or I noticed them anyway, and a long, thin park which I thought we could go and sit in, and plenty of places to eat and drink everywhere, especially down by the canal.

We parked the car and started walking round town. It was a cobbled place of narrow streets, old when you got up close to it, really old, with a great big tower called the Dom in the market square, which we decided to go up on another occasion because you could see the surrounding countryside from it. The new town was industrial, like a big version of Harwich trading estate, just starting and flowing on where the edge of the old town ended, as through a stripe had been painted so that you could walk down the line and have one foot in the future and one foot in the past.

We slid in there slow and comfortable, sort of planning it all in our minds, giving ourselves time to do whatever we wanted to do.

We wandered around till we saw a narrow old hotel. It was overlooking a canal, not too far from the centre of things. Obviously it was going to cost an arm and a leg, but it weren't our money so what the fuck. We walked in there. Will done the negotiations again, two rooms, a single and a double, and asked them if there was anywhere we could leave our car. The bloke asked to see his passport, which Will produced with a flourish, and he left with some Guilders as a deposit while I went to fetch the motor. Charley stayed with him this time, so I hurried back, parked the Peugeot, picked up my door keys and headed up to look for them carrying a couple of cases while a bellboy carried the others.

No problems. They was standing at the window of the double room looking out across the city centre, an amazing view of canals, half an ancient church and winding cobbled streets with happy laughter floating up from them. It was like looking out at a picture book, one where everything is made of gingerbread, and all of it so close you could reach out and pull off one of the painted bosses on one of the beautiful houses and pop it in your mouth like a Smartie.

"We made it," I said.

"Fairytale land," Charley said.

"I could eat a horse," Will said.

"You are a fucking horse."

We just sat there. It was like being given what you suddenly knew your heart has always wanted—and not really knowing what to do with it. There was a telly in the corner of the room. I walked over and turned it on, picked up a controller lying next to it on a lace doily and flipped through the channels. They seemed to go on forever. The only one in English was of a permanent rave party going on in Amsterdam. The people talking on it was Dutch but sounded a bit American. A band I'd never heard of came on and I left them to thrash away and threw myself back on the bed to watch the amazingly clear picture, which was enormous compared to ours at home. Two presenters, a girl and a boy, flopped their heads from side to side in time to the chink-chink-chink of music.

"Let's go out," Charley said. "I'm starving hungry."

The restaurant we found was down by the canal. There was loads of these places along there. Fortunately they could tell we was English and give us a special menu. We had chicken and a beer each. It came with a few potatoes and a salad and tasted a bit different but nice—and there was a lot of it, loaded right up to the edge of the plates. We ate in the shade and looked out at the sunny canal, at the boats gliding past, the people looking out at us, the ducks. Next to us was a big table of English people, all of them eating the same thing. They was different ages and all had badges with their names written on pinned to their shirts.

I heard one of them mention Colchester. "Nothing like this in Colchester," or something. I looked away from them at the others. Will and Charley had heard it too and we all automatically talked a bit quieter so they wouldn't hear our accents. Theirs was quite posh but not local Essex. They'd come over here together for some special purpose, not on holiday like us. I couldn't quite work out what it was, but it seemed amazing to me that we'd come so far away only to sit next to some people from Essex. They was all laughing and talking, enjoying themselves, making jokes about what one or another of them had done or said back at their hotel. I couldn't work them out.

They kept butting in on each other in a way which would've been rude if any of us had done it, to them, I mean, but they listened carefully to each interruption and found them funny sometimes. What it was about I don't know. You could hear all the words but I can't remember them now. At the end of the day it doesn't matter. A couple of them had T-shirts on that said LOGIC. Some was quite fat and some was quite thin.

After we'd ate the chicken up and drunk up the beer we paid up and went for another look around. The sun was quite hot—it was about two o'clock in the afternoon and we flopped through it wondering what to look at next. We walked past a corner café and smelled the clear strong smell of waccy baccy. That took me back home with a jolt. The others got all excited.

"Let's get some dope," Charley said. "It's legal here, ain't it."

"Do you like dope?"

"Of course she likes dope."

"That stuff makes me feel sick and paranoid," I said. "My Mum smokes it all the time."

"Does she?" Charley's voice was full of warmth and admiration. "She must be really cool, your Mum."

I didn't say nothing. It was obvious we was going to be getting stoned at some point in Holland, so we might as well do it properly. We walked straight in there and up to the counter. A thin bloke with a head like the pointed end of an egg with grey tufty stubble around it was stood there in front of the coffee machine. I held up three fingers.

"Three coffees, please," I said.

"And?" he asked.

There was a flat wooden case beside him on the counter with all different types of dope in separate compartments, like a case of fishing flies. Charley and Will inspected them with me, little curls of stuff in plastic bags. We went for the black, a thin tube of it, bought a gram for a few Guilders and a packet of Bob Marley rolling papers and took our coffees over to a table by the window to skin up. Charley looked at me in awe as I quickly produced a quite thin cherub with one of her Dutch Marlboros. I didn't put too much in, so I thought. I passed it across to her to spark it up.

"Sorry," said the bloke from the counter. "I can't let you do that in here."

"Why not?" Will asked.

"Because you are too young," he said. "I could lose my licence. Go back to your hotel, or walk down to the canal. No one will stop you there."

We was a bit disgruntled at that, but we drank up and done as he asked, passing the cherub between us in the sunshine as we walked down to the canal and went to a bench and sat there and smoked it. I was glad we done that anyway, glad we wasn't walking far. The stuff was incredibly strong. I'd put far too much of it in and soon all three of us was hanging onto the slats of that bench as though it was a pedalo that had been swept out into high seas.

We grinned at each other, at everything, our skin stretched tightly back on our faces, the reflections off the water was a dazzling mobile mosaic of the colours of the painted old buildings, tiles of oil, and the sky, if you looked up, was somewhere your eye could travel up into, measuring distances by the motes of dust its beams passed along its way up to the highest little tail of cloud where God lived, or behind it somewhere, as we now knew but had never before believed in. We knew this, we all knew it. I thought we did anyway, I could catch it in their eyes, and then there was a kind of panic in her face and she turned and buried her head in my shoulder.

"This is too fucking weird for me," she said. "Take me home."

Will was looking in the opposite direction, at some people walking over the small humped bridge across the canal, his lips moving slightly as if he was having a conversation with them, holding up a gingery nicotine-stained finger to make some point. Actually he looked like he was talking to me. He looked normal, for him, the most normal he'd been since we got off the boat yesterday, or was it the day before. It helped me pull together a little bit, to remember that we hadn't been sitting here forever, but only for a few minutes after smoking a powerful cherub of black from a café that was still in our sight.

"Will," I called out. "We've got to go back now. Charley's not feeling good."

"I'll be all white in a limit," she said. " I mean, I mean... I'll be a light in a mint. A night minute. Look at that! look at that!" She was pointing at something, at another boat gliding by on the canal, the people in it staring out at us, not at us in particular, but at anything that might have been where we was sitting. Men in bright shirts and sunglasses, a sullen old woman just staring ahead, a lot of couples with their arms around each others shoulders. "Where are they going? I want to go to where they're going."

We stood up again and she clung on my arm, half-buried, peeping out as we stepped back towards the bridge and the road to the main square, where our hotel was nearby. Will walked as an outrider, quite normally, then she perked up again at the sight of so many people. She started to stare at them all as they went past, smiling sometimes, but mostly just staring at the people with wild red eyes, and people stared back at us as we went along. She was holding my hand by her fingertips, straining off like a dog or a kite, and I held on to her because I didn't want to chase her like a balloon.

Will came round and saved me, hemming her in on the far side. She staggered and put her arm on his shoulder to steady herself. Then it was alright, we was held together again.

"I'm alright now," she said suddenly, straightening up, holding back a laugh. "Wow! My head!" She shook it. She was talking much too loud for my liking, but it was a busy sunny afternoon of holidaymakers and everyone was moving along and pointing at nothing and yakking. They didn't want to see us, I knew that really, and then we slowed down and we was somehow or another on our own again and everyone was moving along independently.

We came back into the main square. It just opened up suddenly like when you've found your way to the centre of a maze without trying, because everything leads back there and that's truly how it is. The tower of the church shot up in front of us and we looked up to find its point, travelling up to it without moving, rooted to the cobblestones.

Will and myself looked at Charley.

"Let's go up there," Will said. "It'll be amazing."

Charley shook her head. "I can't," she said. "Another time. Tomorrow maybe. Not when I'm feeling like this. I might fall off."

"You can't fall off," Will said. "It's impossible."

But what did he know.

"Why is it impossible?" Charley said.

Right. Neither of us believed in him.

We staggered back to the hotel, walking in carefully through the panelled reception area, politely picking up our keys and up to the room again where we flopped on the big double bed. All of us was thirsty, parched beyond belief. Charley had a giant bottle of warm coke in her bag from the last pit stop and we took it in turns to pour some of that down us, which had a calming influence on all of us, and then there was nothing for it but to turn on the big telly and watch them dancing to the music for a while, doing a cage dance in some underground garage somewhere, which we soon got totally bored of.

"Let's watch something in Dutch," Will said. "It might make more sense like this."

"Okay."

"Let me do it."

I tossed the controller over to Charley and she flipped through all the channels slowly so that we could see what was on all of them.

There was nothing much on and anyway it didn't make much sense. But we had a good laugh at it, all these people talking their language: Bart Simpson, Lieutenant Columbo, Harrison Ford, Wonderwoman, all of them, even Van der Valk, the Dutch detective, talking in actual Dutch. We rolled another cherub and that was the end of it. We didn't care what we watched. Then it was Neighbours. Harold sounded like a complete prick in Dutch, which he is anyway, and then we stopped laughing. There was a football match on, but Charley wouldn't let us see it. I never cared much for football anyway.

"Boring, boring. I didn't come here to watch that."

"Oh. Go on. It's…"

No way, and she flipped it over, and we had no choice but to sit and watch the shopping channel, which was some Dutch woman demonstrating an egg slicer on a saucepan full of eggs boiling beside her. It was a magic egg slicer that shelled hard-boiled eggs first then cut them into neat slices, heaping them up on a plate next to her, then she picked up the shell, which had come off in one piece, and tossed it in a bin. Charley was fascinated. Okay, so it was watchable the first few times, but how long could it go on? Until they'd sold a billion egg slicers, that's how long.

She flipped back past the football—crowd roar—and on back to the dancing party we'd been looking at earlier and we was stuck on that again.

"Do you know," she said, "If I was back at home I'd watch any of that for as long as it was on."

"In English," I said.

"I'd watch any film," Will said. "Whatever it was, I'd watch it."

"But over here it all seems so boring," she went on, "Do you know what I mean?

"What about that," I said as some sex flipped by. "You don't see that at home. In England." All of a sudden I felt very English, very proud of it.

"Sex anyone?" Charley said.

We watched two blokes with enormous ding-dongs giving it to some lovely woman. I'd never seen nothing like it in my life. But Charley didn't want to watch that either. It made her feel uncomfortable, which was strange since she was into the exact same thing herself; so we slid off again, back to the endless party and the women prancing about in a cage. We was totally smashed again and we just zoned out to it, hypnotised by the flashing lights, unable to say a fucking word. This to us was like being together in paradise. We fell asleep propped up on each other. We fucking loved it.

In the night I woke up with my mouth full of cotton wool. I staggered over to the sink and ran my mouth under the cold tap, gulped some water, splashed it on my face and rubbed my eyes. I looked round and saw that I was on my own in the room. I put the bedside light on. It was around midnight. I went out into the corridor and along to Charley's room and knocked on the door. No answer. I went back to the room and slipped my coat on and went downstairs. I fancied a breath of night air, you know. I thought they was probably asleep in Charley's room—bastards— and I headed out for the front door and the people I could see out there stepping past in the street with smiles on their faces, out for a laugh and a drink at the midnight hour. I joined them.

It was brilliant out there, crowded as day, full up of people trotting off to places unknown. Some of the bars was still open. I had a powerful thirst for a long cool glass of foamy beer, so I went in the first one, on the corner opposite the hotel. Even though the big doors was open, so the place was open to the street, it was still hot in there. I didn't need my coat. I went up to the bar, ordered a lager and took it over to the only empty chair I could see, rejected from one of the copper-topped tables everyone else was drinking at, on its own, like me, next to a pool table with a bright blue cloth and a couple of young blokes circling it, making shots. I sat down and put my glass between my feet, shrugged my coat off and watched them playing, picked up my glass and downed half of it in one. Nothing ever tasted so good as that.

I had a fistful of change from the bar and plunked a likely looking washer down on the edge of the table, supposing it meant the same here as it done at home, which it did, because after a few more balls their game was over and a tall thin kid, about the same age as us, with floppy blondish hair and a face like a scrubbed potato, smiled over at me and held up a spare cue. I stood up. He picked up my coin from the edge of the table, added another one to it from his pocket, put them both in the slider nd held it in till the balls came down. He set them up in the normal way and we started playing pool.

I broke. Got nothing down. Left a stripe over a pocket for him and he cleared half the table before missing a long corner shot where the ball bounced back and rattled in its pocket like an argument that won't sink in and I stepped in to make my bid at fame It weren't a bad game as it happens. I surprised him by replying at all, let alone my riposte of a run of lucky trick shots I'd been practising in the shed for a year. Only two colours and a black left, and a chase you round the houses finale, which admittedly he won but raised his glass up at the end of it and pointed it at mine in an inquiring way.

"Yap," he said when he'd passed me another Dutch beer. "You?"

"Lee," I said.

"Lee Marvin," he said. "Cowboy."

"That's right," I said. "There's a lot of them where I come from."

He laughed at my joke. "Here also."

"Everywhere."

I said something else but he strained his ear forward as if he couldn't hear or understand me, and I realised his English weren't that good, not as good as the other Dutch people we'd met. We solved it by playing another game of pool on the blue table. It was weird in a way, the blue cloth. Playing on green baize was like playing on grass, it seemed natural, but the blue made it different, made it like a toy game in a toy world, like you was pushing the balls, these shiny new balls across a sky like rolling planets, or rolling them across the surface of a still pool. But it was still pool.

He won the second game. We shook hands, I offered him a beer but he held up his palms. He'd had enough.

"You stay in Utrecht?" he asked.

"Hotel," I said. "Over the road, with my friends." I pointed through the front towards the hotel. "Big hotel."

He looked impressed, but he was breaking up his cue and putting it away in its case. I finished my beer, said goodnight to him. He shook my hand. "Yap," he said.

"Lee," I said.

I went out onto the street again. I felt swimmy and a bit bloated in the gut region, burping on the too quick beers, just wanting to lie down and go to sleep. Sweat was pouring off me. I was sweating like a pig in my coat and the gun knocked against me: an extra weight, a worthless thing I was carrying that only slowed me down. Every time I moved I felt more tired, something heavy swilling around in my guts. It was a hot night, the hottest yet in a summer that was going to be one of those summers you never forgot. But I wanted to forget. All of a sudden I'd forgot who I already was—or maybe I'd never known who I was after all. I climbed up to the hotel room.

Charley and Will was back, again watching telly. They said something about having been in the hotel bar, but I didn't care much what they said. I just shrugged my coat off, dropped it on the floor and laid back on the bed, dizzy and a bit sick. Charley went to pick up my coat. I could feel her there beside me, stooping and picking it up.

I heard a clunk. The gun had fell right out my pocket.

"What's this," I heard her say, picking it up in its plastic bag.

"It's a gun," I said. "I found it one of the cases."

"A gun?" Will said. "Why didn't you tell us about it?"

"Don't touch it," I said. "It's got real bullets in."

"I don't like this," Charley said. "I don't like it." She was lying on her side, rubbing her paw as she sometimes done, and then her shorter, thinner arm, where it used to hurt her, then staring at it for ages like it was someone else's hand. She could never get out of thinking she's a freak, I thought. But she isn't really a freak. She's a beautiful girl.

"Don't worry about it," I said to her. I snuggled into pillow world. I wanted to say something else but I couldn't. There really was something wrong with me. The dope was a lot too strong and the beers had set it off again. It wouldn't have mattered what either of them said. I was spark out and gone into a fast slide show of some temple full of lovely cloths and all shining things, and then I was falling through it all straight into a dark, swirling toilet. It was his face I saw there bobbing around in the bottom of the bowl.

ELEVEN

It was brilliant waking up in the morning in the big bed, all three of us stark bollock- and cunt-naked, three bodies on top of the thrown back covers, not tangled together, lying more or less straight up and down, almost like dead. The room was half-dark, just a glimmer of sun through the closed green shutters. I looked over at them, both in a space of their own. Charley was on her front, her left leg cocked over to one side. Will was flat facing the wall. Three young bodies. Even mine was worth a second look. I'd lost so much weight. I couldn't believe the human body needed such a small amount of food; it was something I'd never known before.

I was first awake, but I wasn't in no hurry to wake anyone else up. I laid there. On my mind was these words I'd come around thinking about something about a small box someone was trying to give me, which had something—or nothing—inside of it. I looked at the outside of this box, which was made of a shiny polished walnut. I was saying to this other person—I don't know if it were a boy or a girl, no a girl that was it—what was I saying? I remembered it only for a micro-second and it was gone; another micro-second and the box itself was no longer a box but first a box-shaped blank and then nothing. I sat up, and looked around for the gun.

It was there on the small chest of drawers beside the sink. I got up and went over there, quietly splashed some water over my face and looked at it careful. They'd left it lying on the carrier bag, which was folded underneath it. I picked it up. The safety catch was off. I wondered how that happened. I wondered what they'd been doing of with it. Fucking idiots. They could easily have shot someone—me, for example, or one of each other. I clicked the safety catch over. Before I put the gun back in its bag, I pointed it at both Will and Charley in turn. I put it back in my coat pocket, which Charley had hung on the back of the door. I looked down at the two of them, sprawled out naked. I put all my clothes on and went out quietly to the toilet.

They was asleep when I got back, but I could have sworn they'd moved. They hadn't. They was definitely spark out. I slipped my clothes off and got back on the bed. I liked myself now. I liked the way I looked: a bit beefy, a bit short in the leg but more or less okay in proportions. I felt more myself, more comfortable. I also had a bit of a bone on from looking at Charley. I edged myself towards her and let it rest against one of the cheeks of her arse. She squirmed, and then, in her sleep, her hand came back and swatted it like a fly. I rolled away on my back, lying there for a few seconds; then she flopped over, put her arm across my chest and snuggled up. She was still asleep, her mouth half open against my shoulder, and I felt a thin line of dribble from her mouth run down into my armpit. I didn't move.

She was pressed against my side, a hot slab of girl's flesh, and sweat was running down between us. I carefully picked up her arm and moved her hand down so it fell on my prick, which I tried to manoeuvre in between her fingers and her palm. For a minute it worked and I felt her grip tighten on my todger, but then her hand seemed to know on its own it weren't where it wanted to be, and it jerked away, back up to where it was before. I moved my left hand across and pushed back her hair from her eyes, pushed a hunk of it back behind her ear and stroked it a couple of times. That was okay. She made a small encouraging, comforted sound and moved her leg over mine.

She was still asleep, but she knew, knew exactly what she was doing. I felt sloppy in the head and sank my head back in the pillow to rebuild itself around whatever was left of the contents and the shrivelled half of a walnut that held them in check. Chess was a game I played with Mum sometimes, but she didn't like it much when you beat her. I looked down at Charley out of the corner of my eye. Her eyes opened and her mouth was coming up to meet mine in a wet open kiss. I kissed her mouth back and reached over my other hand to stroke down her body, which she slid over on top of me with an oof from me and a sort of chuckle from her as she nuzzled in for a bite of my neck.

It was fairly easy by now, and we done everything slow and quiet, looking across at Will, who was still asleep and face to the wall. Doing it behind his back in a way that seemed to take an aching long time and was about the best thing I'd ever experienced so far, secret and dangerous, although it would have been okay too if he'd woken up and joined in with us; but she was trembling all over not to wake him, making precise small movements, as I was, which only goes to show, don't it, that however much you might be all in it together, there's always going to be a big kick to be had out of putting one over on the other bloke. Nothing like flooding up into her and her flooding down on me, her small mouth open in a silence, then holding on to me tightly, then rolling off and burying her head in the pillow making a quiet muffled screaming sound, tensed all over for a minute then all sloppy and happy against me.

We laid there together silent for a time. I was disappointed Will didn't wake up straight away but he was well gone. Bit by bit we started talking—about him, about him. I even started it.

"Will's right out," I said.

"He smoked a bit more of it," she said. "He was sick."

"I wonder if he's alright."

"He's alright."

"I wonder what we're going to do today."

"Same as yesterday, I suspect. Walk around. Perhaps we can go up that tower thing."

"We can do anything you like."

We whispered together as if not to wake up the big angry giant, but suddenly it didn't matter much if he woke up or not and we started talking normal; but then normal weren't good enough either and we started talking loud, then we was shouting at each other, laughing.

"THAT WAS A GOOD SCREW WEREN'T IT?"

"YES, CHARLEY, THAT WAS A VERY GOOD SCREW. THANKS VERY MUCH, CHARLEY."

"HAVE YOU GOT A HARD COCK AGAIN?"

"Sshhh!" I looked across at Will. He weren't stirring.

"WHAT ARE YOU GOING TO DO WITH THAT GUN?" she said. "SHOOT SOMEBODY WITH IT?"

Charley crawled over me and sprang up out of bed, giving me a good eyeful of her bent over bottom as she went round and pulled on her clothes. I done the same. Then she went to the bathroom. Then she came back. Then there was nothing for it. We went out together into the new morning light to get something to eat.

Not many people was about this time of day. I was thinking we could go to the bar where I went last night but the shutters was still down. Somewhere else then. One thing I did know as Charley took a hold of my hand: we was all stars. Even Will. Didn't we know it. We was the three stars of this film we was making up ourselves as we went along. A film about a runaway train in tulip land, off the tracks and bumping across the flat fields to anywhere. And, so the story went, once a star, always a star, coming up every day at the same place, shining down on a world that has only turned over in its sleep. Wake up you silly world, I thought.

I wanted to do it with Charley again. It was different on our own, better, and I temporarily forgot she had also done it on her own with Will, and she wouldn't have minded that much if it was him walking beside her in this pale morning sunshine in Utrecht. She looked innocent, but she knew things a girl of her age shouldn't know. I don't mean about sex and that. Other things. I could see it behind her eyes and in the troubled way her clear forehead would buckle in half sometimes. I wanted to know what she knew, but, like everything else about her, I thought it would be easy enough to find out by asking her questions. I felt pleased with myself, thinking them up as we walked along looking for somewhere to eat in, somewhere open.

"Charley," I said to her. "Can I ask you something?"

"Of course you can, Lee," she answered me.

"Who do you think the boss of this trip is?"

"You are," she said, then: "Is that all you can think of to ask?"

"Why me?"

"You just are, that's all," she said, and hesitating: "Where did you say you got that gun?"

"I found it in the bloke's big case."

"Why didn't you tell us about it? That really freaks me out, that does."

"I dunno." I was being honest. "I was going to throw it away, in case anyone got hurt."

She nodded, feeling a bit better about it, so it seemed. The gun was still in my coat pocket, on the back of the door. "Have you fired it off?" she asked me.

"Yeah," I went, "in Delft, down by the river—there was an old warehouse or something." I decided not to tell her about the tiles. "I fired it a few times. It was really fucking loud."

Her mouth was open in a round and her eyebrows had shot up, her staring eyes about to fill with tears—a peculiar expression that was amazing, tragic, over the top: it made me want to laugh till I realised she really did feel so desperate, uncertain. All her fear and her loneliness showed through in that look—it was a frightened answer to my last question. I thought what it said was that she was in my hands, I weren't in hers, like she said.

And then, as if I could conjure up whatever was wanted by thinking of it, a café was open right there, a few early birds drinking their coffees at the bar, and we slipped inside its shade. We sat down, ordered the full English breakfast. I can't remember much about the place. It was just another place to eat and drink in. Charley had her bag with her. I hoped she had a few Guilders in it to pay. I was cleaned out from the bar.

"I met a local last night," I said. "He said his name was Yap."

"What sort of name is that?"

"It's a Dutch name."

"And was he yappy?"

"No," I said. "He didn't speak much English."

"Pity," she said.

And soon we started chewing our food. The same food with subtle differences of the sort which don't make something worse, they make it slightly better if anything, but I can't remember it as nothing but the usual English breakfast anymore than I could describe the smell of our having had sex that surrounded us as we sat there noshing on Dutch bangers and back bacon and free range eggs hatched in the shade of windmills, collected in a basket by a milkmaid from the wrapper of a caramel, cracked in a sizzling pan by a little Dutch boy with nothing else to do with his fingers and served on fresh white bread, all fluffy, all sopping from the bread cow.

But there's some things you can't forget. With me it was Warren Hopkins, Les Hopkins, and my Mum. With Will—I didn't really know—something seemed to have pulled him away from himself, the self he was as I knew him, ever since we'd got in to the car and picked up Charley. With her it was a straight don't know. It was her who'd made this trip into what it was, she who was driving it on the way it was going, by coming, by having sex with us. Me and Will would do just about anything to just to keep this situation going as it was going, that was the truth. She weren't hard to understand in a way. But I had no idea what had made her come with us or be the way she was with us. Without trying to be, trying to be the opposite, she was a complete mystery.

She looked across at me over her half-demolished plate, her mouth bulging out on one side, held her hand up over it in a gesture of being polite. I sat back, looked away, and next minute she was throwing up over the table. She grabbed her napkin, held it over her mouth, stood up. She looked at me and fled towards the back, towards the toilets. I was stood up too and the bloke had come round the counter with a big cloth and he whisked her plate away and wiped the table.

"She isn't well," I said. I went to go after her.

"Let her," he said. "Let her."

I took my coffee over to the bar and sat there sipping it while he finished cleaning the table. He finished it off briskly, matter of factly, without seeming to care that much about what had happened. It was all in a day's work to him. He looked up, done.

"You are out late," he said. "She is not used to drinking. You must look after her."

I looked innocent. I was innocent. "No." I said. "It's not what you're thinking."

"Never mind," he said. "It doesn't matter." He scribbled out the damage and now placed it on the counter in front of me on a saucer.

I looked at it. Quite a hefty slice of Dutch change. I pointed to Charley's bag, which she'd left on the back of her chair. "She's got the money," I said.

He picked up the saucer, screwed up the bill and tossed it away in the bin behind his copper counter.

"We'll pay," I said.

"This young lady should drink some water," he said. "Perhaps drinking another cup of coffee, too."

I sat there, waiting. Eventually she reappeared, pale and tottering, her head hanging low. She picked up her bag and came to my shoulder in a way that said she wanted to go. "I'm so sorry," she said to the bloke.

"It's alright." he said. "Would you like some coffee? Some water?"

Charley shook her head.

"Have a coffee," I said. "Sit down for a while."

"No, I'm fine now." She reached into her bag. "How much?"

"It's alright," he repeated. "No pay."

And then we was outside again on the cobbled street and heading back to the hotel.

"Do you want to go in somewhere else?" I asked her.

"I want to go home," she said, and burst out crying. "I know I'm being pathetic, Lee, but I just want to go back home to my own bed."

"Well," I said. "You can't, can you—and that's that. None of us can, not yet."

"What's going to happen to us?"

"Nothing," I said. "We're just having fun, that's all."

"Look—we've got to go back sometime."

"True," I said, "true. But meanwhile we've got to enjoy ourselves with what time we've got left."

"That's like saying to, to a sheep or a pig that it's got to enjoy itself because it's going to get slaughtered later."

"Well, they do, don't they."

"But they don't know what's going to happen."

"Neither do we."

"It's not going to be good, is it, Lee. Be honest."

"It might be—you don't know that."

"Hold on, hold on—you're not stupid, are you?"

"I hope not."

"Well stop pretending to be," she said. "Because we are going to get slaughtered and that's real."

"Not necessarily."

She looked at me. I couldn't think of a way out, of any way we was going to avoid getting into a massive amount of trouble for what we had done.

"It might not be that bad," I said. "I mean, what can they do to us?"

"They'll put us away, you mong."

Back at the hotel we went up in the lift in silence. Charley went to her little room, stepped into the darkness of it and closed the door. I went into the big room. Will was stirring in bed. He turned over and looked up at me, half-blind without his specs on. I could see his mind trying to form something to say, but he flopped down onto the pillow: what he was going to say was half-formed then half of nothing again, and he plunged back down into the best place for him.

It might have ended there—just petered out in a hotel in Utrecht, Charley whining us to a standstill and Will and myself fighting over her but never getting to understand what made her go. Okay, you could say it was the truth she was speaking in a way and in another way she was only pointing out that we wasn't going nowhere, there was nowhere further we could go, and we hadn't got very far in the first place.

It was impossible for us to think of nowhere to go because anywhere we did go would only be a way of putting off going back, which we had to sometime, she was right. I laid there thinking about this. For me it didn't matter much. I was happy to play the delaying game, forever if needs be, and whatever you was handed out at the end would turn out to be the price, and however much it was somebody was sure to be on hand to make sure you paid it in full. So maybe she did have a point: if we went back under our own steam they might let us off lighter. The ideal would be to drive back the way we'd come down, up onto the ferry and over the water, off at Parkeston Quay, down Clacton and back in the same parking spot, then lock up the Peugeot, leave everything as it was and stroll back into our normal lives.

Charley could just put on the Woolworth's uniform and come back in from lunch. Will and myself could get the bus back to Jaywick, maybe have a Wimpy and chips on the way or stop off in the arcade and play Bash-A-Mole for an hour or two first—and who would know we'd been away. It almost fitted, except for the more spectacular part of our getaway. Charley weren't going to get away with a plea of amnesia. Will's explanation of multiple personality syndrome—or alien abduction—was unlikely to be acceptable. My plea, my defence. I ran away because I was a feared of the Hopkins family. But I couldn't say it, no way.

We couldn't go on, but we had to—there was no way off the roundabout except right onto your head. The gun was an even worse thing. I wished I'd lobbed it into the river in Delft. I wished I'd never found it. I wished it hadn't fell out of my pocket last night. I thought it was the gun, really, that had upset Charley. We couldn't go on, but we must go on. I turned over, deciding to get in another couple of hours shut-eye before getting up to face whatever it was that had to be faced. The immediate future and where it was going, probably somewhere not too good.

I was woken up by Will. He seemed in a good mood, the room was spick and span. He'd picked everything up, refilled the suitcases, cleaned up last night's mess. He sat on my edge of the bed and started talking as soon as I was awake and he sounded like the old Will I knew. Will wasn't downhearted at all. He was absolutely fucking full of it. Full of plans, full of weird little things he'd thought of to do in town—and what we should do next.

"We've got to head for this place—" he said a name "—it's where three countries meet, on top of a hill in—" he said the name again "—I think if we make it there we'll know what to do after that."

"Drive home?"

"No," he said. "We've got to get to somewhere we can get jobs, maybe as farm helpers or something like that. Charley could work in a bar, easily."

"We can't stay away forever and ever," I said, "We're going to have to go back and face it."

"Don't be stupid," Will said. "Why would we want to do that?"

I got up again, hopped into my clothes, "Because sometimes you've got to face reality, Will. "Okay, we've had a bit of fun, maybe we could have been a bit more careful about it, but its obvious that, sooner or later, we're going to get caught—and even if we don't we'd be better off going back ourselves and facing the music. Charley wants to do that and I think she's right. I mean, it's not perfect, but what else can we do?"

"I just told you."

I was on my feet. His enthusiasm was an infectious disease—it injected me with great annoyance. I sprang round the room, looking for something to throw at him. How could he believe in such crap? It just came out of his mouth and he expected you to follow it. To follow his example, for no reason other than because he was following it himself. But in this case there was a lot to be said for looking on the bright side, for heading on to wherever it was. "We'd never get jobs," I said. "They'd sus us straight away. We ain't got no passports or nothing."

"Yeah, we have."

"Charley hasn't."

"We've got these." He reached into the top of the big case and pulled out two passports from a compartment in the lid. "More Spanish passports, one for you and one for Charley."

"When did you find these?" I opened one—it happened to be the woman's. She had dark, shining hair.

"Just now, when I was tidying up. When did you find the gun?"

"In Delft," I said. "I was going to chuck it away."

"You should have done," Will said. "But I suppose it might come in useful."

"For what?"

Will laughed, shrugged. "Bank robbery?"

"Jesus."

"Joke, joke," he said. "Look, I've got it all worked out. We can definitely get somewhere with these. Charley can dye her hair, you can—" he laughed "—lose a bit more weight."

"I've lost loads of weight." I looked down at the bloke's passport. He was as thin as a wafer, in a neat, dark suit, his short hair combed straight back from a face nothing like mine, about forty-five, with a moustache. His name was Ramon Rodriguez. "I'd need plastic surgery to pass for this bloke."

Will said, "It's all method acting. You can make yourself become anyone—" he snapped his fingers "—just by assuming the correct mental attitude. By controlling your emotions, and directing them into another person you want to be."

"That's impossible, Will." He was hopeless. He was still back in his Mum's chalet living in his made up, cardboard world. On the other hand—nothing. "It might work for Charley," I said. "She could look a bit like that woman, if she dyed her hair."

"You could use your own passport, or just put the photo in this one."

"Go where?"

"Anywhere," he said. "What about Germany? Belgium?"

"Be realistic," I said. "We're not going to no other countries."

"Why not?"

"You know we can't really do none of that," I said.

"Well, I could."

"You wish."

Will laughed again and somehow that made it seem alright. He was probably half-right, I thought. We should look on the bright side in this life instead of thinking we was fucked before we started, and I hoped we could cheer Charley up and carry on to this place where three countries met on a hill: Holland, Germany and Belgium. It would be something we could tell people about in years to come. I imagined us all joining hands in a circle at the top of this mountain, or hill, or whatever, each of us in a different country not our own and making a sort of United States of Europe.

"What was the name of this place again?"

"Roermond."

In my head I saw us all turning away and walking down different hillsides into separate countries, saying nothing, not even looking at each other, never to meet again. I thought it would be like that whatever happened so I might as well get used to the idea now. We should carry on to Roermond. It would be a good way of keeping our spirits up—it might even appeal to Charley. I definitely wanted to go there. Why not? Charley was right in a way, in every way, but I wanted it all to go on and on forever.

Some people come into this world meek and mild and leave it just as meek and mild when the time comes. I remember my Mum saying that, and your father was one of them, she said. And I thought I was probably one too. Charley you would have thought wasn't one of the meek ones, but she did have that side to her, the side that needs protection in a way a bloke isn't going to get, and in a way she hadn't got much of it either. Charley weren't that strong, I thought.

Charley came in later wearing fresh clothes. Her hair was wet from the shower. She looked a lot happier. She stood in front of us fingering her hair dry and flicking it back behind her ears.

"Feeling better?" I asked her.

"Much better, thanks, Lee."

"Weren't you well?" Will asked her.

"I was sick," she said. "I feel a lot better now."

I was relieved. I like it better when everyone's in a good mood. I hoped we wasn't going to hear no more about us getting caught or having to go back. Instead we could have some more adventures in Utrecht. Lunch for instance. Perhaps we could go back to that place beside the canal and this time we could have something a bit different than chicken and chips.

Which is exactly what we done. I remember once in a class you said something about how your father had been set in his ways. I remember you said that your ways was set too, and if you're not careful you can get too set in their ways, so they become your own, or something like that, and how we should try and find our own ways, ways that suited us not just be our parents. And I remember thinking I wished I knew more about my own Dad's ways than I could remember.

But there we was. Having chicken again. It was tragic but we thoroughly enjoyed it, sitting out in the slight breeze from the canal and licking the fat off our fingers—the fat of the land—because it was true we was living off it and you never quite know how much of it is going to be left nor for how long it's going to go on. The place was buzzing with life and we buzzed along with it, just talking crap, savouring every mouthful of Dutch beer foam as if it was the last beer we'd ever taste on Earth. Will got hyper, going on and on about this place Roermond. I was pleased and happy to see Charley going along with it and asking him questions although she knew full well he'd never set eyes on the place, and between us we knew we was going there next and that helped us feel that, hey, we was still winning at the moment and to see our prime directive more clearly, which was to carry on doing so for as long as possible.

Next to us was a family. Dutch. But that's all I remember now. I remember. I remember. I never did like eggs. Horrible gloopy things that come straight out of a chicken's arse. I remember saying to my Mum once that I must've ate a bad one, but she said no, no Lee, it was your Dad. He never liked eggs. He would never eat an egg and now he's passed that on to you. It's funny what you remember, but the funniest thing about it was how you remembered it all different by being in this other place a few hundred miles across the North sea, almost as if it wasn't real, just something you dreamed, but more real than any dream, and at the same time it wasn't nothing much.

We walked back to the square in the sun. The sun had us in a prison of its own making but not a bad prison, a prison of skin such as you was in when a woman touched you. The hotness touched you all over and you prickled with it, the air brushing past you like a crowd of smiling people on holiday, and nothing bad could happen to you.

There was this church spire thing we was going to go up yesterday. It was still there waiting for us. We was feeling good, so we decided to go up it there and then. We joined the queue of everyone eating ice-cream and talking in languages. Charley started talking about how she could change her handwriting to be however she wanted it to be. This was because Will had showed her the woman's passport back in the hotel and said she would look like her enough if she dyed her hair black. Now I think of it, I think this is what cheered up Charley, because the woman was beautiful and grown-up looking.

People kept tumbling out into the square with excited expressions on their faces, as though they'd been on a ghost train or a helter skelter, and the queue kept getting shorter in front of us and longer behind till we got into the beautiful cool old church, which we looked around for a bit, then climbed up the stairs, which you was only allowed to go up about ten people at a time, and then we was at the top looking out at the furthest away surroundings.

When we got up there you realised what was so special about it—a long view of everything, right out to the edge of the city. It was like being at the top of a lighthouse where we was the lights shining over everything at once—Charley, shorter, looking over the parapet; Will and myself leaning, pulling back from the dizzying look of tiny people looking up, hurrying about in magnetised lines, the arch of our hotel was like something a mouse could run under for cover, the high clock of the town hall was below us, its procession suddenly in progress: a butcher, a baker, a reaper, a town crier ringing a bell for the year to change back to zero. Not likely.

A look out got you over the roofs towards a round horizon in which this little bit of the world was nestling: a shining city of silver and glass spires on one side, on the other an old crooked place where red and grey tiles quilted into one another, fell away to the ground in a series of slopes you could ski down in your pyjamas. You'd land unhurt in a winding cobbled street, jump up and set off in the moonlight for a meeting with an old blind man with a shop window full of puppets. It was a mustard town where lived a dream twister. I was next to still blabbing on and on Will and a happy, smiling Charley, who was pointing out at the distant glass slabs. It shone up there and a breeze kicked air into your lungs and woke you up to the benefits of being alive on a planet full of everything that had been made on its surface by other people.

"We are the Zarbis," Will shouted out. "We are the Zarbis— and its okay."

"Who are the Zarbis?" Charley asked him.

"Ant people," I told her, "on Doctor Who. Will's got every old episode on VHS."

"No I haven't," Will said, "I've only got the annual for 1966 That has them in it— the Zarbis and the Lepidoptera."

"What are these Lepidoptera when they're at home?"

"Blind moth people," he said, "from the planet..." He couldn't seem to remember what planet, which was one good thing. "...Lepidopterus? Lepidopteron?" He insisted, on and on, but I could tell it was all starting to fade out on him.

I didn't want to listen. Nor did Charley neither. We just wanted to look and be cleaned out of all that shit inside us from the below world. All the other people who'd come up with us was a lot more quiet than us, some of them even had binoculars. We didn't even have the right money for the telescope but we could see far enough on our own. We went quiet. There weren't no set time limit for staying up there, but we stayed a long time, till the others was halfway down the stairs maybe, then we clattered down to let someone else come up and have a look at the world from up here. It looked like a heaven where you could do anything because God said it was so easy. Not as easy as thinking about it, but as easy as what we'd done, which was fairly easy, I suppose.

Downstairs we spilled out again on the square looking as dazed and shocked and happy as the other people we'd seen coming out, as if from a Ghost Train. I was slightly wrong there though. It weren't like seeing a painted ghost or a rubber bat or a real skeleton, nor was it like sliding with your heart in your mouth, banging down a blind sickening tunnel to the ground on a dusty old mat. Yeah, it was a lot better than those things, and we felt temporarily cured of whatever made us all feel so confused and fucked up earlier. We went back to the hotel in relief and surprise and we had another smoke and listened to the radio for a couple of more hours.

TWELVE

Utrecht was a kicking little town at night; there was plenty of places to go; plenty of clubs, plenty of everything you could possibly want—and get—if you had a pocketful of free money and no time limits, no restrictions, just as long as it took till you'd had enough of everything, just long enough to spend every last squashed Rolo from the Woolworth's till.

We went to a bar first, then we went to another bar. We walked past the place where Charley had chucked up her breakfast. That was still open but she didn't want to go in there again. Instead we went to another bar with loud music coming out of it. We got another round in and elbowed our way through to the back where there was a little disco playing and strobe dancing lights flashing up the walls, playing hits from the seventies. Charley handed Will her drink and done her dancing queen bit, spinning and strutting round the floor—which was half empty—but we didn't join her.

She came back to join us and drank her drink and laughed at how pathetic it was compared to the Hippodrome; so we drank up there and went on to another place, a place where there was a queue to get in—which meant it was a good place, Charley insisted, as good as going up the spire, except this time it was downstairs—down underground in the cellar of one of these old places which Utrecht was full of. I must admit I weren't expecting it to be nothing too special.

But when you got in the door—minus and arm and a leg—it opened up into a big underground cave that ran off into several different rooms, all with something different happening in them at the same time. In one room was a place where people was playing skittles, in another a disco with everyone going mental on the dance floor, in yet another a bar where you could chill out at low slung chairs and glass tables, and a place where you could get something to eat. It weren't that big down there, and as it was early on in the night, not too crowded.

We walked round and had a good look at it all. People was looking at us every time we went into a new bit, people a few years older than us who was a bit better dressed—except for Charley, she looked fucking brilliant as usual. There weren't nothing for it but to start dancing. We chucked our top clothes in a corner and went out there. The music weren't too bad for dance music. This was the right place and after a few beers we was ready to freak out and make cunts of ourselves—which was good because we was all together, as one, holding hands and going for it. We couldn't give a toss what anyone else thought because we knew we was the only important people in the place—the only ones who'd nicked a car and driven it across the North Sea to get here. Charley was beaming a smile and twirling around.

We sweated some of the drink out of us and went to get another one in. There was a bit of a crush at the bar by now. Will pulled out a little cherub he'd rolled up earlier—and after we caught a whiff of it from elsewhere we sparked it up and passed it around. That was even better. We took our drinks back to the dance floor and started at it again, really going for it by this time. Charley broke free and done a brilliant turn on her own, dancing like cat woman, drawing her forked fingers back from her eyes, pointing to each of us in turn to come forward and dance round her, which we both done.

We took it in turn to go round to the bar and we made a little nest for ourselves in a corner by an arch against the roughcast cellar wall and it turned out Will had brought the dope with him and we rolled a couple more of the little cherubs. We couldn't talk in there, it was too loud and it took you over and—like it should be—there was nothing anymore; it took your cares away. Mum's cares got a little bit lighter when she toked up on her key-ring pipe and flopped out not giving a shit about nothing, and I saw for the first time that this was the secret of happiness. Happiness wasn't to be expected except by forgetting the truth.

"I know," Will shouted in my ear. "Let's do a pyramid."

"What do you mean?"

"We'll be the bottom and Charley can be the top. We'll lift her up on our shoulders."

"Okay," I said.

Charley weren't up for that. "Fuck off," she said. "I'm not making a complete tit of myself."

We respected her wishes of course, and we played at the cannon instead, charging each other and bouncing off our shoulders, spinning away and laughing and doing it again till we could feel the tenderness of bruises we would remember this night by in the morning like blood coming up under a new tattoo. We was gladiators in a friendly fight and as the music broke off into segments of an equal juice content we was strongly moving forward from one bit to the next in a timeless time of our own greatness and splendour in the cellar of a bar that had filled up with people looking for the same thing. We stepped aside for them, we wasn't greedy.

We went round to the food part and held up three fingers for three burgers. When we'd ate the burgers we went round to see if we could get a game of skittles. It was weird to have a skittle alley in a place like that: an old one such as you might see a few old boys playing in a pub in Essex, people who'd grown up casting wooden balls down a narrow sluice to knock down a few bashed up lumps of firewood, chalking up scores they crossed off in batches of five, bundled up like years as they lived and died over weighty matters like who was going to be top dog. I'd never played before. I knew I'd never be good enough.

A small group of neat looking types was playing quietly, sipping their beers, in buttoned down checked shirts and pressed pre-faded jeans. We sat down on a bench at the side of the alley, mainly to chill out. We was a bit dazed and stoned and drunk and sweating. We cheered a bit every time one of these blokes let go of one of the wooden balls and it clattered down the alley. They was intensely deadly serious about it. One of them looked across at us, a bit annoyed, but then a wide spotty smile broke out on his face.

"Lee," he called over to us, "The cowboy."

"Yap," I lifted my glass, bowed slightly.

He came over and stuck his hand out; I stuck mine out and shook his. "These are my friends," I said. "Charley and Will."

He looked impressed that I had any friends and the others looked impressed that I knew him. They shook hands with him as well and he beckoned us over to meet his mates.

"Yop," he said, and pointing to the other one, "Yip."

We shook hands. Yop and Yip were mighty impressed with Charley. She just sort of floated up in front of them like a dancing balloon, her mouth open, her teeth carefully arranged around her mouth and her eyes lit up like a little doll that's had its tummy pushed in the right place, and her head bounced from side to side like the animated head of a just hatched raptor with drool falling out of its mouth, blinking and sizing up its first strike, but there was something else we knew about her: she was only a grass snake.

But she made them start back, as if a torch was being flashed right in their eyes. They give her three balls anyway and she got first go at the skittles Yip scurried down to set up for her. She scooted them down there in a pretty straight line and we leapt up into the lead. Yap chalked up the scores, England against Utrecht united, but they didn't let us have it our own way by no means. Will almost had to be sent off for throwing balls down the alley in sheer violent frustration. I weren't too bad. Charley occasionally lived up to her fluky beginning. Yap, Yip and Yop was more consistent players, so they won the day, as such people tend to, but it was a brilliant laugh anyway and it kept us out of trouble for the rest of the night.

We kept telling them how good their English was, which it was compared to our completely non-existent Dutch, and they asked us the obvious questions about ourselves and we tried to find out something about them in turn. It was easier asking the questions than understanding the answers, because we wasn't used to listening to foreigners trying to talk English. They wasn't used to trying to understand real English people either, although they must have had some sort of practice. We answered slowly.

"You are on holiday with parents?" Yap asked me.

"No, we're on our own," I said. "All together."

They thought it was a really weird set-up.

"You like Utrecht?" Yop said. "Is nice place, yes?"

"Yeah, it's great," Charley said. "Really lovely."

"You have job?" Yip asked. "You have good job with money?"

"I'm a policeman," Will said.

"I'm a fireman," I told them.

"No," said Yap. "I think you are not. Charley, you have job?"

"Yes. You are model?" Yop asked her in a shy way.

"I am secretary," Charley mimed typing with her eyes closed. "I work in office."

He looked at her hand, which obviously didn't belong to no secretary. "You come on train?" he asked her.

"Car."

"You have car?"

"In England everyone has car."

"Child has car?"

"We are not children."

"No, you are not. But you are young. You must be rich to have car."

"Do you have car?"

"No," said Yap.

"No," said Yop

"No," said Yip.

They was natural questions, nothing wrong with them, but they sounded a bit nosy to us. We didn't want to answer but we didn't want to piss them off either. I could tell they wondered whose girlfriend or sister Charley was, but they didn't tackle that one head on. They took it in turns to ask us about everything. When I asked them what they done for a living they slid away from it. Maybe they was students or something, they looked a bit like students, or maybe they was still at school. Finally we decided to head off back to the hotel. We'd lied to them a lot but we knew we hadn't been good at it.

We shook hands again. They seemed to like doing that.

"Tomorrow," Yap said. "You will come to my house, if you like it. I show you Dutch people house. Have a drink. I show you some things in Utrecht."

"Thanks, we'd really love to come," Charley said nicely.

Will put together a smoke as soon as he got up. Charley told him he was a thicko weirdo. I laid there on the bed waiting for peace and quiet to break out. She went back to her room. I watched some crappy cartoons on the kid's channel till it was time to go downstairs. It was better out in the sunshine again, but not that much better. We waited outside the hotel. We was looking forward to meeting up with Yap, but for some reason we'd had a bad morning.

"Hello," Yap said. "You have been waiting long?" He had a big smile on his face. He looked so pleased to see us that we had to start acting happy so as not to seem like miserable cunts.

We shook hands with him again, it seemed to be just the right thing to do.

Yap lived in a new part of Utrecht, so the first thing was to step over that line between the cobbled, twisting roads of the old town onto wide streets between tall glass buildings and all the rest of new Utrecht. I thought it was funny how they hadn't tried to blend it in at all, hadn't tried to do none of it in roughly the same style. They started building modern next to the old, somewhere that looked a bit like America, or the industrial estate on the other side of the river in Manningtree. In a way it was a giant, older Jaywick. I wanted to tell him about where I came from, but I felt ashamed of myself. How could I say anything about Utrecht when I myself came from a shithole like Jaywick?

We walked past some big ugly blocks of flats.

"Do you live in one of them?" Charley asked hopefully.

"She wants to go up in the lift," I said.

"No," Yap laughed. "It is not far by now."

We turned by what looked like a big new college building towards a street of small low houses—bungalows. "This is like where I live," I said.

Charley snorted with laughter.

"I live there too," Will said. "In my head."

But they was a bit like a row of Jaywick houses. A bit bigger of course, a lot newer of course, plus they looked like they'd been thought out by somebody who could do a bit more than measure off a few lengths of four by two and lash them together with a few Irish jays. With these houses you couldn't quite see what they was made of. There we was, all the way out to sea, if you see what I mean, and more nervous than at any time so far in this weird story we'd thought it was going to be perfectly okay to make up as we went along.

Yap lived in one of the bungalows, which was slightly up on stilts as some of them are at home, and it had a high roof on it as though they just couldn't stop themselves turning it into a three floor house after all. He unlocked the door and we followed him inside, back into the kitchen where it turned out he had prepared a salad meal for us to eat, all laid out at a low pine table.

"What a lovely place," Charley said, doing her woman duties. "Do you live here with your parents?"

"I am living with my Mum," he said, "she is out working in the day."

"What does she work at?" Will asked politely.

"Software engineer," he said. "She is working at the University here—making a storage for their ethnic music collections."

"What sort of music is that?" Charley asked.

"Africa—those places," Yap shrugged.

"I know what that is," I said. "She puts them on a computer."

"Yes," he said, "you are right."

We sat down. It made a change from chicken and chips. We dug in straight away, cutting up fresh bread and dolloping things onto our plates, some of which I fancied, some of which I didn't. There was some salted sprat-type things there that made me feel a bit rough even to look at them; but on the other hand there was some sheets of ham, boiled eggs (don't touch them) and a good selection of salad items which looked fresh; some partly boiled potatoes with the skins still on and some other sort of fish lolling in tomatoey blood with its guts hanging out. Yap popped one into his mouth and started crunching up the bones. I got my head down, tucked into what was in front of me, which, as I say, was a fairly good spread. Mum says I'm just like Dad in that way—I prefer tinned peas to frozen ones. But she's not much different. It's like when you go around the supermarket with her, she's saying, "Well, I'd like to try all these things but we just can't afford them—what if you didn't like it, Lee—which you wouldn't."

Will helped himself to anything and everything, as oily as you could get it and more. He wolfed it all down. Charley took a peck at everything in turn, a couple of spoonfuls of this and that. Last night she'd been bold as brass, today she was timid for some reason, and I realised if there was one thing I was never going to understand, it was the ways of womankind, mainly because I only had my own Mum to go on, and if that was how it was, I didn't want to know much more about the subject.

It was brilliant how he'd gone to so much trouble over us. I couldn't remember when I'd ever done nothing like it for someone, in fact I knew I hadn't. But I made a mental note to be more like him in the future, because it seemed to me that the way he was were a better way to be than anything I'd ever seen or thought of. There obviously weren't a catch to it either, because there was three of us and we could easy have robbed him of all his earthly possessions, if he had any we wanted to take away with us. And just as this thought was crossing my mind, he said, because we'd all finished eating and was sipping some beers he'd got out of the fridge:

"Come on, please. I have something I am wanting to show you."

We looked at each other and followed him up a flight of steps to the upper deck into the roof of the bungalow.

"This is where I live most of the time. I have my bed and my things—it is very large."

He clicked on the light and we looked around the large low space. It smelled a bit musty. Charley sneezed. Most of the floor was taken up by an amazingly complicated four-lane Scalextric track. It was fucking fantastic, full of hairpin bends, crossovers, chicanes, little humpback bridges: a huge wobbly figure of eight with one long straights and a few shorter ones. There was a grandstand at the start-finish line full of tiny spectators, and a man in the act of bringing down a checkered flag. His layout had other features too—like banks of plastic straw bales at the corners, plus a sliproad in the centre where an ambulance and a fire engine was parked. Next to the bandstand was a tall commentary box, a man bent over a microphone inside it; on the roof was a TV camera with a cameraman looking into its viewfinder. I looked around for the pits. Sure enough a team of tiny mechanics in pale blue overalls was servicing one of the cars, changing a wheel, refuelling.

"That's incredible," I said.

Yap laughed quietly. "Now you can see why I have brought you."

Will was also entranced. "Did you make it yourself?" he asked.

"Not all," said Yap. "It was my father's. He started to make it when I was very small. For himself, in a way."

"I've never seen nothing like it," Charley said.

"So," Yap said. "Would you like to have a race or two?"

At the line four mini-coopers lined up across the track.

"An English car," I said.

"Yes," Yap said. "An old one—of the nineteen sixties. My father liked English things very much."

I wanted to ask him about his father. He sounded like an interesting person. I tried to imagine what sort of job he'd had. I wondered when he'd died. Whether it was a long time ago or a fortnight. But it would have been out of order to ask those questions—I wouldn't have liked it if it was myself—and so we all at down beside the transformer, picked up our controllers, squeezed their creaky spring-loaded triggers—and immediately threw our cars off the track from too much throttle. Yap got up and put them back at the starting line.

"I think we could do with a few practice laps," I said.

"Of course."

We started buzzing our cars around the track, or trying to anyway, flying off at every bend at first while Yap cruised around the whole circuit in a smooth, effortless exhibition of high-level driving skills, slowly getting the hang of it. I weren't having that. He couldn't even drive a car, so far as I knew, whereas I'd piloted us across half of Holland, and so I hung on his tail and tried to copy the precise amount of ease-off at the bends, till on about the fourth lap (they was big) I was blipping ahead of him on some of the straights, getting too cocky sometimes and coming adrift, putting myself back on and idling till he came past, then boot hard down to the next bend, blasting Will off at the chicane, leaving the track on the hump bridge—getting myself unslotted, blocking the track for Will—who tried to blast me out of his way but came off as well. Ha ha.

Charley had a natural gift. She just sat there cross-legged in her jeans, holding the controller in front of her in two hands, squinting at her car—the yellow one—with a look of intense concentration. First time she came by me my finger went sort of berserk on the trigger and I was straight off at the next bend. I looked across and she was smiling slightly. Will was trailing far back. The best he seemed to be able to do was a slow steady cruise, so he just done that. He couldn't be bothered to keep getting up to fetch his car—the blue one—or that's how it seemed to me. He weren't trying too hard, just looking glum and plugging on to the bitter end.

"Okay," Yap said, "I think that's enough practice. Now for the first race."

"I need more practice first," Charley said. "Otherwise you're just going to win every race."

"You can have as much as you like," he said, "but it doesn't matter, it's not serious, only having fun."

Charley nodded. "Okay," she said. "I'm ready." She took a deep breath and lowered her head, frowning in her concentration.

"How long is the race?" Will asked.

"Five laps," Yap said. "It is not too many, I think."

We raced each other around the long intricate circuit in the roof of Yap's Mum's bungalow. We raced for hours and hours, till our fingers went numb on the triggers, till our arses went numb, till our legs seized up from sitting cross-legged and our backs ached from hunching forward and our eyes ached from following the darting little mini-coopers, till we was sick of fetching them, till Will had clipped the grandstand with his foot and knocked it against the control tower and the TV crew plummeted to their deaths on the track; till the mechanics in the pits wandered off for a fag break and didn't even bother to come back to witness the outcome.

It weren't like nothing like that. Like anything. Like anything you gradually got better at it, till you didn't give a shit anymore, you was just a husk sitting there, a wired bored machine, removed, looking down on it all from no great height, a finger on a trigger— which took a bit of getting used to at first.

I remembered it as a thumb on a plunger, as it was on my old one that my Dad got out of the local paper and brought home in his boot in an old suitcase, with heavy old fifties cars, motors that worked by an electromagnet that made a row of steel teeth judder up and down on a spline of brass cogs on the back axles, cars that made a real racing racket as they slammed around a metal track—fucking amazing, especially the AC Cobra that blew away the D-type Jags, heavy so that when they flew off they could really hurt you, or hurt the dog, old Mick.

But we was soon all equalised to an extent so that we could give one another a race, and everyone's luck had run out, it was just pure concentration of four similar machines, even Yap was floundering in the end in a few dices with Charley. Will picked up the controller of the fastest car, but that only gave him a temporary advantage because his was the most wandering mind of all of us, always off somewhere else, twitchy at the best of times and unable to make full use of his available equipment. Charley had the disadvantage of her bad hand, but the advantage that it had made the fingers of her good hand stronger. We did about ten races and we all won some of them, if only by the others not being quick enough to find the slot, till the overall winner—Yap, of course—got up with a shy laugh, and said:

"I think it is time now for refreshment of the racers."

We got up and left the wrecked grandstand behind us and went downstairs to the kitchen. We sat at the table where what was left of the meal was still there. Yap got a big bottle of Coke out of the fridge and we rinsed the track dirt out of our mouths with it and picked at some of the leftover food.

Will laughed as he slurped at his glass and folded the last sheet of ham into his mouth with his fingers. He ate it in about five seconds. "That was great," he said.

Charley looked as happy as I'd seen her. "I feel like I've been off somewhere else," she said. "I feel like I've been miles away."

"You're like Penelope Pitstop," Will said. "Except—"

"You're a wanker," she replied to him. There was no arguing with her. Because she had been miles, we all had, and she was out in the lead, and there weren't nothing you could compare it to really. "I'm the best driver out of any of you—except Yap." She flashed him a big smile.

"It was good," he said, "Very good." He beamed at her, smiling all over his face, and it was obvious he thought she was a very nice girl. He wanted to marry her. We all did.

We sipped at our cokes and sat there waiting to be chosen. But no, no. It weren't really like that. In fact, there must've been something about the way the three of us was together that made it obvious to Yap exactly how we was together: what the situation was between us. And as I think back on it now I almost think I can see him guessing. He suddenly went red. He got awkward, stood up, walked to the sink to start washing up—to hide it from us. Charley got up too and went to stand beside him to help drying. We cleared the table, passing empty plates, wondering where to put everything.

"Thank you, my friends," he said. "But it doesn't matter—I can do it later."

We helped him anyway. We soon cleared everything up; there weren't nothing else to do and not much to talk about, at the end of it all, except the mystery of why he was so nice when he didn't have to be, which isn't such a mystery after all, unless you haven't come across it very often. Otherwise it was making us feel a bit awkward, because we had nothing to give except our good wishes, which we did, because it was right obvious we would have to go soon and have to say goodbye to him. I knew it, anyway.

"Your father," Will said. "I think he was a very clever man."

"My father died," said Yap. "Three years ago. We used to race a lot on this track."

"My father passed away," I said. "Eight years ago."

"Mine's dead too," Will said. "It's only me and my Mum."

"How weird is that," Charley said. "My father—I don't see him anymore, never."

Yap seemed surprised. It was a little bit strange, wasn't it. There we all was and none of us had a Dad, just memories. We sat there not saying nothing about it. There weren't much to say really. It was something we all knew about but there you are: there didn't seem all that much we could say to each other about it. Perhaps we didn't need to say nothing— we didn't. We was suddenly bound by that one thing, as if we was the only ones who didn't have Dads anymore. It felt like it should mean something though I couldn't say what it was; but it did seem to mean that Yap was one of us for now.

We was still sitting there when his Mum came in from work. She was a small, stocky lady with short grey bushy hair. She didn't seem tired from work—she looked busy, ready to get on with something else, and surprised to see us sitting around her kitchen table. She smiled in a friendly way and shook hands with all of us. Yap quickly explained who we was in Dutch. She put the kettle on, then started asking us questions about what we had done in Utrecht. Her English was perfect. She asked the same questions about ourselves as Yap had done, but she didn't seem so happy with the answers. She crossed her arms and nodded. Charley explained she was a secretary. The kettle boiled and she poured it into a white pot in which she'd shaken some loose tea-leaves. Suddenly she seemed to lose interest in us.

Yap was hovering there, a bit awkward like. We took the hint off him and stood up, said goodbye politely and stepped out in the sun.

"See you soon." Yap waved. "Tomorrow perhaps. If you have a car, I can show you some interesting place."

We said that sounded like a good idea and we headed off down the road to find our way back to the centre of Utrecht. It would have been good to spend another day with Yap, and at that minute it seemed likely that we would. That's one of the things I regret most about all this. I wish we'd spent more time with Yap when we had the chance. He was a nice bloke and I wouldn't have minded finding out more about him—and his Mum—and his Dad.

THIRTEEN

As soon as we got back to the hotel we started having another barney. It was about something stupid of course, but it went on and on, as they tend to, and by the time it calmed down we didn't want to do nothing except get in the car again and leave, forget about the place where it happened and put it far behind us as everything else, as far as Jaywick itself, far away as my Mum and hers—and as far as Will went I could've well done without him being in the car, but there you go, there weren't nothing I could do about it. He was in it for the duration.

When we got back he just kicked off for no reason, he just started getting gobby for nothing. I think it was Charley who started him off. No it weren't, come to think of it, it was me.

"Here, Will," I said. "Why did you tell Yap your Dad was dead when he's just gone to live in Lowestoft?"

"I can tell him what I like, can't I?"

Charley chipped in. "Is that right? You told me he was dead too you lying little toe-rag, just so..." She went quiet, remembering when he'd said that—back in Clacton when she was hero-worshipping him for saving my life.

"It was less complicated to say he was dead."

"No it weren't," I said. "You said it so nobody could have one up on you. You was lying to make yourself big, as usual."

"Yeah, well," Will said. "I am big, compared to you. Warren Hopkins was..."

"You just stood there," I said. "You didn't do nothing, not really."

"Anyway," Charley said. "I can't see what you've got against Warren. He ain't that bad. I would've come with him if he'd asked me—at least he's got his own car."

"Yeah," I said, "I wonder where he got the money for that."

"What do you mean?"

"Well, he's only the same as us. So where did he get the money for a motor like that."

"Saving up."

"What, from his weekend job in Asda?"

"So where did he get it?"

"I don't know," I said. "I'm only asking the question. Thieving, I suppose."

"Well, I don't have a problem with that," Charley said. "He's still got the car. It's better than not having one."

"Depends what you think about thieving," Will said. "I think it's disgusting myself."

"So what do you think this is then?" she said. "You've just done the same thing. So have I. So has Lee. What's the difference?"

He didn't have no answer to that. There weren't one. But I didn't want to put us in the same category as the Hopkins. I didn't want to be associated with them and it bothered me that Charley thought we was the same. The thought of her going with him—which I expected she must have done—made me feel sick to my stomach. Because as far as I was concerned Warren Hopkins was a fucking animal. You could say he didn't know wrong from right, but you wouldn't be saying much. He didn't know nothing.

"You're just a pair of silly little boys." Charley stuck the knife in: "Warren Hopkins, he's twice the man compared to you two put together."

There weren't nothing we could say to that. We just had to take it. We just had to accept that was the way she saw things, but not only that. We had to accept that the way she saw things was the right way, because we might have liked to think we was better than Warren Hopkins but we didn't have a leg to stand on. Shitty though it all was, every time after that when something came up which I had to make a decision on, I found myself thinking, well, what would Warren do if he was here, let's look at it from Warren's point of view, and Warren's answer would be so and so, as if Warren was really something, as if he had some sort of secret code to crack everything, when in another part of my brain—the good part—I knew Warren Hopkins' way was just to hit somebody and try to make them do what he wanted, or to nick something, or just be an out and out cunt to everybody, even when it would be obvious to most people he weren't going to get away with it in a thousand years. Except he usually did get away with it.

She weren't going to change her mind. She weren't even in two minds about it. She thought what she thought, and I've got to admit it was what most people think: that winning is the most important thing, that what you've got is the truest test of what you say, and by those standards everything I thought, which was only what I'd like to think, was a complete and utter load of fucking cock.

"Well," I said. "You're here with us and that's that."

"Worse luck," she said. "Well, I'm going out on my own to get pissed. And I don't want neither of you two trailing after me." She pulled on her shoes and slammed out of the door.

What now? A couple of minutes ago we'd been full of it, but all of a sudden we had nothing at all to say to each other. Surprise, surprise. Charley had won the argument—and I knew it weren't going to end there. She was going to prove it to us over and over again.

"All because the lady loves Milk Tray," Will said. "Methinks she likes it a bit too much that damsel."

"All because she was good at Scalextrix," I said.

The way how he said it was like he knew what he was talking about, but I knew he didn't know. He didn't know nothing that I didn't. It annoyed me. I laid on my side, away from him, closed my eyes. There weren't nothing to do except stay there and wait for her to come back. Will rolled a cherub and we smoked it watching some programme on telly—more music, more football, more of anything that took us away from what Charley was doing. But it didn't. We sat there, walled in, silent, feeling fucked up and trying hard to pretend it was a normal, good-time feeling.

After a while he flicked round a bit and found a film on. Goodfellas, in Dutch. I must know that film back to front by now. It's a bloody good film as it goes. It was funny hearing Robert DeNiro and Ray Liotta and that other nasty little cunt talking in Dutch-speak. They all had gravelly voices, but funny ones, making sounds that didn't quite seem to fit on the film. After a while me and Will started copying them, not the words but just the sound of them. The little one had a high squeaky voice and Robert de Niro had a deep one and the one who was telling the story had the weirdest voice of all. You couldn't imagine it coming out of him except it was, and the women all sounded like screeching puppets. We was laughing at it, but we wasn't laughing that much. We watched it right through to the ending, where he comes out of the front door in his wife's dressing gown and picks up the milk and the paper.

Watching something like that can make you feel better about yourself and put a whole different light on things so that even though you know it ain't true you know it might be. If we was the goodfellas we could have just slapped her around a bit. Everything would have been alright again after that, but it was difficult to see what would make this situation better. I wasn't thinking straight—you wouldn't be wrong to say that—but I thought none of it would have happened this way if it had been just myself and Charley on our own. We'd both have got along fine. Everything would have worked out quite easy then—ignoring that it wouldn't even have happened and her being the sort of girl she was, ignoring the reality.

After that there was nothing much to watch and we both just laid there on the bed, really zoned out by this time, wondering what had become of young Charley Price. I looked across at Will. He was fallen asleep. I got up and turned the telly off and turned out the light. My head was full of rags, stuffed full of choked up nothings. I flopped back on the bed and laid there. The room was turning, I felt a bit sick and when I closed my eyes there was purple dancing lights and at the bottom of a deep hole a few little figures I couldn't quite see was moving around on the stage of a toy theatre, moving in a circle like the models on the clock we'd seen from up the church spire. It was a dream. I didn't want to fall into that one. I didn't like the sound of what was going to happen in it. I kept pulling myself away to where its perfect sense turned back into a few pieces of wood propped up in a shed, or something similar.

Then I heard voices outside in the corridor. One of them was Charley's. The other one was—you guessed it—a bloke. Then they went off like a light that has lit up something for a minute and I felt better somehow, released from wondering what was going on, and I fell asleep because it was a lot easier than laying there thinking about what was definitely happening in Charley's room. I didn't need to find out nothing. I guessed she'd brought back somebody she knew. Not Yap, but one of the other ones. Yip— there'd been a spark there, I remembered. He was the best looking one. So much of life was simpler than you thought. All you had to do was think of the most obvious thing. She'd gone out looking for him. He'd been around waiting for her somewhere. There was no secret to it except maybe one between them, no real mystery. I fell asleep, happy I'd worked it out.

But when I woke up I felt like shit again. I'd been dreaming of Charley, the little bitch. Will, who seemed more and more of an arsehole to me, was still in dreamland. As ever. It was light outside, getting brighter. I got up, got dressed, went out to the toilet, washed myself in the bathroom. Sat on the end of the bed, listening for tell-tale sounds outside in the corridor. Which I didn't have to wait for for that long.

As soon as I heard a noise I went out there. I must've had my bat ears on because what I saw was Yop closing the door of Charley's room as quiet as anything and turning away to walk downstairs. He looked me full in the face. I forced a smile at him. He smiled back.

"Yes," he said. "I know. You are Lee. You are Charley's friend." He looked awkward, but he couldn't help sounding pleased with himself. "I am going home now."

"I'll come with you," I said. "I was just going outside for a breath of air. Thought I'd go and see if the baker's is open."

"Bakers?" he said. "Ahh, yes, yes, I think they will be open by now."

It was a beautiful day out again. We walked along in the beginning of it, not many people about, as I had with Charley a couple of days ago. Yop looked a bit rough. He obviously hadn't got much sleep.

"You going to work?" I asked him.

"Not yet," he said. "I have to go home, to clean myself. Then I will work." He let his shoulders sag. "I am tired."

"Where?" I asked. "What do you do?"

"This," he said, and he made a sort of pointing movement with two of his fingers. "All day—in factory. It is very boring."

I wondered what it was he was trying to show me. I didn't matter though. Soldering probably. Soldering some electronic gadget together in a factory, that's what it looked like. It didn't matter much. I didn't bother asking him to explain.

"I was with your friend Charley," he said awkwardly. "You don't mind?"

I shrugged. "Charley does what she likes," I said.

"Yes, yes, I see that. I am thinking I might be able to see her again."

Just then we passed a baker's shop, the smell of fresh bread wafting out the door.

"It is here," he said.

"Okay," I said. "I'll walk along with you for a bit and come back. No hurry."

"Okay," he said. But he weren't very happy about running into me.

He was a shortish bloke, a bit different from the others. Where they was blond, his hair was darker. He had a sort of thick neck though he didn't look strong with it. I noticed he had small hands, big eyes, and a thin quite cruel-looking mouth. I couldn't stand him. He was the sort of bloke who wouldn't give you the time of day if he didn't have to, but who would prefer telling a lie to the truth even if it was going to be more difficult to get away with a lie. I could tell these things about people.

We turned and went down onto the canal bank, near where the restaurant was where we ate. We walked along the opposite bank, along the path. There was nobody about, just a few ducks, and it was too early in the morning for them to even quack when they saw me.

"You live near Yap?" I asked him.

"Quite near," he said. "Not really." He was trying to avoid something, but I couldn't quite see what it was.

"So you met up with Charley," I said.

"Yes." He beamed all over his face. He obviously couldn't help it. "She is an incredible girl. But I think—" He laughed "—that you and your friend must already know that."

I hated him more than I'd ever hated anyone before. I couldn't believe Charley had it off with him. She must have been pissed out of her brains; that was the only excuse for that one. He speeded up, trying to get away from me on his short legs. Anyway, he didn't manage it. Because I pulled the gun out of my pocket. It was just there, I had the opportunity to use it, and as we walked I found it and I clicked the safety catch off and I held it there ready.

He seemed to think it was a toy. He put his hands up. Then he put them down.

"She likes it," he said. "She likes it in every way." He laughed nervously. "I like it too." He laughed again. "I like her hand especially."

There was something weird about the way he said this. Something that made me feel gutted inside, a sort of lurching feeling that you get when can't believe in something no more. He was talking in a sick way. And he was staring straight back at me, there was no escaping from it. I mean, I don't know why but I just pulled the trigger and shot him straight in his stupid grinning face. There was hardly any time for him to put his hands up or say nothing. His face came off in slow motion, and the bullet smashed out of the back of his head. He exploded backwards and fell into the canal, made a big splash, and he turned over like a log and that was him done for.

The noise echoed around and around, like it does, and for a few seconds I was trapped inside it like a wisp of smoke, rooted to the spot till a wind came to suck it away. But at the end of the day it was too soon gone. Nobody was about. I climbed up the steps back up to street level and slipped the gun back in my pocket.

I turned and ran, ducked off as soon as I could down a street I didn't know. No one saw me. After running for a while I turned round and walked back the way I'd come, to the bakers, and I bought a few fresh warm rolls to take up to the room, but I weren't really hungry and before I got back to the hotel I chucked the whole bag in a bin. I walked to the corner by the hotel, then I went back and put the gun in the bag with all the rolls and left it nestling there for someone hungry to find later. I swear I didn't know it was going to happen. Just because I was jealous? Just because I had it in my pocket?

I went upstairs and straight into her room. She'd got up and was standing there in a t-shirt, looking at herself in the mirror. It was only a second or two before she turned around to see who'd come in, but in that time, that split-second, I felt the whole laziness of her: she didn't care who it was really, she was lost in her own reflection—that was the main thing for her and it always would be. She'd never break out of it. I saw she had a black eye: a real shiner, a whack.

"Hello, Lee," she said.

Something about the look of me must have frightened her—but it was myself, I was the one who was scared utterly shitless, scared angry. I thought of Yop, turning there in the canal. I'd somehow known he should be there. How did I know that? I walked right straight up to her and I grabbed hold of her by her shoulders. She knew what to do then. She went weak between my hands, as if it was me suddenly who was holding her up, and she pushed her mouth against mine.

She was ready for it, ready for more of it. She wouldn't have minded taking a punch in the other eye. I realised then she was mad. I pushed her over onto the bed, and she fell back, laughing, opened up wide and squirmed so I could get into her and I punched my cock straight up into her and I came straight away in two pushes, not enough to drain the anger out of me, not enough to stop her bucking and pushing for more, but there weren't no more. I rolled away and shouted into the pillow. She went still beside me, limp.

She was lying on her side, holding her left arm with her right, rubbing it, more stroking it, as though it hurt her, which it obviously did, flexing it. She moved down to her cat's paw and rubbed that too. It was hurting, I could tell, and I thought maybe she'd banged it against him too hard.

"Did he hurt your hand?" I asked her.

"Yeah," she said, "he did. He grabbed hold of it really hard and he really hurt me." Her eyes filled with tears, she started sobbing into the crisp blue pillow.

I put my arms round her and held her.

"I'm a flid," she started babbling, "I know I'm a flid. I can't help it, okay? Why does everyone have to be so horrible to me? It was the same at school. They took my dinner money and I couldn't get it back. Flid, they said, Charley is a flid. Nyah, nyah, nyah."

I didn't know what to say. Her eyes was swollen red. She wiped her paw across them and sniffed up her tears.

She reached over and lit up a Dutch Marlboro. "Do you know who done this to me?"

"Some bloke," I said.

"It was somebody you know," she said. "Someone we both know."

"Who?" I thought she meant Will, but it couldn't be him.

"It was Yap's friend."

"Which one?"

"The smaller one—I can't remember his name." She looked at me. "He just kept going on and on, asking me if he could come up for a minute. I said okay just to keep him quiet. But I didn't want to do nothing with him, because of you. He got frustrated and hit me."

"And that's what happened?"

"Yeah," she said. "It didn't hurt much at the time, it was just a sort of slap. Then when I woke up this morning it was like this—Mike Tyson." She give a short laugh, liking the sound of what she was saying.

"We're going today," I said. "We've got to get out of this place as soon as possible. It's not safe no more, I can feel it."

"Yeah," she said. "I think you're right, Lee."

We laid there. I was wondering where we should go to next. I thought that the place Will had been going on about sounded okay, but I was a bit dubious about it being so close to all those other countries. Didn't that mean there would be border guards. A lot of police around and everything. But it would be a good way of getting Will up and going. I didn't want an argument with him for hours and hours.

"What are you supposed to put on a black eye?"

"Steak?" she said.

"Everybody's going to think we hit you."

"I'll get some sunglasses."

"Good idea," I said. "I want to do it again before we go. Is that alright?"

"Yeah," she said. "You know me, Lee. Of course it's alright. Sometimes I think I was born to fuck. Do you think there's anything wrong with me?"

"No," I said.

Will was coming round when we went next door, rolling an early morning cherub to get him going. Needless to say he was none the wiser about nothing that had gone on the night before, this morning. Dope seemed to make him forget himself, but wherever he went to in there it weren't somewhere he was capable of telling us about, and it did make him quite easy to get around if that's what you wanted to do. Just press the right buttons and he was like putty in your hands.

"Wake up mate," I said. "We're all going to Roermond."

"Oh, great, great," he said vaguely.

Charley sat on the edge of the bed. He sat up, the sheet falling down around his middle. She put her hand on his bare shoulder and kissed him on the cheek. "Look at this," she said, holding up her head and showing him her bruise.

"What happened to you last night?"

"Some bastard hit me," she said. "That's what happened."

"Who?"

"Just some drunken bastard in a bar," she said. "What does it matter? I want to get out of this dump."

"I thought we was going to see Yap," he said. "I like Yap."

"I like him too," I said. "But we've got to go on—furtherer than he can go. We wouldn't be able to bring him back again if we do what he said."

"Besides," Charley said. "If he sees this he'll want to go to the police—which we can't do, right?"

"So whoever did it is going to get away with it." Will was really angry at the sight of Charley's black eye. He jumped out of bed and got dressed. "Come on, we've got to do something about it. You must know who it was, we'll find the bastard."

"Of course I do. I'd recognise him anywhere." She hesitated. "But we'd have to find him."

"That's what we should do then," Will said. If it was an act he was putting on I've got to admit it was a bloody good one. But it weren't an act. It was just his good side showing, which is just the side he wanted to be same as anyone. "Where's the gun?" he asked me.

Charley looked around. "It was on the side. No it weren't, it's in your pocket."

"I went out this morning and chucked it away," I said. "In that canal. I decided that was the best place for it. In case we have to say nothing about it later, I can say that." I kept my voice perfectly calm but I weren't calm inside. I was jumping with fear. Any minute now they was going to ask me the wrong question. I had to calm myself down drastically. It was like practising for the police.

"Yeah, yeah. Good idea," Will said. "They can't say anything to that, can they?"

Charley looked at me.

I turned away, started packing things away into an open case. She helped, taking things out and refolding them, slowing me down. Will said he needed to get something to eat. We was hungry too so we stopped what we was doing and we all went downstairs to the hotel dining room. I hadn't realised you could get breakfast there, but Will was an old hand, a familiar face to the girls behind the counters. He'd been down while we was out wandering in search of an open café. I thought they should see as little as possible of us, ask themselves as few questions as possible. That made me nervous, like Yap's Mum, because you never knew what they was thinking or when you was going to start acting guilty. Charley had a black eye now, and I, remember, I had this fucking great scar on my left cheek.

The girls stood behind counters. You took a tray and filled it with what you wanted. The room was still half-full but there was only scrambled egg and toast left, cereals and coffee, fruit. We filled our plates, gave our room numbers and sat down at a free table. I got to work on a bowl of cornflakes with dried bananas on top. Charley munched a bit of toast, Will demolished everything in sight in a whirlwind, slurping at his coffee between courses.

Straightaway some people at the next table was looking over at us. Some nosy sort of people from somewhere or another. Belgium it turned out. Friendly enough people.

"You are late," the bloke said. He looked us over and made a sleeping sign, cocking his head to one side on a pillow made of his praying hands. His wife and little boy was nodding and smiling. "You are English?"

We smiled back.

"English football," he said. "Very bad. Beckham—he is shit."

Will laughed. "That's one way of putting it," he said in Spanish. "This is my wife—and my young cousin from England," he introduced us with a big build up, a flourish we didn't want.

The bloke was taken aback at first, but accepted it easily enough. He spoke back in a bit of Spanish and Will chatted to him. Then he turned to Charley and tried it out on her. She smiled and nodded, keeping her mouth shut. Then they all said their names and that they was from Belgium.

We ate in silence, not wanting to give ourselves away. In a way it was a relief because it meant that all we had to do was whatever was necessary to get out of there, which we done. We filled ourselves up and went back upstairs, smiling goodbye at the Belgian family. Will also lifted up an arm to wave at the girl on the hot food counter. She laughed, waved back.

"She thinks you're a dashing Spaniard," I said.

"I am," Will replied.

"You're not like other people," Charley said to him. "There really is something weird about you."

"Glad you noticed," Will said. "It's really about time somebody did."

"Everyone did," I said. "That's why you're so popular everywhere you go."

"I never go anywhere. Anyway, who'd want to be popular with the vermin I have to associate with?"

We laughed, went upstairs and finished packing. Then it was the easy way out of there. Will paid the bill, picked up the passports, I picked up the car from the carpark, half-surprised to see it there again, our old dream-wagon waiting for the off to parts unknown, and we loaded it up with our fancy-dress costumes and set off up the road for somewhere else, somewhere beyond our dreams.

One way or another we was all glad to get out of Utrecht, which I must admit was one of the most interesting places I'd ever been to so far, and I knew I would have lots of memories of it coming back, but for now I was happy enough to leave it far behind. We all was. We opened the windows and let the air blow through us and blow it all away, peel it off and throw it away like the skin of an orange, or a banana. It was a great feeling, and like a lot of things in life, it seemed worth its price while you was there feeling it.

Charley was in the front seat. I loved the way she rode in a car, with her legs apart, one of them always propped up on something, so that her skirt fell back, always making sure that whoever was with her got a good view of her minge. We was great. We was fucking untouchable.

Will was counting up the money in the back seat. "I hate to tell you this," he said. "But we're going to run out if we're not careful."

"What if we are careful?" I said.

"We should buy a tent," Will said. "And get to where we can find some work. Anything, picking tulips or something."

But we all knew that didn't exist and I turned on the radio and we listened again to whatever was in the charts, to old hits from any time that was always playing somewhere or another. Will found that Brimful of Asha and that one still sticks in my memory from leaving Utrecht time. Leaving a mess behind I could only hope I'd managed to clean up as best it could be, because with the road coming up under me for mile after mile it weren't long before that grey canal was in my mind, and Yop floating in it, turning over lazily like a big turd while I watched with the gun in my hand, unable to pull myself away from him.

Charley picked up a pair of sunglasses from a chemists near the hotel, and with them clamped on her face her narrow features was a perfect mask as she turned away to the wound-down window and let the breeze pull back her mop of blonde hair like Marilyn Monroe.

FOURTEEN

There was no real reason for us to go to Roermond, the only one being that we'd already decided it and it was Will's biggest idea so far. Apart from the tent and finding work somewhere; but I thought it might turn out that we done that too, because myself and Charley hadn't turned out to be so good at coming up with other suggestions and here we was, still going, waiting for the world to fall down on top of us and it hadn't done, not yet, not till we'd gone on a bit further and got into a few more scrapes. As for Yop. Well, he deserved it. I deserved a medal for saving the world from any more trouble with him.

For Charley he was gone, so far as you could tell from anything she said. Nothing. I think she was a bit ashamed of herself. It was her fault after all. She didn't have to go out looking for trouble, looking for a shag, and now she was going to lay low and make do with whatever she'd got. Us, in other words. She was one of us, in other words, and like us she was going to have to wait and see what happened next on our journey together across the Zone.

I sounded like Will to myself. William Woody-Gomez, my mate. He was going to pull us through to safety, if he could, and I forgot about my mean thoughts about him of last night and earlier. It's different after you've killed someone. It's like you've fed. You feel lazy, you just want to stretch out on a rock and bask in the sun and let your dinner go down, and then you come round and you feel refreshed but sort of slack, not quite so much whip in your tail, you're quite happy to slither along in a friendly world, and you don't want nothing else to bother you.

Maybe if you was a snake all that would just be till next time you was hungry, but for me there weren't likely to be a next time. It was a freak thing, like a flood that came over the wall, or a finger of fire that just happened to point at your bungalow, or somebody like Charley walking into your life and turning you from a boy to a man. All those things was near impossible but likely to happen in the long run, especially if you kicked a bit, made them happen. Don't be afraid of nothing, I wanted to say to anyone. Just kick out and hold your breath and flap your arms and legs about. It's alright kids because I am one of you who is actually doing it, I am

146

someone who has won their way to the top at an incredibly young age and against the most incredible competition.

Lee Hookaway of Jaywick Sands, *This Is Your Life*. Michael Aspel walks forward with the glowing pale blue book, coming at me from behind as I warm up onstage in an empty theatre. Mum and me snuggle up in front of the telly. I wonder who it's going to be tonight. Oh, I heard it's that bloke who plays the mad sergeant on The Bill. What do we want to watch that for? Because I like seeing all their mates and hearing all their stories, Why? I like hearing about when they was young. I like imagining they're talking about me. But. But not this time. This time it's my turn. Mum turns to look at me in amazed amazement and then we're sucked away, into the back of the telly, along the tubes, like genies into a bottle.

"You've forgotten something," Charley broke in on me. "There's the travellers' cheques. I can write that woman's name on them no trouble. I can do any signature you like."

Will perked up. "You're right, I forgot."

"So we're not too bad off then, I said.

But it didn't mean that much to me really. Just another bit of unreality to toss in the dream-basket. I tried in vain to get back to This Is Your Life. Who was going to fill up the empty chairs opposite me? Who was the first mystery guest behind the curtain, just about to speak into the off-stage microphone? I hoped it would be my Dad. I had him walking through the curtain in his old overalls, smiling his special smile, but I couldn't hear him speaking. I'd missed that part and now I couldn't make that part up, or he weren't coming through or something.

I got annoyed and done a little nose twitch on the old Peugeot to scare them. Someone behind saw us swerve and leaned on his hooter. Someone else in the opposite lane on the dual carriageway flashed their headlights at us. To wake me up. The others remained quietly in their seats and we drove on in a bubble of silence to where something might pop it suddenly and we'd tumble out onto the grass to a round of applause from the teachers, and the pigs, and you as well. Yeah, because it was me who was driving this car and I didn't want no more distraction from them.

"I done that to get your attention," I said. "Has anyone looked at the map? Does anyone know where the fuck we're going?"

"Roermond," Will said. "Like we said."

"Yeah, but where the fuck is it?"

"I thought you was heading towards it."

"Well, I'm not, I'm just fucking driving. That's my job, in case you forgot. Keeping this fucking car on the road while you sit back and enjoy yourselves."

It was too much of the same fucking thing. We hadn't been out on the road five minutes and the same problems kept coming up. Will got the map out on the back seat, batted it straight as if a bluebottle had settled right on the spot where we was meant to be going and had decided to sick up its dinner right there. Roermond, I didn't like the sound of that place, I didn't want to go there, but Will soon had it identified as being in the opposite direction to the one we was going. Not too far though, just a sign that must have flashed by and I'd missed. I took the next exit and turned round and we barrelled back to where we should have turned off.

We was zigzagging around on roads where we didn't know where we was, we was nowhere, a bunch of nobodies in an old Peugeot family saloon from the sixties, going off at a weird angle to everything. It was Yop, turning over lazily in the canal in Utrecht and suddenly putting up a wet hand, beckoning me back. I felt sick inside because I weren't going to get away from what I had done to him for no good reason, not this way. It weren't any way I'd ever thought of going before. When we got to the turning I turned down it and we was off down another open road, more tulip fields falling off to either side so we could be seen for miles and miles: runaways.

Runaways. It came from Will, who had been singing that song off and on all the way out of Utrecht. He was trying to get on the good side of Charley, his little runaway; but he didn't know how far we had come, not yet. It struck me that we'd been walking around in a dream world, doing whatever we liked, without realising that we was runaway slaves, more or less, even though useless ones that no one would bother to look for very hard; but they would look, they would definitely find us. That's what was in the zone. Us. And Them. They was trying to catch us and send us back to Jaywick, which was a place that kept pulling on your leash for as far as you ran and as long as you lived. We'd come unstuck. We was flapping loose, that was all, like a flysheet whose peg has come out of its ground.

Open windows and the wind blowing in done their magic work again and blew it all out of our tiny little heads. Roermond was ahead of us. Will managed to convince us that something special awaited us at the spot where those three countries met. It was like they shook hands on a deal, which he hoped would make it a lucky place for us, as we all did. Before we got there the car had to break down. Lee Dorsey sang that one—one of Dad's favourites. Fifteen miles from town, my old car broke down. Battery's dead, man like I said. Just my luck, I got the fuel pump stuck. And that's what happened: the motor was straining, gears grinding, then we jerked to a stop, changing gear and hopping along as the motor died, failed, and we coasted to a stop in a handy little lay-by on a country road miles from anywhere.

"This is where you do your mechanical stuff," Will said. "I noticed a tool kit in the boot, next to the spare wheel."

"Yeah, I saw that too."

Charley said nothing, hooded in the passenger seat in her sunglasses. I got out and opened the bonnet. Will reluctantly followed. It was like taking the lid off a kettle that was boiled dry: scalding acrid steam, a burnt plastic smell, and we stood back to watch it blow away in a cloud of low-hanging poison over the tulips. Tulips are things that really exist in Holland. There are a lot of them. I looked down at the motor: a bombed city, presided over by a giant air-filter bird that hadn't drunk up enough of bad things to keep our wheels turning, its great funnel beak dripping with black water. I found a rag in the boot and pulled out the dipstick, wiped it and put it back for a true reading. Truly we was out of oil. I done the same with the radiator cap and yes a final bullet of steam shot up in the air.

"We're fucked," Will said, "and all due to a lack of basic maintenance, I'd say."

"You cunt."

Charley had stirred herself to get out of the car. She stood back a little way, watching the little cloud scudding away over the tulip fields. The soul of our car, its driving power force, had

149

left us and gone off on its own journey over the low countries to some far-distant sea where the spirits of dead motors congregated to talk about their adventures at the hands of the humans who'd imprisoned them in tin boxes, not even bothering to check they was properly fed and watered in such a way as to ensure they enjoyed a full active life-span.

She didn't say nothing. She didn't have to say a dicky-bird. I knew what she was thinking and I knew that she was right.

"Right," I said. "We've got two choices. Either we stay here or we push the car to the next garage."

"Let's stay here," Charley said. "We can have a picnic."

"What with?"

"You two are so stupid. I don't know why I bothered bringing you."

"Well, you wouldn't have got far on your own. You're the car bloke—you should've made sure it was okay."

He was right. But he just had to stick the boot in. I was gutted. They had no suggestions to make. There was none, apart from just walking or trying to thumb a ride. I didn't know if the car would start again, but I hadn't heard no major clunking or grinding; so it was fair possibility she might go if we filled her up with water and oil. I thought so anyway.

"I wonder how far to the next garage."

"Miles. A few miles, probably. Could be even further."

The long road stretched ahead of us and it didn't look in the slightest little bit promising. We was stuck and there was no Lee Dorsey to sing and joke us out of it.

"What about turning round and pushing it back," Will said. "I thought I saw a Jet station by the roundabout back there."

"I didn't."

"Neither did I," Charley said.

"What roundabout?" I asked him.

Will said nothing. He weren't exactly the best person in a crisis.

"I know," I said. "Why don't we just walk up that magic stairway that was in the fields back there and ask the man in charge of it if he knows where to find a good mechanic?"

"What shall we do then?" Charley said.

"Walk," I said. "You stay here, I'll walk."

There was a big empty plastic water bottle in the boot. I got that out and set off on my own. I didn't even turn around. I heard the doors slamming behind me. They'd got in the car to wait. I walked on. The sun was high in a clear sky, traffic streamed past my left shoulder, the road long but with a slight curve in it that meant I'd put them out of sight in half a mile or so, and then, who knew, civilisation might suddenly start up again, because we'd just happened to break down on one of the blank spots that had been reserved for cultivating useless plants.

I walked on up the road. Sweat was stinging my eyes. I wanted to cry. Why not. I let it go, there was no one to see me here, and no tears for long. That meant I weren't allowed to cry, not for myself nor for anyone, and nothing I ever done would make that no better in the eyes of some people, even though none of them knew about it as yet. Somehow I knew they would find out and I knew what their reaction would be when they did. I didn't want to think about it at the minute.

Nothing appeared. I stuck my thumb out without looking round; but no one stopped. No one cared, basically. I suppose they must just have driven past the car, thought oh look, they've broken down, then saw me trudging along, thought, oh look, he's got a long way to go, and then drove on having a good laugh about it. I've had cans of beer chucked at me for waiting for the bus to Clacton, believe it or not, just because some arsehole in the passenger seat thinks you're a wanker for not being in a car.

A tree. That was interesting. I walked up level with it and then past it. I walked and walked. I remembered the tree, but only for a minute. I remembered climbing it even though I hadn't climbed nowhere. I'd just dropped off a tree like everyone else, hoping to roll as far away as I could from the Mum tree, out into the sun. Well, I had got my wish alright, it was baking me like a potato and in the end I would be all fluffy inside. The water thing was a big square thing, yellow and red; I couldn't believe nothing could be as heavy as an empty water bottle. The grip kept digging into my hands, a protruding ridge of plastic digging in, a seam, badly made. I swopped it around, banging on my legs, timing myself by a count of two hundred when I could change hands. I was going to need a lift back. I needed a lift now. Finally I stopped and turned around and stuck my thumb out properly, smiling, not quite looking them in the eye, something which I suddenly knew was the best way to approach the public.

A car pulled in. "Se habla español?"

"English," I said.

He drove off as quick as he'd stopped, a right little prick in something I didn't recognise, *el toreador*. I supposed he must've seen the Peugeot's Spanish plates; but why stop and drive off again? What's the difference? Then I tried to look at it from his point of view. Maybe he just didn't speak no English and he knew he wouldn't be able to talk to me. Maybe he hated the English people.

Another car pulled in, a Citroën 2CV, a really beaten up one, driven by what looked like a couple of farmers. There was a bloke behind the wheel, a middle-aged bloke with long greasy hair. His Mum was in the passenger seat. They didn't speak no English either. I pointed at the water container and said garage. The bloke got out and let me climb in the back. It smelled of earth. There was earth in there, all over the floor and scattered over the narrow back seat, which I shared with a sack of something or another. I leaned over to see what it was. Tulip bulbs. It smelled of petrol in the car, but the windows was as wide open as they'd go and you could see the road through the floor, and that carried some of it away.

The driver seemed to be operating the throttle with a lump of string he held in his left hand, steering with his right. His nails had dirt under them, skin rough and torn as if he'd been scrabbling in the dirt all day. The motor was labouring, dying, picking up, racing as he eased his foot off and on the clutch till we'd picked up enough revs to lurch out into a gap in the flow of holiday traffic.

They didn't say much, not to me. They didn't say nothing in fact till we was miles up the road, then they started talking to each other at the tops of their voices. They wasn't shouting, just making themselves heard above the motor. I couldn't understand a word they said, of course, but after a time it became obvious they was discussing some subject that had nothing to do with driving along a road with a bag of tulip bulbs and a hitchhiker in the back in a car that didn't seem like it wanted to go nowhere. They was talking about something else, some debate they'd been having for years, or maybe just some telly programme they both watched. That was my guess, anyway. The way they talked was nothing like the way I talked to my Mum, but in a way it was, there was that in it: a situation I recognised. I felt comfortable with it, it had a calming effect on me, and the whining drone of the motor and the petrol smell let me huddle into myself. I dropped off asleep for a blink of shut-eye.

My favourite place to be was between asleep and awake, straining between these two main places so that the outer world was just something thrown up on your inner screen, something you can ultimately control, which you can if you can take the frighteners, because you can make everything they throw at you dance to your tune, and just for a minute or two it bleeds over and makes perfect sense of everything, and it really does if you manage to keep hold of it and carry it with you throughout your movements in the small world we live in by day.

I was adrift again. I thought that I was in the other car, our car, still in the back seat, but Charley was behind the wheel, crashing the column change, Will reading a map, turning it around on his lap because he weren't sure which direction we was going in. But I knew. I was steering from the back; I didn't have to think of where we was going, just be there vaguely thinking of what would be the best thing to happen, and lo and behold, a perfect turn-off appeared and we turned down it past some cabins to a long lake surrounded by woods, and along the banks of this lake there was people fishing.

We pulled up past them and stopped at a cabin that was our own, where we would be staying for the night. It was dusty and no one had been there for years, no one would ever look for us and we could stay there as long as we liked and cook fish on a fire beside the lake and kick the ashes out afterwards. It was the sort of place you look for all your life, the sort of place Mum looks for and pretends she's found every time she goes down the creek with a few of her own mates and they all get stoned and sleep out in tents. But this was different. It was just for us and you didn't have to listen to anyone's stories around the fire. There wasn't no stories and you didn't have to go home either. And when it started to get boring—but it never did, because you was always back at that moment of pulling off the road, driving past the lake to the perfect place for the first time, the minute of getting there before you unpacked everything you'd brought with you and turned it into a place like any other.

"Garage." I opened my eyes. The old lady had spoken. She'd turned around in her seat and was holding up one finger in a way that might have meant one mile or might have just meant be patient, wait for it. Her face was incredible. She looked like an witch. Her hair was a tangled mess of fuse wire pulled back in a piece of rough string, her features criss-crossed by thousands of major and minor roads and she had relied on surrounding her teeth with their own healing fluid instead of going to a dentist, meaning there was almost none left, and she had an old green farm coat on with cow-muck crusted on it.

Her son concentrated hard on the road, the throttle-string wound round his fingers, nodding his agreement with everything she said.

True to this promise we pulled into the Jet station, I hopped out, said goodbye and went over to the tap beside the carwash I left the container to fill under it full blast, I splashed some of it on my face and went over to the main bit to buy a couple of cans of oil. When I got back the top was overflowing; a water-lake spreading across the forecourt like a speeded up country swallowing the dusty world in one gulp. The 2CV was parked in it, her motor running. The woman beckoned me over to them. I capped the water bottle and struggled to their car. Amazingly they'd decided to run me back to the Peugeot.

I rode all the way back alert with my arm around the water bottle, we was really clipping along at 45, the little motor singing away to itself like a forgotten song that has been remembered suddenly from a long time ago, in my case before I was born, because I'd never met people like them before. I wished I was one of them myself; anyway, they wasn't like people from around home, people I would be one day, people like I was now.

We couldn't do nothing except nod, but I tried talking to them slow and in English, with many hand gestures, touching my heart, and pointing to far away Essex, a flat country like Holland, and they seemed to catch my drift because they done their own version of this back to me, the old lady wheezing and showing her broken teeth, the bloke chuckling from the side of his mouth as he bent forward over the wheel of the little 2CV, which was corrugated and rusty: a piece of old farm equipment that only went if you was friends with it. They was part of the car and it was a part of them, they was welded together in it, and I could see them riding up and down this road looking for people to help on a permanent basis. They dropped me off by the car, still standing with the bonnet up and no sign of the others; they waved off my thanks, turned in a circle across two empty lanes and sped home.

I wrestled the full water container to the car and filled up the radiator, which took up about half of the water. I put the rest in the boot and found a small funnel in the tool kit. I went back to put in the oil. There was still no sign of Will and Charley, the car was empty, so was the road. I busied myself pouring both cans of oil through the funnel, replacing the oil cap, wiping everything off with a rag and hoping for the best, praying the motor weren't seized solid due to my carelessness. I chucked the empty cans into the shallow ditch beside the field in time to see them approaching along a narrow path across the field fifty yards down the road. They was miles away, walking back lazily through the tulips. They was carrying something.

I got into the car. The key, our magic key from the jam-jar in Will's room, was no longer in the ignition. They'd taken it with them. I sat behind the driver's seat and waited for them to arrive. It seemed to be taking forever, but, you guessed it, my eyes closed in the beat of the sun, and I dozed off, sweating, in the soft muggy haze in the car, till they woke me up ten minutes later, waiting for an opportunity, a twenty year stretch without interruptions to grow a long beard of lies, like you, like you and all the rest of them, but no such luck.

"We thought there might be a farmhouse back there." Charley leaned in over me through the open window, kissed my wet forehead.

She'd caught the sun a lot in the cotton dress, slightly too big for her, which she'd put on in the hotel before we hut up the cases. It brought freckles out on her skin, her face red and shining, raw and inflamed looking down to where her tits swelled out, a bit like an allergy rash when your skin comes up, and I suspected they'd been rolling around in the tulips, rubbing the petals all over them, or fucking in some barn somewhere.

"So what was back there?" I said. "A barn?"

"A shed," Will said, "full of these." He held up a battered plastic bag he was carrying, full of dead-looking tulip bulbs.

I got the key off him and stuck it in the ignition, hoping for a first time start, but the engine wouldn't turn over. All my worst fears was coming true. The motor was seized up. I put the Peugeot in first gear, told them to get behind it and push, which they done, but when I let the clutch out the car just ground to a slow halt, hardly turning over. Then I thought of what Dad would have one, and I stuck her in reverse and got them to push on the front end, and it was true, it worked better to turn the engine over backwards, I could feel it freeing off, saved in the nick of time from seizing into a solid block. Then forward again in second and she was turning over, then she fired and I sat there giving the motor a few revs to get that black blood and that white water pulsing round, till I thought the insides was wet all over.

Will and Charley was flaked out on the verge, chests heaving, covered in sweat. Served them right, the dirty bastards.

"Come on!" I shouted out the window, "Get in the car. We're going. Quick, before it dies again."

They dragged themselves up off the grass and got in the car, flopped into their usual poses and we was off again. I put my foot down, thinking we might be able to catch them up, the farm people in the 2CV, overtake them and give them a last wave, but we didn't, unfortunately, and I didn't ever see them again. But it didn't matter for now, or forever probably, because we was all shouting with happiness at having escaped, having got away with it again, and we turned the radio up and shouted some more.

What we did come to was a small town, a place with one main street, quite long, and a few bars and shops along it. Can't remember the name of the place, it's on the map somewhere, the town with no name. We stopped there and took a double room in a bed and breakfast place and got blind drunk on a few beers in a little bar next door. There didn't seem no point hurrying to get to Roermond, so we decided to slow down and take it easy. This seemed to be just as good a place as the others, in its way. But it closed down early. When it did we rolled out into the street, dosed up to the eyeballs with beers and chicken and chips, but we didn't want to go to bed yet.

"Let's try that place," Will said, and so we decided, without discussion, to make our way towards the only light that was still on, the lit up sign of a bar further down the street.

The blinds was pulled down, but behind them people was moving around; a bit of music seeped out under the door. We pushed it open and went inside. First thing I noticed was a couple of chairs had been pushed over; a lot of very drunk people was lurching around pointing at these chairs but not picking them up; they was in the middle of an argument, but it looked like a friendly argument, or maybe. I wanted to turn round and walk straight back out he door but the others was behind me so I pushed on up to the bar to see if they was still serving.

The bloke behind the bar was a thin, punkish type of about thirty-five with a half-smile on his face and a raised eyebrow expression that said he was about to think of some smart put-down, probably by referring to something you hadn't a hope in hell of ever having heard of before, a fair bet in my case.

"Yes?" he said. "How may I help you?"

I was right. He was English as well, which surprised me a bit, and so was several other people in his bar, as I discovered when they started shouting over my shoulder for drinks.

"Three pints of lager," I said.

"Sorry," he said. "You're not old enough."

Someone behind me laughed at him. "Serve 'em, Pete. Go on, you bastard."

"I'm not serving underage drinkers and that's that."

I turned to leave, he caught sight of Charley behind me, and immediately pulled out three fresh glasses. "Oranjeboom?"

"Yeah." I pulled a note out of my pocket and put it down on the wet bar. He whisked it up and rang up the sale on his till before carrying on with the order.

"Just this once," he said. "As you're passing through, like." He give me a dubious glance. "Lollipop with that, sir?"

I picked up the three glasses with splayed fingers and shooed the others back. They found a small wet table off to the side. We huddled round it, trying to make ourselves invisible.

"That bloke's a right pillock," I said.

"How can you tell," Charley said, "They all look the fucking same to me."

"He's English."

"Can't you tell?"

She peered over at him in a way likely to attract attention. "He looks like a weasel."

"More of a stoat, " Will said.

"More of a rat."

"Probably a gippo," I said. "You can never get rid of that lot."

"My Dad's a gypsy," Charley said. "He got rid of himself quite easily as far as we was concerned. Arsehole."

I hadn't known this. "Where was he from then—all over?"

"Yeah," she said. "But most of the time they was in Kettering. There's loads of them out there. He went back there for a bit after him and Mum split up. I went to visit him there when I was a little girl."

"What did you do?"

"Ate a lot of ice-cream. I stayed in his Mum's caravan. She was a real old witch. She's dead now. She looked after me when I was down there."

For some reason—she didn't talk much, really—we both wanted to hear more about this, but her look had done its work and the bloke from behind the bar was wending over, a half-full glass in his hand.

"Come far?" he asked

"Utrecht," I said.

"Nice place," Will said.

"Yeah," Charley said—and he turned his full attention on her.

"Have a good time there, did you?" He had an easy smile when he tried, looked a harmless sort of bloke.

"Yeah," she said. "We met some locals."

"Can you see with those things on?" he said. "You're supposed to take them off at night."

But she weren't rising to that. She shrugged and looked away. "You live over here, do you?" Will asked him. "What's it like?"

"It's okay," he said. "Provided you know the right people."

I expected it was, but I couldn't bring myself to believe he was one of them. "This is a busy place you've got," I said. "I suppose a lot of people must stop on their way through here."

"No," he said. "I see the same crowd every night."

"That must get a bit tiresome," Will said. "I would think."

"You could say that."

"Is it easy to find work over here? We wondered if there was any seasonal work, like there is in France or Spain."

"Not really," he said. "I've never heard of anyone doing that, unless you've got a skilled trade. Where you going next?"

"Roermond," I said.

"Oh, it's nice there. A few hills, some woods."

"What's the town like?"

"Okay. Just a little Dutch town."

"Like here?"

"No, a bit different. Did you know three countries meet there?"

"Yeah," I said. "That's why we thought we'd have a look at it."

He looked like he thought that was interesting, but he weren't giving much away; maybe he didn't have much to say. I sank down into my pint, and the others done the same.

"Someone was killed in Utrecht today," he said. "Shot dead— it was on the local news. It's a mystery—a local boy was found dead in the canal."

"Blimey," Charley said. "When was this?"

"About lunchtime."

"We left early," Will said. "We had some car trouble on the way."

The barman shrugged. "Just thought I'd tell you. You look too young to be out on your own," he smiled at Charley.

He wandered off, and we never did find our way back to Charley's gypsy Dad in Kettering, not that night. Somehow he had put the cap on our nightcap. We talked for a bit, finished up our drinks and left, then walked up the road to our room.

"Utrecht didn't seem that sort of place," Will said.

"We might get stopped," I said.

Charley said nothing.

"If we get stopped, that's it," Will said, obviously enough. "One way or another they'll crucify us."

"Did you get rid of the gun?" Charley asked.

"Yeah, yeah," I said.

FIFTEEN

Next morning we was up bright and early on the road to Roermond. It weren't bright and it weren't particularly early. It was an overcast day, a sheet of cloud had blown in from somewhere, and we slept through till about eleven, dragged ourselves out to the car and drove off almost without caring if we did or not, the only thing being we was glad to get out of this little dump of a town, whatever the fuck it was called. The others seemed to have forgot about the bloke in the bar, but I couldn't stop thinking about him. He weren't the sort of person you want to talk to nowhere—even though he didn't mean no harm something about him give me the creeps. He was too curious. He knew too much, or thought he did. I thought everything was closing in on us, and the longer we stayed here the quicker it would come.

A bit of sunshine makes a lot of difference, don't it? All the difference in the world between happy and sad, good and bad, going somewhere and going nowhere, which was what I felt we was doing. Still, you shouldn't blame other people for your problems, especially if they're your own fault. And it seemed the sky had blown over dark because of me and my bad actions. I wanted to go back to the canal and rub that out but I knew I never could. I half wanted to turn myself in to the police, because I knew I'd done a bad thing.

The rain came hammering down on the roof of the car, covering everything else too in a swift downpour, as if the low skies had opened all at once and dumped a hopper of golf ball sized raindrops on everyone's head, so that you thought it must wash away the fields, the few strung out farmhouses, and the road, which slowed down into a wide river bed that everyone nosed along with their lights on. I managed to find the wiper switch, and the wide blades flopped slowly back and forth, up and down lightning danced across the horizon, and we was all in a submarine in an electrified goldfish bowl. The radio went static. Charley turned it off.

All together again, me at the tiller, Captain Nemo sat in the back seat silently looking out of the side porthole, enjoying it passing, enjoying being on the inside with us as another big gust of wet sky ripped a trembling scar across the fields, which rose a little bit at the edge of horizon in a sort of lip of capillary action on the inside of a glass to hold it all in, so that you might be scared of drowning on dry land or being washed away to fall off the edge of the world when the surface tension broke.

"This is like being in a submarine," Charley said.

Then Mr Sun came out and chased away Mr Rain, who ran off over the fields flapping his big black umbrella, off to look for something dead or dying. We came through it suddenly. I imagined the car streaming and steaming as we speeded along, glowing as if it had been charged up by lightning, and it was as if the countryside sprang open again and you realised why Holland was so lush and green and although it was flat it was built on a hidden curve to a perspective that could pivot and change it all round in a minute's time.

The storm whipped away behind us. They both turned round to watch it racing across the fields in a band of darkness. I caught it in the mirror: a black shadow world collapsing into nothing, turning over once, then just going out like a piece of wood that has carried on burning for a few seconds underwater, giving off a white glow before it surrenders and dies. I sighed with relief, letting go of the wheel slightly as the road dried out; it was like we'd bounced up onto it like an amphibian: a duck.

On we went past a sign that said Roermond 15 kilometres, down a dip into a puddle of lightness and up again through woods, as if all these borders had to be shrouded under green shade. I was on the lookout for a signpost that pointed three ways, to three countries. I wondered what had happened in these woods during the war, when Europe was under the jack-boot of the Nazis. It weren't that hard to imagine people running and getting shot, trying to get up maybe and falling down in fresh snow, covered up by more snow and blown away. But it was even worse than you could imagine. I imagined a big black Swastika on the town hall in Utrecht, but I hadn't when we was there. The woods made me think of that. Everything can be easily hidden in the woods where everything can be easily hidden.

That's why my Dad died. He was old, an old Dad looking for a second chance, but he didn't really get that chance. He got Mum instead. She was young, a bit crazy—she must have been to go for an old bloke like him: older than you, even, when they first met, and he was too old to handle her, that's what I think, if anyone could have done anything about what she's got inside her.

I used to ask him how old he was when I was really little, and he said he was as old as the hills but he didn't know as much. He only knew about cars. That's what he liked about Jaywick. It reminded him of the olden days, he reeled off the names of the roads and told you a story about each one of them, every car on the road was a road there, but it didn't lead far, not nowhere really. That's why I feel so old. An old soul Mum called me, and she said it was because I had an old father. Good old Dad. Dead, before I knew much about him.

Then we was in the town itself, another big old place, a bit like Utrecht and Delft rolled into one, a couple of tall churches side by side, just there to be the last one before Holland finally petered out. The last knockings of a clogged clog. Will wanted to find this place he'd read about, where three countries met on a hill. I didn't know how you'd find something like that. Neither did he. We didn't stop there, just circled around it while Charley tried to work out the map.

"Where do we want to go, Belgium or Germany?"

"Germany," Will said.

"Belgium," I said.

Roermond was a two-river place, I remember. I remember going over a bridge over one of them. The two rivers merged together like the countries, invisibly, first one then the other. Somehow we found our way out onto a little road going somewhere. I was expecting to be stopped by a border patrol, but there weren't one: there was no border, just a couple of circles painted on the road in some little place I don't recall the name of, an old stone by the side of it, then we was in Belgium. We hadn't really crossed nothing, but it was like we'd made another escape.

We talked about how the border ran right through the town—what it must be like to have neighbours on the other side who spoke a different language. What if you went into the wrong shop and bought the wrong newspaper and you wouldn't be able to read it. Ha ha ha ha. We wouldn't be able to read it anyway.

It was Belgium not Germany. But no one seemed to give a toss where we was, really.

"Come on, " I says. "Where we going next?"

"I don't know," Will said. "You're driving."

"What's the capital of Belgium when it's at home? Luxembourg?"

"Brussels," I said.

"Let's go there then."

"How much money have we got?"

"Some," she said. "Not much. We should go into a bank. We should change the travellers' cheques over."

"Yeah," I said. "We'll stop in the next reasonable-sized place. We need juice. We need to get something to eat. I wonder what the Belgians are like compared to the Dutch?"

"About the same, I expect," Will said. "How should I know what they're like?"

"I think they're nice people in this part of the world," I said. "They seem alright to me." I meant it as well. It was just a shame I'd gone and killed one of them.

"I think we're protected," Charley said. "Sort of by magic."

"Don't say that," I said. "Because we're not protected."

"Well, why else are we bowling along through Belgium instead of getting nicked?"

No one said nothing.

I pulled into a garage for a top up. I looked at him to see if he looked any different to a Dutch person. He didn't, so far as I could see. A bit shorter than most of them maybe. Still, that could due to other reasons. He happened to be a short one. He was a midget in a land of giants. He was a young bloke, a bit of a scruff with all over the place greasy hair. Something about him looked slightly familiar.

"Here," Charley said, "that bloke looked just like you, Lee."

"Yeah, I thought that."

"What, him?" I looked over my shoulder as we pulled off, but he was walking back to the office and I couldn't see his face. "Let's have another look at him."

I turned left and circled back into the forecourt, whereupon the bloke looked up in surprise as I drew up in front of the office.

It was true, I thought, although I couldn't see it as clearly as they could. Charley and Will was practically wetting themselves in excitement. I stopped the car and we all got out. Charley was pointing at my face and at his. Will was nodding.

"Brothers," he said. "You are brothers."

The bloke understood me. A smile cracked his face and he looked at me. He put out his right hand and we shook hands. I automatically put out my left, for some reason, and we shook again left-handed, a sign we just invented on the spot that we was twins. We all stood there laughing, trying to think of something to say. Pointlessly, because it was obvious that he didn't speak no English at all. He tried saying something, but it was in a language we had no chance of understanding. It was Flemish, a language that made you sound like you was just about to gob on somebody. Unlike the Essex language, our language. Suddenly he turned away and beckoned us to follow him.

He led us around the side of the office. We followed him past the toilets towards a bit of waste ground at the back. He pointed up at the roof, which sloped backwards. The garage building weren't much more than a fairly recently built large shed. Where he was pointing up the plastic guttering had come away in the storm, the same one we'd driven through I suppose, and it was hanging down the wall, broken in half by the force of the water that had flooded over it. Underneath it was a big painted oil drum stood up on bricks, full to the brim, overflowing with dark rainbow water. He stepped up to it, mimed grabbing hold of it, and made a tipping gesture. He wanted us to help him empty it out onto the ground.

Will and myself stood on one side and he was on the other. Charley was in the way at first, but she stepped aside quick enough when she realised what we was doing. My Belgian twin was sort of at the front, his hands over the lip of the drum, which sloshed water everywhere—just feeling it you could feel it was heavy, and the ground was muddy already. He kicked at the front bricks, which was solid under it. We rocked the drum back as far as we could and he kicked them away. We lowered it as slow as we could, letting it go, and the water slopped out and slopped back all over us; then we let it go some more, till we all let go and leapt back and a great tidal wave of water was released over the back yard, like Niagara falls or something, and the sheer weight of it and the forward movement sloshed most of it over in a river towards a steep ditch with a few rusted wings and old tyres in it that dropped down to the wire fence; but plenty of it splashed back over us—we was drenched below the knees—and the drum crashed to the ground.

We didn't mind. It was something, something to do. We laughed at it. Then he put the bricks together and we got under the rusty old drum—which was heavy, even empty—and we hoisted it back onto them. It was a messy, dirty job, more than he expected it to be, I think, and he looked a bit taken aback at the mess we was in. Charley had missed most of it; she just got the pleasure of watching. We laughed. We thought it was funny somehow. We paddled over to the edge of the ditch and looked down to where the water had flowed away, to where it was laying in the bottom in a shallow moat.

We paddled out again and went round the front to where some idiot was waiting for petrol by the pumps, looking a bit irate, and ready to drive off. He served them while we stood beside the car, our shoes sodden and squelchy. When he'd finished serving he shook hands with us again. He was laughing now, pointing at our shoes. He ducked inside and got us a coke each out of the fridge, and a big bar of chocolate between us. And that was that. We said goodbye to him, we got back in the Peugeot and carried on.

We drove on, across Belgium, as far as we could get before tiredness and the feeling of afternoon and wanting to stop made us slow down. Once again it was a country we knew nothing about; it had no milestones for us, and no milestone inspectors, nothing to aim for except Brussels, which was only a point on a map we didn't have and the name of some vegetables we usually avoided eating except at Christmas, before lying down to sleep it off, hoping someone would come round, even someone you didn't like.

After a time we found ourselves crossing some more fields on another flat empty road, not a main road but one we'd turned off onto because we thought we might as well go the long way around, and the sun had come out again, and this little road led across bare fields of which the hay had been scraped up into haystacks such as you might see anywhere, and we stopped by the side of the road to eat a couple of bag of crisps we had left and pass a bottle of coke between us and stretch our legs.

"Let's go for a walk." Charley said. "I want to go and look at a haystack."

We followed her, of course, down a stubbly row of stalks, to the nearest one, thinking—I was, anyway—of the first time we'd stopped in the cornfield back in Essex, and wondering what she had in mind for this time. By the time we got out there we was all sweating. We walked around the back of the haystack away from the road and threw ourselves down against it and finished the big bottle of coke. Will stood up and threw it up over the haystack. It rolled down again. Charley chucked it too, and back down it came. Then I had a go, lobbed it as high as I could, and this time it got stuck in somewhere in the middle and didn't come down again.

The three of us stood there looking up at the side of this haystack, then we looked at each other, and it was like the first time again, although a bit different, but the shine hadn't rubbed off Charley at all—she just got brighter and brighter there in the sunshine, between the two of us both giving her our all. I remember she had a cotton dress on from the dress-up suitcase, small blue flowers swarming all over it as we pushed it off her here and there and swung her between us like partners in a rock and roll dancing competition. Her period was ending and she pulled out the last tampax of it and lobbed it up in the direction of the coke bottle, never to be seen again, the tampax that flew away.

That was it. We carried on till we was all spent, then we went back to the car. We was getting hungry and ready to carry on our journey to wherever it was going to carry us to next—who cared anymore, we didn't—a place on the map was just a pinprick for sunlight to come through it and make upside down pictures of us in our memories forever, and what happened in these special days would always be with us, and we all knew that without having to say nothing about it.

White lines flickered underneath us like a film, like arrows pointing the way for a few miles, changing colour, disappearing, coming back to make sure we was still headed in the right direction—going somewhere pretty quick, the radio chirping away, always the same old songs, the country flat, the sky low. Well well well. It went on after all. We hadn't dropped off the edge. We was ready to stop. We was going. We wasn't happy or sad, not really, just floating in our box along the great river, and the stars came out, rushing past in the shapes of all those little places that was announced and crossed themselves off in the blink of an eye, leaving a few pictures behind for the empty miles— someone crossing the only street, leaning outside a bar; a dog barking at us as it must bark at everyone passing all day long, a kid for no reason at all suddenly sticking two fingers up, or one, or a girl anyone would like the look of who looked like she might like to hop in if you slowed down for her; someone clipping a hedge, painting a wall, smoothing concrete over a path, mending a roof on a little house that weren't your house—as if the whole place had stirred itself to life for a moment to be seen by us as we went by.

Charley was looking at the map. "It's run out," she said, "we've gone off the edge of the world. We'll have to get another one."

Will was excited by this news. "Don't bother," he said. "Let's just follow the signs and see where we end up."

"How far do you think Brussels is?" I asked him. "About how far?"

"No idea," he said. "Two hundred miles? Three hundred?"

"And what's in between?" Charley asked.

"A few places, I expect," I said.

"How do we know we're going in the right direction?"

"We don't," Will said. "That's what's so good about it."

"I think we should get a map," Charley said. "And don't forget about them travellers' cheques."

I pulled over when we came to a place big enough to have a bank. A pretty little town called I can't remember, just the sort of place you'd want to stop if you was on holiday. A river. Lots of old brown buildings with carved fronts that looked like they came from a long time ago and been deliberately kept that way, for the tourists, or maybe the Belgians themselves actually liked living in something that looked like an old photograph of itself. I didn't blame them. I would have liked to live there, in none of these places we seemed to pick. They was all better than anything in England. Anything I'd seen anyway. When you come right down to it, England ain't nothing special, not really. I didn't know why people go on about it so much. Belgium was better. So was Holland.

We parked and started to get everything ready. Charley had done the woman's signature over and over again. She had it down perfect. All she had to do was write it on a few of the cheques, which she done in that spiky little handwriting, and try to look as much like the woman in the passport photo as possible. She didn't look unlike her. The main problem was that the Spanish woman had dark hair and Charley was a blonde. I thought she should dye her hair. We could get a room and she could dye it black, then we should be able to get away with it, just about.

But she didn't like that idea. "Lots of people dye their hair blonde," she said. "I'm a real blonde, I am, and I'm not going black just so we can get some more money. I'll get it anyway, just watch. It's easy."

She was lying. She'd forgotten the old photo she'd shown me with her boyfriend. In that she had brown hair. "What will you do if they start staring at the photo and looking back at you," I said.

"In disbelief," Will said.

"I'll just shake my head and laugh," she said. "As though I just dyed it blonde to go on holiday."

"That'll work," Will laughed. "I know it. She's a genius, Charley."

"What else can we do?" she asked. "We ain't got enough money for a room."

"What about your eye?" I said to her.

She still had her sunglasses on. She took them off. "Is it bad?"

It was pretty bad, a real shiner that sat on her face almost as fresh as it had been, only faded out a bit round the edges now to the colour of an egg yolk. It looked tender to touch.

"Does it hurt?"

"Not really," she said. "Stop it! Stop looking at me like that!"

She put her glasses back on, squirmed her shoulders and looked out the window. It'd started to rain again, spottily, then drizzling down like tears. I thought, it always rains in this fucking country. The Belgians was obviously ready for it. Umbrellas at the ready at all times, bobbing along the pavement. Pity we didn't have one, I thought. Pity our plans had run out. But they had, well and truly squeezed dry. Also everyone who passed had an unfriendly look on their face. I realised we'd just been lucky with the bloke in the garage. This lot would be on the blower to the pigs as soon as they looked at us. They was looking at us already, just for being in an unusual motor. Suddenly I hated their fucking country. What a dump to end up in. Now I realised what everyone was always going on about. We was subsidising these bastards and they didn't feel in the least bit grateful for it. They didn't give a shit.

We sat there listening to the rain. It was hammering on the roof so hard you couldn't even hear the radio properly. I turned it off. I opened the door and got out.

"Where are you going?" Charley said.

"For a walk."

"You'll get soaking."

"Leave him."

So they left me to throw a moody and I walked away from the car. Not too far. Far enough to get them out of my sight, around a corner into a shopping street, which was nearly empty, hard rain running off the awnings over shop fronts, splashing in torrents onto the pavements, off into the gutters, flowing away down the street towards the river, the drains. Far enough to get soaking wet. Even the Belgians wasn't out in this lot. They'd scuttled for cover indoors. I couldn't blame them. I stood under the awning of an old-fashioned tobacco shop, its window full of pipes, brown shag spilled out from a horn. I wondered what animal it was from. I stood there because I had to but it was too late. I was soaked to the skin. When it eased off a bit I went back to the car.

"We've got to get a room," I said. "We can pay for that with the travellers' cheques. What are they in?" I'd been worrying about that one. "What money are they in?"

"Pounds," Charley said.

SIXTEEN

The Belgian police was waiting for us—and that was that. There was about six of them hanging around outside the little place, looking at the car. We was coming down the road. Charley was wearing a brown scarf over her hair and one of the woman's dresses, and some make up over her black eye. But it was no good. It took us ages to find out where the bank was and when we did do it was shut. We couldn't very well turn and run, could we, so we just had to walk towards them, and they grabbed us, rougher than they had to be. Charley started crying straight away and didn't stop, but we couldn't do nothing. It was the people in there who'd got suspicious, because of the car, and made a phone call to check us out. Bastards. Or maybe it was the bloke at the petrol station, the one we helped, as quick and easy as that. But I never did find out how they found us.

They didn't rough us up, or slam us down on the pavement, but they did search us. They took Charley into a back room— one of the pigs was a woman—and made her take her clothes off. Then they made us go upstairs and bring the cases down ourselves—we hadn't unpacked this time—and put them in the back of the Peugeot. They didn't say much. They put us in the back of a police wagon and took us to the station. As we climbed in, I looked over my shoulder at that beautiful car, knowing I'd never sit behind the wheel of it again.

This bit is actually terrible. But the way it was at the time was we just had to hang on and go right through the middle of it, and that's the only thing I can do now; but I have to tell it exactly as it happened because it's part of the whole thing of what we done, and what happened later on is also a part of it, and so was this part where we totally fell apart and acted like kids.

The wagon they had was this big black 4x4 Renault, and they had the uniforms to go with it, funny little light blue hats, fucking great truncheons. All of them had guns in buttoned down holsters, and black gloves on. After the main one had spoken to us a few times and we didn't understand none of it, the rest of them never said a word, but they did talk to each other in Flemish, laughing and joking about things we didn't know; which puts you off a lot, people laughing when you've no idea what's so funny. We wasn't laughing. We was petrified. They didn't even let us sit together. Will and myself was on two single seats on one side, three pigs staring straight at us. Charley was at the front next to the woman. We could only see the back of her head. She didn't turn around. I thought they must think one of us had hit her. What else could they think?

The police station was one of the old buildings at the edge of this town, one of the brown buildings. We was taken inside it, sat on a bench for a little while, and then taken into an office where a more friendly sergeant said hello in English. He was laughing. He seemed to think it was funny, what we'd done. But I knew it weren't really. Especially that bit by the canal. But the funny thing was that never came up in their trained minds.

"You will go home now," he said. "You want to go home?"

I don't know what the others said, but I didn't say nothing. I didn't know if I wanted to go home or not. Not, that was the real answer. But the main thing for him, and the rest of them, was getting a cup of tea down us and putting us in cells for the night, because tomorrow morning they was going to take us to our home. We was tired, too tired to take it in properly, so we just shuffled away wherever they told us to go. They took our photos, took our fingerprints; afterwards I laid down on a shelf in the cell they put me in and fell asleep straight away: that was one sure way of getting out of it.

In the morning we was given breakfast and coffee, but there was no use hanging about nor was there no more talk. Just a lot of smiling as if they thought the whole thing was some big joke, which made me think something bad was about to happen. Well it would do wouldn't it. They let us stand close together, and we hugged each other as if we hadn't seen each other for a hundred years of hunger and strife—and it made us all realise how scared we all was and how close we'd all got on our little moving island. We'd floated a long way together, we'd seen and done a few things, some bad, some good: we was two brothers and a sister, and we always would be no matter what happened to us any further.

They ushered us out to one of their wagons, another Renault 4x4; but before we could climb into the back of it, one of the pigs turned, turned round and pulled his handcuffs off his belt.

He made me and Charley stick our hands out, as though he was going to yoke us together, but then he laughed, said something, and clipped them back on. There was two others. One for each of us to make sure we didn't get away, a woman cop for Charley, and I thought this is going to be a mighty weird trip back to Essex. I wanted it to be over and for whatever was going to come next to be got on with and take place back there, but I knew it was going to drag out for ages, over every step of the way back over the ground we'd driven together.

I say that because I was pleasantly surprised, as we all was, to find ourselves driven to an airfield a couple of miles outside town and put in a two-engined red and white plane, a Cessna, small but not too small, with a couple of the pigs and a police pilot in the front with a cap and a big pair of headphones on. We got in the back, fastened our safety belts. They handed us a paper bag each and we was soon up and away over the fields of Belgium, alight with something or another, up into the grey cloud covering them over, and through it into a blue space where the sun came through more bright than ever and we was skimming along over the surface of a meringue: a toasted layer of fluffy egg white and sugar rushed by with our shadow on it running beside us.

Charley spoke. "I feel sick," she said, but she didn't throw up into the bag. She just sat there, looking out, not speaking to us again for hours, as though we was the cause of her problems. Will looked out the other side—thinking about something, I suppose—and I tried not to, because this was one of the best bits of our whole trip, and it weren't something we could've got otherwise than by doing what we had done. I wanted to laugh out loud, to say well, it was all worth it, weren't it boys and girls. I didn't, but that was what I thought to myself. Forget it, I thought. Forget it and enjoy yourself while you can.

The pigs was quite happy. They was smiling at each other, laughing and talking, pleased with themselves to have got such an interesting day instead of handing out parking tickets or telling teenagers not to ride their bikes on the pavement or whatever else they might have been doing instead of flying to England in a light aircraft with three frightened, harmless kids who wasn't going to give them no trouble. They both spoke a little bit of English.

"You are brave," said the man. "You are strong. Now you are going back to your country. You are pleased?"

"Your Mother will be happy to see you," said the woman.

Charley managed to do a half-smile. "I don't think so," she said.

Will and myself felt the same way. We didn't answer. We knew what we had to look forward to weren't going to be good. It was going to be as terrible as the reasons we left behind, but even more so. There was no point looking forward to getting a clip round the ear—you might as well pretend it weren't going to happen. But up there in the clouds that weren't too difficult. The plane kept droning on and on.

We went down for refuelling in Holland, and we got out to stretch our legs and have a drink in a long corrugated hut at the edge of an airfield somewhere. I thought about how much this must be costing, to take us all the way back home by a police plane; then we got back in and took off again, a bump up into the air, and we was like millionaires going wherever we pleased in our own private transportation—I imagined like The Stones or someone like that flying in to play somewhere or out to a studio on some island where they lived.

I fell asleep for a while, and when I woke up again we was way out over the sea. "Look," Will said, "it's the ferry."

I looked down, and there, a tiny glittering dot with a faint white trail behind it, was the boat we'd come on, or another one like it. There was other boats too, big ships, although they didn't look much bigger, sailing on their long curving ways across the world, like boats in the bath, and you couldn't quite believe they was nothing more than toys, which they obviously was, and we was no bigger to them, if they could see us at all, than a tiny buzzing toy plane high overhead with no one inside except ideas of people, not us, and like all sickening ideas you couldn't look at it for long, and like all amazing sights it soon stopped being amazing, but stayed nice, and there weren't nothing to say about it, we gaped out.

The pigs had a flask of coffee and some sandwiches. They handed them round. I wanted to go to the toilet, but it was okay, there was one, and I went down there and came back to my seat.

"This I'll never forget as long as I ever live," Charley said. "This is fantastic."

She'd brushed her hair and fixed it back in a ponytail. The bruise around her eye had faded but was still visible against her fair skin. I didn't know what she'd told them about it, maybe the truth, but anyway myself and Will hadn't got blamed for it. She looked tired but all of a sudden young, about twelve years old, and I felt about the same age myself, and Will didn't seem that grown-up either. Whatever else we ever done, none of us would ever be able to fly a plane, or order one to be flown, and all we could do was behave ourselves and be small and keep still in the palm of someone else's hands, in their sky.

The coast came up into view in the end, and as soon as it did it seemed to rush towards us, reeling us in to England, and to see the loading cranes of Parkeston Quay brought a lump to my throat, and we skimmed along the coast to Clacton and dropped all too quickly onto the airfield beside the road we'd travelled down so often on the bus, its windsock billowing out in the breeze. The Essex police was there to meet us. We soon said goodbye to the friendly Belgian pigs and the pilot, then we was whisked away to Clacton police station for questioning. We was cautioned and made statements and we was told it was a very serious business and we was going to be charged with theft of the car and of the money which Charley had stolen, but which all three of us had spent.

One thing you can say about the Essex police—they really do know how to make you feel welcome in your own country. I mean, really. They handled us with kid gloves when the Belgians handed us over; they coaxed those statements out of us like friendly uncles who couldn't wait to hear about our naughty adventures. We was interviewed separately of course, but there was nothing to go wrong on, not for the others. It was a fair cop, straight up guvnor, and all that bollocks. All I had to do was not mention a couple of things. They could see I was nervous. They always can. I was nervously waiting for something to come up about the gun, but it didn't. Or something about... what happened in Utrecht, but that didn't come up. I was told they was bringing the car over on the boat, so they'd see the luggage then. But they didn't say nothing about the Spanish people.

If anything it went too smoothly. I was suspicious about this. They'd phoned our parents straight away of course. They was all there waiting for us: Will's Mum and my Mum and Charley's Mum (who didn't know them)—but they wouldn't let us see them till they'd finished talking to us for now. Then they let us go—we had to come back the next morning to be formally charged for some reason—and it was when we first set eyes on our Mums that we really started shaking.

They was all in the waiting room—Jennie as well, who'd given Mum and Mrs Woody-Gomez a lift in from Jaywick, and Charley's Mum, who was standing a bit apart from them and looking pissed off. Will's Mum starting crying as soon as she set eyes on him, which set Mum off, and as soon as she starts crying she gets angry to go with it. She started shouting at the cop who brought us in, as though it was his entire fault, because of something the one who spoke to her on the phone had said to her, but it was impossible to work out, because she was crying as well and not making much sense. Will put his arm around his Mum. Charley done the same with hers. We hugged our Mums.

Charley's looked well pissed off with us—and we soon found out why it was.

"You kidnapped her, you did," she shouted at Will and myself. "You dirty little pair of bastards—you should be locked up the pair of you, not her."

Charley tried to pacify her but it was no use. I was surprised about the way her Mum looked. She was nothing like Charley, who was tall but with a big bum, a shape that sort of sloped downwards like an upside down ice cream cone. Her Mum was short and stocky, wide shouldered. She had the same nose though, like a long spoon, which was something I realised I especially liked about her. Now she turned away from us, going out with her Mum without a look back, her whole shape going with her, and my heart was going out the door with them. Her Mum had short, wiry grey hair, brushed back. She was wearing a pair of earrings like blazer buttons. She was older than our Mums. She turned back at the door, held up a finger, about to give us some more gob, but changed her mind at the last minute and left. That was the last I saw of Charley that night. She towered over her Mum, but her head was well down, her blonde mop hanging over her face, hiding in shame.

We was left alone with our two Mums and Jennie. We went out and got in her Landrover. Will and myself climbed in the back on sacks and she drove us back to Jaywick Sands. Not much was said in the front, mainly because Mum and Jennie didn't know Mrs Woody-Gomez very well. Me and Will sat on our wheel arches getting covered in dog hairs. We could just see one another's faces in the spill of oncoming headlights, looking straight across at each other, secretly smiling undercover of darkness because whatever happened we'd done it, what we said we was going to do, and had a bloody great time of it. What could be wrong about that?

Jennie dropped us off at the door. She didn't come in, just drove a little bit further down the road and let off Will and his Mum. Once safely inside, I relaxed. Mum put the kettle on for a cup of English tea and I sat down in front of the telly and waited for it to arrive. Before long she came through with two mugs on a tray and a packet of chocolate digestives. A big smile plastered all over her face.

"So," she said. "You didn't mess about, did you, you and Will."

"I brought you a present, Mum. But I left it in the boot of the car. Some tiles from Delft."

She laughed. "You didn't nick them off a roof, did you?"

"No," I said. "I bought them in a shop."

"I didn't know you'd been to Delft," she said. "I went there once."

"It's a really beautiful place," I said. "The best place we went to."

"Come on," she said. "Tell me everything about it—tell me everything you did. You didn't make that girl do anything she didn't want to, did you?"

"No, Mum, we didn't."

"I knew you wouldn't," she said. "Go on, tell me all about it."

I didn't know where to start except at the beginning. I reeled my mind back to getting into the car and went on from there, onto the boat, over the water, all the places we went to and all the things we'd done—most of them, anyway. Some was too embarrassing, and some I just knew not to tell my Mum. Because you never know quite where you are with her, you never know when something's going to be flung back in your face, added to which I was feeling very tired and wobbly. It was so weird to be back home. Although we'd only been away for just over a week I felt like a different person to the one that had went; but at the same time it was all crashing in on me again—everything I'd tried to forget, every reason I'd had for trying to get out of there.

I talked till it was over, which didn't take as long as you might think, and the very fact of telling my Mum about it put it in the past, made me realise there was no way I could ever get back there, to where we was, and now the same place I'd tried to get away from was going to crush me—maybe forever—so perhaps there weren't so much to laugh about after all.

"I've got it all worked out," Mum said. "I know exactly what you should say to the police—especially if that woman says anything."

But I was too tired. I couldn't listen to her plans anymore. "Tell me in the morning," I said. "I've got to sleep, my eyes are falling shut."

*Okay, dear," she said. "I've made your bed up next door."

"In my room."

"Yes, in your room."

Well, at least she hadn't rented it out. I crawled under clean but slightly damp sheets and I fell straight asleep.

I'd been dreaming about Charley. In my dream she was stood beside me at that moment on the bank of the canal, both of us looking down at the Dutch boy, his shirt bloated out behind him in the flowing water, bobbing in front of us like a great turd. I was trying to say something to her, to explain it away and make her go off with me somewhere. In the dream I was getting my own way, managing to persuade her nothing was wrong. It was the anger I was putting into insisting on it that woke me up. As soon as I was fully conscious I pushed it all out of my mind.

I got up, put some clean clothes on and went out to make myself a cup of tea. Mum was still asleep. I let her sleep on, just stood on my own in the kitchen for a few minutes, drinking my tea by the draining board and looking out of the steamy window. There was a tight lead knot in my chest. I wanted to phone Charley to see if she was okay, but I didn't even have her phone number. I put my cup in the sink, slipped my coat on and stepped outside.

Same grey morning light. Same old Jaywick. What a fucking dump it was. There was a Beautiful Jaywick boat still washed up on its bed of gravel in front of the sea wall, full of red geraniums, but they looked fresh somehow. The earth was freshly turned over, as if someone had emptied it out, laid a body in it and repacked it with the dirt and flowers. Charley had died, a dream carrying on in a warm clinging way. I'd buried her in that boat. I decided to plant her like a big limp tulip. I carefully, gently laid her to rest, her knees crooked slightly to one side; I packed in the earth around her so she'd always be close to me, right there with the same burnt out car next to it as a marker of my love for her. I kicked across the loose road and climbed the wall; looked over at the grey heave of sea, tide half out, the sands glistening a bit. I walked along the wall, hands in my pockets, wishing I was still somewhere else, wishing I had the keys to that motor in them. Not in one place or another. It was the saddest, loneliest feeling.

I looked down at the landside—and who should be walking along, staring at his stupid shoes, but my old mate Will coming to see me. He couldn't keep away if he tried.

"Will!" I shouted to him.

He looked up, waved, changed direction slightly. I walked as far as the steps and he came up to meet me. Together we got down onto the beach and walked out towards the sea. It was a gusty morning, too early for anyone to be out yet, so we had it all to ourselves, and we carried on out to where we could begin to feel the spray.

"So it's over," he said. "What do you think we'll get?"

"You said six months," I said. "Or maybe we'll get away with community service."

"My Mum says she's going to kick me out whatever happens."

"She won't. Mine doesn't seem to mind all that much."

"Your Mum's weird."

We stood there. Either we was going to walk all the way out

to the sea or just turn round and go back. But I walked on and Will followed. I felt like I was in charge now. Really I felt like we was two different people who'd met up after years and years, in the future. Much older. It couldn't be that we'd only been away for a week, and all this stuff about what our Mums thought just seemed to come from somewhere else.

"I wonder what Charley's going to say," he said.

"She won't say nothing—we didn't make her come." I was positive about that. I knew her Mum couldn't make her say nothing she didn't want to say. Will didn't answer. I was glad. I didn't really want to talk about Charley no more. I wondered if we'd get a change to talk later at the police station. "I wonder what's been happening here," I said. "Nothing I expect."

"You're wrong there," he said. "There's been four more fires."

"Anyone hurt?"

"Yeah," he said. "I'm afraid so. This place is totally mad. And while we've been away it's gone even more madder. That's why my Mum's so upset. She's getting out. That what she says. She says she doesn't care if she has to sleep in a field. Who do you think is doing it? Les Hopkins? Warren?"

I didn't say nothing. We looked at the sea for a few minutes, then we turned round and walked back towards the concrete sea wall. We climbed up on it and there we was again, looking over the roofs, looking for new gaps. Everyone knew it was the Hopkins family. Someone's paying them, I thought suddenly. Someone who wanted to get rid of some people they didn't like. It was going away and coming back. I could see it all a lot clearer. The bungalows along the front looked like an unbroken row of patchy teeth; the cavities started behind them: Jowett Road, Standard Road, Vauxhall Road—all broken by black stumps, sumps, pits. Holes where the houses of unwanted residents had once been rooted or had stood up on their little crutches out of the drained marshland.

"It's all the old people—they think it's their paraffin heaters. I've had an idea about it though."

"What's that?"

"Well, what if they're burning their own houses down—to claim on the insurance. I mean, you can't insure a place in Jaywick now, but they've got policies going back donkey's years. They want to sell up but they can't. So if they burn the place down they can use the money they get to buy something somewhere else."

"Who told you this?"

"No one," he said. "It's just something I thought of."

Will and myself kept walking. I told him my theory, all the ins and outs, whys and wherefores, before we even made it to the sea wall. As I was talking I realised it really did make perfect sense. He seemed to think the same way. I knew I'd bring him round to my way of thinking in the end. But no, somehow it didn't add up to as much as I thought. He kept arguing back at me until the plainly obvious was about as clear as a bubble of dubious substance.

SEVENTEEN

We'd made our statements, but they still wanted to go over and over them again before formally charging us with nicking the car and being accessories after the fact to Charley taking what had gone through her till during her shift at Woolworth's, which meant we'd more or less encouraged her, and helped her to get away, and helped her spend all the money. There was going to be other charges, they said, like wasting police time, if we turned out to be telling any untruths, because we wouldn't get away with it. White lies was really dirty lies. One way or another we had to pay back every penny we spent.

They made it sound like we'd be sold into slavery for the rest of our lives. But wait a minute. It was only couple of grand at most. Between the three of us that was pocket money. But I decided not to make too much of a nuisance of myself. I was very open with the pigs. I shrugged and said whatever they wanted to hear. I knew I'd done wrong and now I realised I had to pay the price. They seemed to accept that I was being sincere, which I was being, although not totally sincere of course.

It turned out they'd got the car back. A Belgian pig had driven it all the way to the ferry, and someone from Harwich took it back up to Clacton. They said they was surprised by the state of the car. It weren't beaten up or nothing and had been kept in fairly good order. The clutch weren't burned out, which was the usual thing with joy riders. They had me there. I couldn't stop myself from letting on that I was the driver. They said I seemed like a good driver. Why didn't I take my test, then I might be able to get a driving job. They didn't say nothing about the luggage. They didn't say nothing about the gun, which made me think the Spanish people hadn't told them about it. I mean, why would they? It was illegal. Why did they bring a gun into the country anyway?

It seemed this was a question that would never be answered—it weren't asked, that's why not.

We'd ruined their holiday, did I want to think about that instead? They had to go all the way back to Cordova, now they'd have to wait months before getting their car back because it had been impounded as evidence in our trial. I didn't know the rules—but they could seem unfair sometimes. What would those people think of England? They wouldn't be coming back here in a hurry, would they? With those stern words the pigs let me go.

I waited for Will for a couple of hours while they put him through the same thing. I was hoping Charley would turn up— even if it was with her Mum—but no such luck. When he came out we done what we always done, walked down towards the front, went in the arcade and had a game or two of Bash-A-Mole. The moles go up and down. You try to bash them with a hammer. We got quite a few, imagining each one was a pig's head, then we went down to the sea and tromped out over the pebbles to look at it.

It was an overcast day, very few people braving the water. Most of them was wandering around town eating chips. Summer was in full swing, college had broken up—and we'd missed our exams. We didn't care. We knew neither of us was going to pass the fucking things, no more than a flight of pigs was likely to come wheeling in over the waves, round the corner from Walton-on-the-Naze and drop fruit pastilles into our mouths. But what is likely after all? I realised by now Will hadn't any idea what was likely or not, no more than I did. Nothing we'd done was no way likely. How long before they realised we hadn't come back?

We chucked a couple of pebbles and turned to walk back, just like we'd done that morning in Jaywick, because that's where we wanted to still be, far away from here. But there was a girl leaning on the white railings, I noticed as I looked up towards the prom. It was Charley. She waited for us, her stiff hair pushed back in the breeze. We ran towards her, shouting, ran up the steps, and she held her arms out to us and we both grabbed her and lifted her up in the air.

"Hello boys," she said. "I hope you two ain't been getting up to nothing naughty while I was away."

We linked arms and walked on down to Guzzlers, a fifties-style place on the front, to get a Coke, and we sat in the window as she told us about what had happened to her in the past twenty four hours, like it was some epic journey where every step had to be prepared for and explained in full, and we wanted to hear about it to an extent. We also wanted to hear about her Mum: but it was obvious her Mum weren't going to make her say we'd raped her.

"I've just been into Woolies," she said, "to ask if I could have my job back."

"And?" Will asked. "Forgive and forget, is it?"

"No," she sounded surprised. "They wasn't interested at all."

Charley, I realised by now, was someone who has to try everything out. She didn't know what will happen, only what has happened, that's if she bothers to remember. Now she wanted to have a laugh and we was more than happy to have a laugh with her. We drank up and went outside.

The clouds had blown away and the sun was hanging down low in the sky, tickling the tops of the waves, like a great big beach ball. We walked down the front arm in arm, the three of us together, like I say, feeling it was for the very last time we'd be together like this, feeling weird, special again. The sun really was amazing, as though it had floated down closer especially to have a look at us. We walked towards it, drawn right to the end of the railings where we hung over and looked up into the sky. It was hovering directly over Walton, so it must have looked even more spectacular from there.

Trouble was, there was nowhere further we could go. We snuggled together in our own sunset, trying to make a little nest out there, kissing and cuddling and rubbing her special hand as if it was going to get us out of trouble by her magic.

Will and myself went down the shed for a game of pool. We wasn't expecting no one to be impressed, we just wanted to show them we was back. It would have not been a surprise if they ignored us. But it was. Warren Hopkins and a couple of other kids from down the bottom seemed mighty friendly all of a sudden, saying things like good shot, challenging Will to a game of table tennis, even letting him have the blue racket if he wanted. They asked us when the court case was coming up, in a month's time, and it was all turned around just like that because we'd got as far as we had, with a girl with us, Charley Price.

If you believed any of those little tossers meant you any good you would believe anything, which you would be right to do wouldn't you basically, because the news was true, although how true was another matter, what with all these people putting their oar in and muddying up the clear water which enables you to see right to the bottom of everything. It don't do you no good, does it, although I don't know nothing about the subject, because in everything all of these things was always a little to the south of where you said they'd be. Does that make sense?

"I reckon you'll get three years apiece for what you done," Warren said suddenly, revealing just the sort of well-wisher he really was. "They're going to crucify you for that one mate." He laughed at me.

"Yeah, yeah," said his mate.

We was getting slaughtered in the usual way at the shed, passing a big bottle of Ice Lightning between us. We played a game of doubles with Warren Hopkins and his scrungy sidekick, that floppy-haired streak of piss Mark Hallow in his Motorhead T-shirt, a flushed pale face full of red volcano spots, and scuffed pointed boots courtesy of Mrs Selfish, Will's tailor, one of several Clacton places specialising in dead people's clothes: dead tasty.

They was up on us and then we was all over them, but it didn't matter a fuck really, did it, who won what. It meant we had to have another game as a decider and then another decider after that when they won it and the games decider we had won over them, which it were obvious they would do from the start, but it was still quite a nice friendly thing and a way to show what had been decided so far by our actions, by which we had pulled ourselves up considerably in the world. But really we was just passing the time away, spying out the lie of the land, so we thought we better go home before it got too aggressive. Neither me nor Will had a folding cue and I didn't fancy trying to fold one of those knotty old sticks around Warren's great fat bonce.

"What's been going on here then?" I said, more or less as a parting shot. "Been playing with matches again, have you?" It was the exact right-wrong thing to say to him.

"Don't get too gobby, Fat Boy," he went. "Your Mum likes the taste of my dick too much." Something pathetic like that.

"Watch it, feller," said Martin Harrison.

Will looked like he didn't want to get into all this. He was standing in the door with it open, letting a North Sea draft in through it, so I said the only thing I could think of, which was: "Anyway, your Dad's a fucking cave dweller, Warren. He thinks he's invented fire by rubbing two sticks together."

Warren laughed, believe it or not. "You don't know nothing, Lee. Your mate here knows more about it than what you do."

"I know nuzzink," Will said. "Nuzz-zinc."

"I know your family is bad news," I said. "Whatever bad happens around here has always got the smell of your shit around it. You're even worse than the JRA. At least they don't burn your fucking house down."

"You don't know what you're on, boy," Martin Harrison said. "You want to keep your nose out of things you don't know."

But for a reason I couldn't work out straight away, Warren was happy to see the funny side again. "Les Hopkins ain't my proper Dad, Lee." He laughed again and I wondered why he'd want to make such a disgusting confession in front of his mates.

"Our Dads is gone too," I said, "both of them gone—one way or another. Do you know why? Because our Mums didn't want them no more. They booted them out, didn't they? Maybe they was right to. They had their reasons."

"Your Dad ain't gone away, Lee, he's dead… same as mine." He laughed again, then could restrain himself no longer. "He was my Dad too, you pillock."

"Don't be so fucking stupid," I said. "You're as thick as a milkshake, you."

He was grinning at me.

No one else, not Mart Harrison, not Will, and not one of the other minor henchmen of lower Brooklands was smiling. They was all just looking from me to Warren, back to me, and to Warren. "You do look a bit alike," said Mart Harrison. "Especially round the eyes."

Warren Hopkins had eyes like a pig.

"It's true," he said. "He were giving my Mum one when your Mum was pregnant with you. In the back of his car, apparently."

"But we didn't live here then."

"But that's how you came to live here, pillock. Later—because my Mum and Dad—Les—come to live here when he got out of Norwich or something. They had to break in and squat it, not like you lucky cunts." He could see I didn't believe him. "Ask your old girl if you don't believe what I'm saying to you. Your old boy and mine are the same. My Dad told me when he was pissed one time. He said he didn't want no trouble between us because we're half-brothers."

"When did he say all this?"

"Just before you nicked that car and fucked off out of it."

"He kept that to himself."

"Well, you would, wouldn't you. Mum never said nothing to me about it. Still hasn't. Les told me not to bring it up."

Will let the door close behind him. "Ask your Mum," he said quietly. "It could even be true."

"Yeah, she knows," Warren said. "She went along with it. She had no choice when he came here with you two to fuck our lifes up. There's no doubt about it, mate. Our Dad was a greedy cunt through and through. He could leave it alone neither. He had to keep pick pick picking at it till it bled again. He was dirty bastard, Lee."

I'd never heard Warren talking like this before. He was nearly crying from the straightness of it, from the effort of talking so long, from the sheer effort of saying it. I wanted to grab hold of him by the neck and start whacking his head on the side of the pool table. I wanted to scream at him to shut the fuck up, but I couldn't do that neither. I knew it was right because he said it all in public like that, otherwise why would he? Why would he say it unless everyone knew it was true already?

It was all too much for me. I turned round and walked out of there, head down, back towards our chalet. Will walked along beside me, but I couldn't bear to have him nowhere near me. I didn't say goodnight, just peeled off and went indoors.

Mum was still up, doing the crossword in the Clacton Courier.

"It is true me and Warren Hopkins had the same Dad?"

"Yes, Lee," she said plainly, like she'd been waiting up for me to ask that question. "It is true."

What I done then, I know it weren't fair. I went over to the three Delft tiles she'd propped up above the gas fire, picked them up, took them out to the doorstep and I smashed them to little pieces there one by one. Then she started crying, but not saying nothing. I felt really bad because it wasn't her fault, she hadn't done nothing wrong. Nothing except not telling me I had a half-brother on the doorstep. It didn't mean to say I had to like him, but still it was something worth knowing, or you'd think so.

I went straight through to the front room, my own room, slammed the door, chucked myself down onto the mattress in one graceful movement, landed on my elbows with my face in the pillow—and I really let go, bawling my eyes out for the first time in years, about everything. Not just that but everything that had happened and was still up ahead. But when I thought about it, after an hour or so, I was alright again.

I remembered about it straight away, pulling myself free of a dream which had it all in of course, only in the dream it was Mum who was Warren's Mum as well, and it was her who was setting all the paraffin fires with Les Hopkins, who turned out to be my real Dad. I woke up muddy and emptied out from it. Nothing is quite as bad as what your mind will do with it, that's my opinion. Mum weren't in, and when I opened the back door all the pieces of her tiles was still all on the step, scattered around like a blue broken picture of milk, a past you couldn't possibly pick up and put back together. I remembered Dad telling me how birds used to peck open the tops of milk bottles. Birds was quite intelligent then. When milk froze on the step a long finger of white ice would poke up through the lids.

I was ashamed of what I'd done last night. It had become a routine with me to be like that when I got in pissed. It was the only way to show how I felt, but it weren't a good way as I knew from when Mum was just the same: it was her I'd got it all from, I always thought. It was just the way she was and the reason why my family was like that. I didn't remember my Dad being nothing else but calm and together with whatever he had to do, but Warren Hopkins was a bit the same, I could see it now I'd thought of it. Now it had been explained to me I knew that was the way it was really.

I gathered up all the pieces and chucked them in the dustbin, put the lid on it. I was soon up and dressed again but there was nowhere to go, nothing to do down here at the big toe end of the sock of nowhere, nothing to do but bang around like a wasp in a sugar jar in a sort of desperate boredom that made me want to go and get Will and go out and nick another car and get going again as soon as possible.

I put my coat on and wandered down to the Brooklands shop, hoping to find Will there again, his coat tails flapping down over Supercar, but it was empty, peeling blue, the slot rusted over, still forever. I looked through the window of the empty amusement hall, at the flexes hanging down like whips from the walls, and not a single machine was left, not even a broken one. I went in the shop and looked around for something to buy. I had no money in my pocket except enough for a bar of chocolate, so I bought that.

I ate it walking along, deciding to do one of my old loops around the place: up, past the Never Say Die and down Golf Green Road, then out towards the Three Jays and cut back and round to where I'd first started. The loop. The loop that I'd stepped into due to being born, it seemed, a collar tight as on a dead boy's shirt that was meant to fit you but it didn't fit you and it never would, no matter what they said. Nobody and nothing was about. The place was even deader than usual for a weekday morning, just dull grey emptiness and the flicker of a few tellies of old people in rooms behind net curtains they bought from Sweet Tina's years ago, 'for all your net and curtain needs', which is one business in Jaywick that never says die.

I passed by the shop-in-a-house, the shop that's never open because it never was a shop really, just a few packets of Daz piled up in a pyramid in the front window on a piece of pegboard, the red boxes turned yellowish green by sunlight, and a few cans of beans with nearly the same but older labels lined up across the sill, a couple of cardboard magazines of wooden clothes pegs—dead ammunition from long times ago. We passed this place, or used to, every day on our way to the bus stop—about halfway down the road, halfway to nowhere, halfway across. All that happened was the Daz packets bleached out a bit more. I thought of getting the bus into Clacton, just to wander around or something, but I had no money in my pocket. I bounced back like a wasp. I'd banged against the glass again, against the sides of the milk bottle: a buzzing little bastard in a yellow and black suit.

189

I got to the end and turned round and came back down the road: the only, lonely, road there was. There was something good about getting out to the edge and coming back, though not as good as getting away forever. I decided to go round and see Will, see what he was getting up to, see what his mad mother had to say, and maybe listen to a few of his scratchy old records. Yeah, Will. Will was indoors. I was so relieved when he opened the door as I knocked, like always, as if he'd been standing behind it. I went in and sat down on one of his old armchairs. Said not a light as one of his singles ground to a last climax: shot down.

Sonny and Cher. It clicked off. We sat there. Mrs Woody-Gomez put her head round the corner, dressed in her usual flashy way, holding her handbag, about to go out somewhere mysterious. I give her a sickly smile, because I knew it was ten to one she would kick off at me, even kick me out the house. But she didn't do that, not this time.

"Ah," she said, "it is these two dangerous criminal back together. Bonnie and Clyed, Frank and Jesse James. Bootch Cassidy and Sundance Keed. What is your new plan? You escape this time? You jump over cliff in raging river?" She laughed drily. "I wait, I see. I go for boring job interview. That is life, you see. Life is boring, yes, I'm afraid so." She left us there to think on this truth of hers.

"What job's that?" I asked Will.

"Secretary," he said. "She won't get it. She never does. She'll come home and cry about it later."

I remembered that about Will's Mum, that special characteristic of hers. I wondered how many times you could do the same things, get the same results from them and carry on, this time, this time: not this time; and wondered how many times we'd had this same conversation and how many times more, if we stayed here, which we probably would, after we'd been banged up for six months each, and come back home, we'd have it again.

"What happened to that gun?" Will asked out of the blue, as if he'd just thought of it that minute.

"I chucked it away in Utrecht," I said. "I told you."

"That was a good move," he said. "Where did you get rid of it?"

"Put it in a rubbish bin."

"I thought you chucked in the water?"

"No, I weren't nowhere near the canal when it happened."

"When what happened?"

"When I decided to throw it away. I chucked it in a bin just outside the hotel."

"That was a weird thing to do," he said. "But it was a totally weird thing that he had a gun in his luggage."

"Because he's a criminal, I suppose—I mean, why else?"

"Do you think he was going to shoot someone with it?"

"Yeah, he was going to shoot someone with it—undercover of having his family with him. We probably stopped that happening."

"How do you know that?"

"I don't."

"I prefer to think otherwise," Will said. "I prefer to think he was on the run from someone, they all was, and he brought the gun with him for protection."

"On the run from the mob, like."

"Right. What else would explain it?"

"I don't know," I said. "He thought it was a cigarette lighter. He picked up the real one by mistake."

Mum was stood on the doorstep talking to that horrible JRA woman. The other one. Councillor Joan Fiddler. Poking her nose in was Joan Fiddler's speciality. If she weren't hassling you for money she was dropping all the latest poison in your ear; and if she weren't doing that she was smiling and nodding her head to extract what she could of your troubles—to add to her stocks of other people's troubles, to see if she couldn't multiply them by a thousand and send them back to you, all in the name of helpfulness and making everyone feel part of the community. So you couldn't get out of it. You always had to give her something. You had to cross her palm with filth of one kind or another, then she'd go away contented.

Mum always seemed to forget this about her, or maybe she just took it for granted as she fished around in her old bead purse for the subscription money, and she dredged up what she could from her conversations with Jennie, because Jennie was her only real friend in Jaywick. Jennie heard a fair amount of what was really going on. I could tell by the expression on Mum's face when she caught my eye, by the way her hip slumped against the doorway, that they'd been talking for ages, a really epic jawing match, and in the look on Jo's face when she turned to see me coming towards them, I read the full tale of my crimes.

I pushed straight past them, straight through into my bedroom.

Mum hammered on the door a few seconds later.

"What?" I called from the bed. "What do you want?"

She came into the room. "Mrs Fiddler said hello to you. Don't be so rude. Come and say hello to her."

"I can't stand her."

"Come on, you know what she's like."

I stood up and went out with her to where Jo Fiddler was still waiting on the step. "Hello, Mrs Fiddler," I said. "Sorry I was rude. I thought you was talking to Mum."

"So," she said. "So you're back from your adventures, Lee. I expect you had quite an exciting time out there, didn't you?" She poked my arm with a finger, her mouth puckered into a fruity shape, and her beady button eyes fixed on my face.

"Well, yeah," I said. "It was alright, I suppose. A bit silly, really."

She stood there, hands in the pockets of her coat, one foot slightly forward, looking up at me in that perky, inquiring way, temporarily gobsmacked. She was about five foot one, her dark hair in a neat short cut, her skin young-looking for a woman her age, a woman who smoked and drank. Mum used to wonder what kept her looking so young-looking.

"You took a young lady with you, I hear," she said. "Kidnapped her from Woolworths, I hear." She said it jokily with her trademark cheeky grin, but it was obvious what was going on in her mind. What had gone on, in fact. What had already been around the town twice and come back on the ill wind that blows down Jaywick Broadway.

"She invited herself," I said. "Then she moaned all the way."

Joan Fiddler laughed. "Just like a woman, eh Lee? I think you'll find they're all like that," she said, as though she was any different from the rest of them, which she was in a way. "We don't know how to enjoy ourselves, do we Angie?"

"Well, you seem to make quite a good stab at it," Mum said.

Joan Fiddler laughed again. "No peace for the wicked." She said it in a self-satisfied way; it was one of her sayings, one she'd thought of all by herself apparently.

But she really was wicked, I thought. Not just mildly annoying but a really nasty piece of work who went around boasting about it, and if they laughed with her they was in. Then they got a treat—a few words of her advice, which, so Jennie said, was guaranteed to bring you to rack and ruin.

"So," she said. "Are we going to see you at the meeting on Friday night? You really should come, Angie. Don't let the bastards get away with it. That BRU lot want to split us up. They'll have the council down on us again like a ton of bricks. If they have their way we'll be back to the days of the Elsans and the Bisto Kids. You've got to give and take a little bit to get what you want, that's what I've always said. I'm all for the pioneer spirit—that's where Maggie Thatcher got it right. She would have been on our side on this one. The ideal of Jaywick is home ownership. We fought for it. Our parents fought for it. Now the council want to build here and start moving in their yuppie tenants onto our land. It's not right, is it, Lee?"

I shrugged. "Is that what they're doing then?"

"Of course it's what they're going to do. They're already done it. That's what lies behind all this. Divide and rule."

I wasn't sure I got her drift, but never mind, Joan Fiddler was absolutely positive she'd got her point across. She give us a final twinkle and headed off to drum up support somewhere else. I'd always thought she was a member of the Labour party. Wasn't they supposed to be in favour of council houses and all that?

"So what's this meeting about?" I asked, "about the council again?"

"It's about these bloody fires," she said. "It's the fault of the police. They don't seem to give a toss about our old people. And the fire-brigade. We need a fire station in Jaywick itself, that's the only solution."

"I don't know why they can't find out who's doing it," I said.

"That's what we'd all like to know," said Jo Fiddler. "We'd all like to know that one. Do you know, Lee, there was a terrible thing happened here when you were away."

"What was that?"

"A couple of boys, about your age, squirted a can of deodorant in a thirteen year old girl's face and set light to her with a disposable lighter."

"Where was this?" I asked her.

"In the alley down the side of Acacia Way. They burned her eyebrows off. She could have been blinded. And then they just ran away laughing."

I didn't know what to say. It was bad alright. I half suspected Warren Hopkins, that little fucker was capable of anything. Scumbag. It got so you didn't want to hear about these things anymore, they was all so typical of round here.

When she'd gone I went back indoors with Mum. I picked up a stack of old Yellow Advertisers that was lying in the corner of the living room, and read through them to see if I could get any information about what was going on. Nothing. Just the usual load of ads for restaurants in Clacton, photos of horse trials and school swimming competitions, births and marriages and deaths. Nothing about us. Nothing whatsoever. They didn't like nothing real to spoil the Yellow Advertiser.

That night I sat in with Mum. I didn't have a lot of choice really. She was well upset with me for smashing her tiles I'd brought her, and for what we'd done and where it was going to end up. If it was just life to us, it was killing her, so she said, and acted it out, but she had her own point of view, and I tried to respect it for what it actually was.

"You're getting out of control you are," she said. "What are you looking in those old papers for?"

"I was looking to see if there was anything about us."

"Well, there was. A little bit. About how you'd gone missing. Can't remember which one it was in though. We didn't know where you'd gone."

"What I can't understand is why they didn't get onto us straight away," I said.

"Because they're dopey," Mum said. "Because they've got better things to do with their time."

We watched a bit of telly, the new start of something, then she turned round and said to me again: "You are, Lee. You're getting totally out of control, if you don't mind me saying so."

"I'm not Mum. I'm totally cool with it. I know what's gunner happen and I know what I've got to do about it."

"You think you know," she said. "You all think you know. You always was a cussid little devil."

"Well, if I don't know, I'm fucked," I said. "It's bloody obvious, innit? They're going to put us away for about six months, three months if we're lucky, or we might get away with community service—that's if the beak's stoned or pissed or something."

"Wherever did you learn to talk like that?" Mum sucked on her pipe, her cheeks going in, and a curl of smoke curled up from it in a thin question mark. Her eyes bulged, let go water as she let go of the toke. That was one thing that hadn't changed and never would change. "You didn't learn it from me or your father."

But if you're asking did none of this bother me unduly, my answer is no, because at the end of the day we'd done what we wanted to do and if we didn't completely get away with it, well, we never expected to get away with it really, so waiting for what was going to happen next was just another part of our roll of the dice. Obviously there was a whole chain of things we threaded that was still settling down, and what happened was partly caused by what we'd done, by ourselves.

"Let's go up the tower," Will said.

"Okay," I said. "We'll do that." A couple of days later we beat a path down to the place where it was. The Martello tower had been broken into and boarded up so many times, locked with padlocks and a steel gate which swung open one day then disappeared, all so long ago we didn't remember, and it was a curious walk down there as we waited to see if we would be able to find our way inside.

The tower was open but the door was rotted and jammed shut and we tugged and strained at it till it came back a couple of foot over the brambles that had grown up to the door, along a pair of fresh score-marks that told us someone else had been up here not long before. A sour reek hit us straight away, and we pushed into the darkness. It was like stepping into a tomb; a rustling scuttle made us hesitate. We waited till they'd taken cover. We stepped in and followed the shafts of sunlight to some narrow, winding stone stairs that led up to the top.

Will walked to one of the slits and looked out at the flat sea. "Goodbye thin white duke," he said. "I have taken down your ridiculous portrait from my wall."

There was a rank smell of stale piss. Dim light, all of it coming in through empty slit windows with bars on, like high castle windows. I went over and looked out at the grey heave of the North Sea. No boats on the horizon, just a long flat container ship, too far off to see its flag, ploughing up to the Hythe to deliver a cargo, coal probably, from god-knows-where, to what was left of industry, places like that industrial estate on the other side of the estuary at Manningtree, with goods trains sliding in and out of it, a wisp of smoke hanging in the still air from a tall steel tower, a fat cube of outside plumbing next to it. Nothing like that to look at here. A pair of swans flapped overhead in a straight line, making their double honking noise, like those wind-hummers we used to whirl around our heads when we was kids, or something, like nothing but swans really. They passed on inland without missing a beat, synchronised, not needing to egg each other on, just together.

"Amazing up here, isn't it?" Will was stood beside me at the next window. "You forget."

We looked out at the sea, the sunlight strong on it, a yacht or two tacking out from Brightlingsea, a couple of retired old boys aboard out for the day, or a family of rich bastards heading for the Mediterranean. I caught the glitter of a pair of binoculars for a second. They was out there looking in on the Martello tower, but too far out to see us.

In the corner there was an old mattress, dragged up here not too many eons ago by some other kids. I didn't remember it being there. I walked over and kicked it, bent down to touch it. Damp, stuffing hanging out, and a big brown patch on it that looked like dried blood, its jagged shape suggesting someone had died here in terror and agony. "Look at this," I said, "I think someone was murdered here not long ago."

Will came over and looked. "Is it blood? Or is it rust?"

It looked a lot like dried blood to me. I supposed someone—a woman—could have bled on it and that's why they'd thrown it away, to be dragged up here by an army of worker ants. I scraped it with the toe of my shoe and some of it brushed away. It was like dry powder. What was it? I didn't really want to know. Just old blood-rust. But there was a powerful bad feeling in the place.

"Look at this," Will said, "right over here."

I followed him over to the corner behind the door to where something more recenter was stashed. It was an old jerrycan. It looked like an army surplus one, rusty but still in use, a roughly folded rag tucked under the handle. We squatted down to look at it closer. The rag smelled strongly of paraffin. I picked it up. Heavy, full. Will unscrewed the cap with the rag and looked down inside, sloshed it around a bit. It was filled about three fourths to the top with pink paraffin.

EIGHTEEN

One day I walked down past the Martello tower, across the middle of the golf course—one or two people still playing at all times—and carried on all the way to the edge of Butlins, round the wire fence, and looked in at the last few holiday-makers around the old blue pools. They was drinking, clowning around some of them, but mostly they was older people just sitting there, and when they smiled at me I smiled back, not looking too closely at them because they could get quite aggressive sometimes about being stared at like animals in a zoo. Or maybe that's what I was to them—a bit of local colour straying up to their compound after a few scraps. I bought me an ice cream in a sweet shop and licked it as I walked all the way back again.

There was a time when we used to collect lost golf balls and try to sell them back to the club, a time after that when we just nicked them and chucked them in the sea. There was also the time when I put one in Dad's vice and squeezed it till it exploded and all these compressed worms of elastic flew out like he said, just like they had done when he were a nipper, just like they always would. Who could guess there was so much gunk, so much violence, in a golf ball. No one would guess, and that's why it's something a lot of people have to try for themselves, just to kill the cat.

Friday came around. It was the big meeting in the Commie Centre. They was all in there, every one of them, every bullshitter and bastard in Jaywick, all the people who was normally too high and mighty to talk to us. Under one roof. Getting ready to give it some in the great cause of the sound of their own fucking voices. The leaders of our community, twats one and all. I recognised Joan Fiddler, sitting right up there at the table on the stage, looking like she owned the place. I hadn't been in there for years, but I remembered the trouble it caused when they decided to ban music on their premises. I think Joan Fiddler must have been behind that, on the grounds that it caused too much noise at chucking out time—and nobody young had no reason to have nothing to do with the place no more. The shed was good enough for us.

Mrs Lambert was sitting in the front row in her Tibetan bobble hat. Mum and myself sat at the back. Will and Mrs Woody-

Gomez sat next to us. The Commie Centre isn't that big, not like an aircraft hangar or nothing, not even as big as the old closed up arcade. There was rows of plastic chairs clipped together, each one with a leaflet on it, but in spite of it being an important meeting there was quite a few empty rows of seats between us and the front two or three, which was basically full. Most residents had voted with their feet to stay away, it seemed, and that made me think it couldn't be that important after all. It made you wish you hadn't bothered wasting your time. But I was wondering if the Hopkins family would turn up.

"I don't know why I bother," Mum said, "I hate these bloody meetings."

She didn't often. I was hoping she weren't going to get worked up again.

Mrs Lambert stood up, pottering to the back of the hall. She seemed to be looking for something, like a cup of tea maybe, but there was no tea available this time. She went through the door towards the toilets, which was out there, and on her way back she spotted us and came over to say hello to us.

"Quite a turn out," she said. "Quite a turn out for the books." She pursed her small mouth in an unconvincing smile. "I must say, I am surprised to see you here." And that was that. She pottered back to her seat at the front, leaving us sorry we'd even bothered coming.

Warren and Les Hopkins came in. Their Mum, Mrs Hopkins, marched down the front and sat in the second row. All you could see of Les Hopkins was the shaved back of his neck, a pig's neck, and his head, also shaved, seemed too small for it. What a fucking animal. Yvonne Hopkins glanced sharply from side to side, angry, as if daring anyone to say nothing to her, and ready for it. Her candy floss hairdo, wobbling ever so slightly, obstructed the view of whoever was sitting behind her.

The meeting was about to kick off. On the platform next to Joan Fiddler was George Spires, Maureen Owen, for the JRA, and a single community pig from Clacton, who sat on the end looking uncomfortable. He was a grey-haired, thin bloke with a little rat-like face, and people had always held it against him, you could tell. He also knew he was in for a right bollocking from the residents of Jaywick, but in his heart he didn't give a shit. The whole place could go up in flames as far as he was concerned, along with all the scum who lived in it. Good riddance. He would be reassigned somewhere else. Brightlingsea maybe. The truth was, in our part of the world, they didn't seem to be enough pigs to go round. It was a rarity that one should show his face, and so it was to him that the curiosity mainly turned.

Joan Fiddler stood up and introduced the speakers, her eye darting around the room as she stood there, the great Joan Fiddler, our saviour, cracking jokes. I remembered how she'd stopped the council building a skateboarding park like the one in Brightlingsea, because she thought it would be a magnet for drug-dealers and child perverts.

But when George Spires stood up to talk it was a different matter altogether. Everyone liked him. Everyone liked George, whether they was on his side or not. He didn't have to try. *Old George has stood up*, I seemed to hear everyone mutter under their breath so that it amplified into words and a can't help it round of applause before he'd even said nothing. He was a red-faced little short-arsed feller George Spires, but there was something about his face that fitted, and his way of standing, holding out his hands as though pushing everyone down into their seats, as if they was about to mob him, pausing, hesitating before he opened his mouth—something that more or less won everyone over straight away, so that even people who totally disagreed with everything he stood for, liked him to stand up. Maybe… but he was better than Joan Fiddler, who couldn't make herself clear on nothing, and who expected you to trust her when it was all too plain you shouldn't trust her an inch.

"Fifty year I've lived here," George said. "I've lived here through the worst times we've had, and some of the best ones and all. I remember Frank Stedman. I remember the Morocco Club. I went away to Aden in the army—and afterwards I come back here. I came back, didn't I. I remember before then when I was a nipper, fishing for black eels under Hackney bridge. I remember before the sea wall was built. I remember people up on their roofs, crying and being swept away. I remember hundreds and hundreds of people drowning over the years. But I've never seen nothing as bad as this. Old people, people who've lived here as long as me, being burnt alive in their own homes, burnt alive like in gas ovens."

He put his hand up and touched his forehead, fell to quietness. I wondered what he was going to say next, but I didn't know it. When he put his hand down again and tried to open his mouth, he couldn't speak. Suddenly there was tears streaming out of his eyes, and he said:

"This could be the end of Jaywick. There's nothing left that I'd want to recall, to pass on. If we can't look after our own house—and I mean catch the bastards who're doing this—they might as well send the bulldozers in tomorrow morning, as far as I'm concerned. That's all I've got to say. Brooklands was called after a racetrack as we know, the drivers used to buzz around it. Some of these youngsters use our Brooklands as a racetrack. I've complained about it, you know I have. But that's nothing much, is it, just kids, not compared to this. Whoever's behind these burnings, they're driving a stake right through our hearts." He said: "and that's all I've got to say." But he added: "I've seen crows dive-bombing a buzzard before now. They all get together, if he's on their territory, and they attack, and the old buzzard, though he's miles bigger, he soon buzzes off.

The hall was hushed. Everyone in there had breathed in at the same moment without letting go. He sat down.

Joan Fiddler stood up again. "Thank you, George," she grated on. "Well, that was a very positive message, wasn't it, from the head of the BRU. I know we've got problems. You know we've got problems. That's why we're here tonight. So I hope our next speaker, Maureen, will have a more positive message for us— about what we can do in a positive way about the plans of the council and the private builders who are building here—and how we can help the police catch these arsonists."

Molly Gower was a large, scruffy woman in a frayed cardigan. She got to her feet and started talking quick in a nervous voice in which no one could hear proper what she was saying.

"Speak up, love," a bloke called. "We can't hear you at the back."

"Can't hear her at the front neither," someone else joined in, and everyone laughed.

"Apologies, apologies," said Molly, a bit louder. "Well, can you hear me now?"

"Just about!" the bloke called back.

"Good!" she said. "What I want to start by saying is—I like Jaywick! I like living in Jaywick! I like my house and where it's situated—and above all, I like the people who live in Jaywick. As Joan says, there are many positive things about the changes coming to this town. But if I was going to build here, well, I think I'd think twice about it. Wouldn't you?"

She was in full flight now, and everyone was listening to her.

"I understand how George feels. I'm sure we all do—that's why its absolutely essential that we pull together as a community—and root out this rottenness in our midst. Because I know the people of Jaywick are good people. Yes, good people. And the sort of people who set fire to other people's bungalows—for whatever reason—even if they don't like them—are monsters. They are murderers."

"Course they are, love," an old bloke shouted. "They're the sort of people who'd pour petrol over a dog and set light to it, just to watch it run around, like happened last winter to my pooch." He shouted louder: "And they want the same fucking thing doing to them, that's what they want!"

"Yeah," said a deeper voice. "They're also the sort of people who hide behind their lace curtains and don't do nothing about it."

"You can't accuse Maureen of that," said Joan Fiddler.

"Thank you, Joan," the woman said, "I don't think anyone meant to suggest anything of the sort."

"Get on with it, can't you," someone said.

"Let the lady speak her piece."

"So what's your idea then?"

"Neighbourhood Watch."

"We've got Neighbourhood Watch," someone called. "See no evil, speak no evil."

"Neighbourhood Bitch," I said to nobody in particular.

"What we need is more proper community coppers. Coming round here on a regular basis."

"They ain't got the manpower."

"They're bleeding useless when they do manage to turn up."

"It's not kids, anyway" someone shouted out. "Not this time it ain't. There's something else behind it."

The meeting was in full swing. Molly Gower was talking away to the crowd, bouncing off them, letting everyone have their say, then coming back again. George Spires sat in his chair, coming to life a little bit, close listening with his head pushed forward like an old, ruffled hawk. And the community copper crossed his thin arms, angled his narrow, dented head. Will and myself looked at each other. We had other fish to fry. None of them, not a single one of these brilliant people seemed to notice when we got up together and slid out the back door.

Will hopped up on the sea wall and started hopscotching along it in his clumsy way. I thought he as going to break his neck. I walked along in its shadow, in his shadow, out on the sea side, soft waves lapping yards away, a sheet of dark water out there, not too choppy, the coldness rising off it even in summer, and up in the sky a fingernail clip of a moon hanged down. If only Charley was there with us, I thought, alongside of us, tromping along and complaining, what a fucking shame.

"Here we are," I said.

He disappeared. I climbed up and over the hand-rail steps, pulling myself up and over like over the side of a submarine, to jump back into action as soon as we synchronised our watches and smeared the black stuff on our faces.

We was right opposite our place. I watched Will heading off down the side, then overtook him at a trot. I unlocked the shed, slipped the open padlock back on, and picked up that old olive green jerrycan from behind the door. Too heavy, sloshing with paraffin almost to the very top, but I stuffed some rags in my pocket, picked it up and ran with it, using its weight as a pendulum to kind of run us down the road. I stopped fifty yards on, picked it up and ran again. Will stood in the middle of the road, walking backwards, my look out. No one else was about.

We stopped outside Hopkins ranch, with its handsome array of dead cars, a sort of circular junkyard drawn up around the main homestead like a wagon train. We walked in past the hulks of motors, a few scalped defenders still holding rifles in their hands behind the wheels, but they didn't give us no trouble, no trouble at all. Straight away I started sloshing paraffin through the letter box, about half a gallon, stuffed a soaked rag in after it like a fuse; then we lobbed a brick through the front window, sloshed another gallon in there. Will got his Mum's household matches out and set light to it. A flame jumped straight up like a puffball of blue light. I dropped it and the dry grass crackled and shot up in a floating pool. I couldn't pick it up. I stamped it back out.

"Quick," Will said to me. "Do another one, quick."

I found another rag. We doused it in the para and set light to it, closer to the window this time. I managed to swing it in through the gap. Light fuse in front door, retire. Which we done, ducking out into as much darkness as we could find, down the side of the caravan site along a dog track into a muddy bit of brush, up over the sea wall that way and onto the dark beach. Nothing but the waves and wind. Totally disconnected from what we'd just done, which we knew was right and could only stop the Hopkins crowd dead in their tracks for good, walking again with a great black sea at our shoulders. Nothing to say none of it was real, I mean. Except for the jerrycan in my hand still sloshing with half a gallon of unused paraffin. I was back on that road again, walking against the traffic along to the last knockings of Holland. Or Belgium.

"Throw it in the sea for fuck's sake," Will called out to me. "We've either got to go back to mine or go back to the commie centre. Which is it? Come on, what do we do now, mastermind?"

"Let's burn the fucking shed down," I said. "They'll never think that was us."

Will laughed a long maniac laugh out of the darkness, going up into a yalp at the end. "I like it, I like it!" And I heard him slapping his two hands together like a seal.

We went back over the wall where the shed was on the other side. Jesus, the Hopkins place was going up like a fucking haystack now, you could warm your hands on it from fifty yards away. Still no one was about. But there wasn't many residents down that end. Everyone was obviously in the meeting, or else they didn't want to get involved. Anyone who did look out and see it was the Hopkins mob that had gone up would be more than happy.

We knew didn't really have no more time. But we done the shed anyway, done it good. It was quite easy to whack the windows in with the heel of the jerrycan, wet another rag, lob the can in through the hole, then set light to it and stuff it through afterwards. The pool table went up in a sheet of blue flame which went tumbling and flowing off it and shooting across the floor and up the side walls, lit up the inside like the inside of a garage. Brighter than it ever was or would be again. I stood there and looked at it for a minute, at what we'd done. My old feller was bulging out of my trousers. I couldn't believe what it felt like.

We went straight back over the sea wall and ran out as far as we could get, myself sprinting after him over solid wet sand, full pelt, then further out past the tip of the town, out towards the marshes where it stank to high heaven.

NINETEEN

Dave Berry really was a two-faced cunt. Face number one was this tough but fair responsible type of bloke who understood you, who was basically on your side and was going to try and keep you out of prison; number two was a feller who was always busy, always on the move, who had a thousand and one threads running through his fingers. Curly-haired, thick-set Dave Berry from up North. All round decent bloke. Everybody's mate. It was so obvious he was going to throw us straight to the pigs. He had a lot of cases to consider, you know, especially his own.

I didn't like the way he talked to you as though he knew you and understood you when basically, he knew fuck all about us. I didn't like the way he thought we wasn't bad kids and that we knew we'd done wrong, I didn't like it at all. Failing that, I didn't think much of his idea that we knew the score. We knew nothing. Or that us and him was basically on the same side, and we all knew what time of day it was etc. I didn't like none of that. So with Dave Berry it was a case of keeping your mouth shut as far as possible, admitting nothing, not smiling, crying maybe. Yeah, crying. He liked getting you to shed a few tears.

Tom Chaser, our lawyer, tried to take you through everything step by step. It was like, if you do this, this will happen, if you say that, they will say this. And this is exactly what you'll get for it. So this is what you've got to say. He was an okay type, a scrawny little feller whose skin seemed to be flaking off in his face in red nervous patches. He had a jerky, nervous way of talking. He believed in helping people so long as they helped themselves, and even if they didn't help much he'd still have a go, a bit of one anyway. He was acting for all of us, assigned by the court, and he talked to us all together. He didn't try to have a laugh and a joke with us. We all knew it was serious, and he seemed to understand that what was happening now weren't something that happened to us every day of the week.

He didn't like Charley much, but he didn't let it show. Except to myself—I can always tell if anyone doesn't like her. At first I thought he was going to be like her Mum and start accusing us of all sorts of things. But it could be he was just shy of her because then he seemed to sit back and look at us as a group, and he could see how we all liked one another, and when we was together we really was. It seemed to please him greatly. He had a thin smile, like he was laughing to someone who weren't in the room, someone always with him, you know, like the only person he could share a special joke with.

Going in to Clacton and seeing these official people, and seeing Charley again, that was good in itself. We was the centre of attention for once in our lives, not rehearsing for a play we wasn't actually going to be in, a true play that would last for the rest of our lives, and then everything would change. I know I keep saying that but it's true.

It weren't difficult, it weren't difficult in the slightest, because we only had to say what really happened, and although we was going to plead guilty to everything it was still important that he said the right words for us. The only thing I wanted to say was I didn't mean to kill that Dutch bloke, but that was the only thing I couldn't say nothing about. And I knew I wouldn't by accident. Will and Charley wasn't going to say nothing about the gun: it was completely forgotten by now that it ever existed.

"That Spanish family aren't coming over, are they?" I asked Tom Chaser out of curiosity.

"Why would they do that, Lee?"

"Well, to see us being punished," Will explained. "To get their pound of flesh. Take some pictures of us."

"Yeah," Charley laughed. "We didn't use his film up. We didn't even find his camera, did we?"

"No," I said. "Shame about that," I said. "We'd have something to remember it all by then."

"This isn't funny," Tom Chaser said. "What you've done isn't a joke. You don't laugh at the court unless you want to be taken to be in contempt of it, which—believe you me—is not what you want. Don't try and get clever with the law. That's my honest advice."

"Did they get their car back?" I asked him. "I mean, I'm only curious, sorry for all the trouble we caused and that, but I just wondered about it."

"Yes," he said, " yes, yes, I think they did anyway. I'm not sure about it actually. And as far as them coming over here, well, they could if they liked. There's nothing to stop them."

"They could pick up their car and luggage at the same time," Will said, "if they haven't already done so."

"Yeah," Charley said. "Don't they want it or something?"

"Of course they want it," said Chaser. "It'll be sent back to them—apart from what the police need as evidence."

"Would they take some pictures of it?" I asked him. "I mean, I wouldn't mind one, seriously, as a reminder of what we done."

"You'll have plenty of time to remember it if you go on like that," he said. "The main thing to remember is to speak when you're spoken too, and to be very polite. Just do it. Do you all understand me? Do it like that and you might not even have to go to prison."

But they couldn't let us walk free from the court or everyone would be doing the same as what we done. We had to hold our hands up and take what was coming our way. Charley didn't say nothing against us, but her story did have to be slightly different to ours. After all, she wasn't involved in actually nicking the car, only the money, which was something she done on impulse because she wanted to go with us, whereas we'd made plans to nick that car. We'd packed our clothes, brought some keys along, and generally gone about it in a way that made it obvious premeditated evil. Charley got too excited, that's all.

"Did he suggest you to go with them?" the woman magistrate asked her. "Was there any suggestion you should empty your till and take it—sort of as a price of your seat in the car?"

"Not really," Charley said. "No, it was my idea, miss. He didn't want me to come at first, I could tell, but I wanted to and he just couldn't refuse me, that's all."

"I see. And what about when he threatened your colleague into handing over her takings."

"He didn't threaten her, miss. It was more of a joke really, to make me laugh."

"But he did tell you what was their intentions."

"Yes, otherwise I wouldn't have known what was going on. He didn't even know I was working, like I says, he just popped in to get some sweets."

Chantel was sitting there in court. She was the only witness they had against us. You remember her. The one you thought was so sweet. She wanted to be an airline hostess. You couldn't tell her she couldn't be, could you? But they made her do it, she had to, otherwise—she told Charley—they would sack her from her job. I felt sorry for her, our eyes all on her, sitting with her hair combed back, her head down looking at her knees, ashamed of herself and praying for it to be all over. Charley came over as trying to protect us. She came over as a good brave little girl, and she held up her dud hand across her thin chest as though she was crossing her heart with it and hoping not to die.

They was trying to say we'd led her astray. She didn't want them to say it. They said it anyway, more or less, by giving us six months each and letting her off with community service—because there was the doctor's report, as well, which said due to her being a flid—which weren't due to her Mum taking some drug when she was pregnant as I'd thought it was, which was years ago in the sixties, but something else, I don't know what—anyway, she weren't completely in her right mind, she was easily led, a bit simple and all that, although a good-hearted girl who hadn't previously done nothing wrong, who was trying so hard to be a credit to the community.

Tom Chaser was another bastard, although he was only doing his best for Charley, so I didn't mind too much. He didn't even look at us when he said it though. It was like we wasn't there. No way, no way was we going to say nothing. But you know the rest of it. Six months each for Will and myself. In separate places too, so we couldn't get together and plan no further mischief together, which we was almost bound to do, wasn't we. We had no fathers. Someone did say that in our favour. But we wasn't going to play on it. We was too proud. But it still counted in their eyes, it counted against us. That and coming from Jaywick. Teach them a lesson they'll never forget.

In the middle of the judge's summing up I turned around, I don't know, out of that feeling you sometimes get which isn't a feeling till you find someone's eyes are boring into the back of your neck:. Sure enough, they was. It was the Spaniard, a dapper little matey with a little black tash. He was staring straight at me. I stared back. I nudged Will. He turned around. We was both looking at him, and he were screwing us really hard, his face not moving a muscle. I couldn't turn away from him. I realised he was trying to hypnotise us. I turned away from his dark, compelling eyes.

"Can I have your attention please," the judge said. "This is a serious matter. I recommend you to take it seriously."

Charley had turned to look as well; she turned back to the magistrate. "Get on with it then," she said. "Silly cow."

"I think we'll soon find out who's silly," the woman said. "You are silly. You are a silly, silly little girl."

I could feel the heat of the Spaniard's eyes on the back of my neck. He wanted to know what had happened to his gun.

I looked around at the courtroom, the pale wood panelling of all the walls, the benches like church pews, the neatness of it all, the invisible lighting at the sides splashing soft halos up on the wood, the whole thing like chosen out of a catalogue in one go, Court 2, pale teak please, slotted together in a few hours by work experience kids or kangaroos. A kangaroo court. Three light green plush covered chairs was behind the magistrates long, empty desk, its shine guaranteeing the total impossibility of mistakes; behind the chairs, on the wall, hung a powerful red shield with three big curved swords with holes in them: the ancient shield of the County of Essex.

I kept my eyes well downcast as we shuffled out and one of the court ushers come in behind us, but near the door I glanced back at where the Spanish bloke had been sat. He weren't there no more. I see him head out of the door on the other side of the room, looking up and smiling at a policeman: a sizeable, lumpy sort of bloke, a sergeant.

Another pig took me by the elbow and guided me down the corridor away from the room we'd been waiting in. I watched Will and Charley disappearing. They didn't turn round. And I was taken into another room, on my own. A sick feeling gathered in my stomach. I thought the Spaniard would be there to meet me. He wasn't. Instead a plain-clothes sergeant sat behind a desk of the same wood as those in the courtroom. I didn't recognise him, couldn't take him in. It was as if he'd sprung out of nowhere into my story. As soon as I'd sat down with the uniformed sergeant at my shoulder, he reached into an open briefcase beside him on the floor, pulled out the Spanish bloke's gun and laid it on the table between us in a clear plastic bag.

"Recognise this?" he said. "Take your time. I want you to think before you answer, Lee, alright? Because at this point it's in your interest to co-operate with us as fully as you can."

"I never seen it before in my life," I said immediately.

"In a few minutes you'll be going back into court. I can't tell you what to do now, but I can tell you that this gun has recently been used to kill someone. In other words it's a murder weapon."

"I know," I said. "There was a fight in Utrecht. I found it in the bloke's suitcase. I showed it to this nutter we met. He grabbed it off me and started threatening me with it, waving it around. I tried to get it off him and it went off by accident. It was terrible, terrible." And I burst into tears, I couldn't stop myself. I put my head down, I had a good cry and I tried to imagine it was all a dream, that this is what had actually happened by the canal. It sounded like it could have done.

"And your friends saw all this happen, did they?"

"No," I said. "They was back at the hotel. They knew nothing about it, honestly."

"I don't think I have to tell you, Lee, that you're in very serious trouble."

I said nothing. I snuffled and tried to control myself.

He looked at his watch. "Time to go back into court, young man. I'm afraid we'll be carrying on with this conversation later."

Then we was sitting in court again and listening to the sentences. Beforehand I'd thought we should all concentrate on going down proud. It was the least we could do, in the circumstances, I thought, but as soon as Charley saw me being led in by this other pig, and she saw the state of my face, she started crying too. Will just stared straight ahead, white as a sheet, and the woman magistrate laid into us one by one, trying to assassinate us, or at least make us feel as low as she could manage.

Will was a weak, self-indulgent boy who'd foolishly given into his fantasies without any thought of their consequences for others, without any sense of right or wrong. Charley—she was particularly nasty about Charley—she was a selfish little person who thought life was all about taking what you could get. She had a handicap to be taken into consideration, but it had been, and there was no excuse for it, nor should she be given no special sympathy on account of it for the terrible things she'd done to herself and others, spurring these stupid boys into even more stupid actions. It could only be hoped that a custodial sentence would teach her belatedly what life was all about, that it contained responsibilities as well as pleasures. Charley's head was down, almost in her lap, and her hands in front of her eyes, rivers of tears was pouring out of her like sweat from her face.

When it came to my turn I wanted to stare straight back at the woman, but I didn't. I bowed my head just as Tom Chaser suggested. I knew it was something I was going to have to get used to in the near future, so I might as well start practising straight away. I heard her saying much the same things about myself as about the others, but I thought she seemed to have run out of anything to say. I could tell by her tone of voice that she didn't think I was the ringleader, that was Will, the good-looking one, or maybe Charley was mainly to blame in her eyes. I might've been imagining it but I thought she sounded a bit sorry for me.

Six months each we got, all in different places of course, which didn't sound as bad as it could've been from her summing up. We got off light. But even as someone tapped a little hammer and we all rose to watch them file out, there was a nasty, unfinished feeling in the courtroom, mainly in my gut, a feeling that something else was going to happen, like a thunderstorm built up that just didn't want to happen yet. I knew what it was, of course. I saw my Mum crying as she shuffled along her bench, past people, hurrying to get out, get out, get out in the fresh air, have a cigarette before she died of everything that, this time, I really had done to her.

They put me in a cell on my own under the crown court. They took my belt and shoes off me and left me to myself, no cup of tea, no comfort, no nothing. Death was staring me in the face, I wanted to make a good friend of him, but I had no way of getting close. How can you shake hands with a man who ain't got no hands? At times like that you just shut off and curl up into yourself. In the morning they give me a cup of tea and that, and I felt a bit better as a result. No one came down to get me for an interview, not for a fuck of a long time.

But it was as though they treated me with new respect when they realised I was going to be charged with murder. They looked at me in a strange, different way, and that in turn broke me down. I sat there in the cell going over my accident story. I wondered whether to tell them that Yop had raped and beaten up Charley. I didn't wonder. I knew I was going to say that, because it had more or less happened. I did wonder if Charley would back me up, and what her Mum would have to say about it.

After a couple of hours someone came to the cell door again. Here we go, I thought, but it was lunchtime already. I took the lid off an egg salad and started picking at it. A pig stayed to watch me.

"You know where you're going don't you, son," he said eventually.

"Where?" I asked, expecting him to say I was going to hell.

"Holland," he said. "I hope you liked it, because I think you could end up spending quite a bit of time over there."

When I'd finished eating he took the plate away and I was left alone again to think about my story.

The gun weren't found in the waste bin where I left it, but instead a few days later by a Utrecht waste disposal worker who happened to spot it down at the town dump. By that time Yop's body had been found in the canal with a big hole in his face. They knew who he was though, from his ID card. And the gun led them straight back to Ramon Rodriquez. It was a registered Spanish police gun, a Spanish make, and they soon found him. The only mystery there was why it took them so long. Long enough for us to hang around in Jaywick and get into some more mischief and eventually come to court.

Ramon Rodríguez was a Spanish copper on holiday with his family in England. They'd only just arrived in the country and had driven down to Clacton to visit some relatives, but they'd only just got there, and had popped out to look along the sea-front when we nicked his car. I don't know why he had his gun with him. Perhaps it was just force of habit, he needed it to feel safe or something, but whatever the reason he was in big trouble for it. Off-duty Spanish pigs bringing their trusty firearms onto English soil definitely weren't part of no EU co-operative policing policy. It was a stupid thing to do and he hadn't reported the gun missing when he reported his car stolen. He felt stupid enough already, hoping it would blow over somehow, it would be alright, basically, and not get discovered.

Anyway, it had my fingerprints on. Rodriguez was from a middle-sized place in the interior of Spain, not a tourist place, but big enough for him to be a detective in it. That's what I thought was likely. Once they got me back to Holland to stand trial I was totally stuffed. I couldn't say nothing about Charley neither, because if I let on I was angry about what he'd done to her, and jealous, that gives me a motive. I'd be handing myself to them on a plate. I had to stick to the accident story, the boys larking around story I came up with on the spot when my brain overdrive was fully engaged.

None of this happened. They had to prepare their case and extradite me first, which, so I was told, they would be able to do quite easily; but in the meantime I stuck to it being an accident and started to serve out my sentence in Chelmsford nick, young offenders suite. I soon found the best thing I could do was to keep my mouth shut, and that helped. If you're not forever talking about a thing, ten to one you're not thinking much about it either. I tried to ignore everything and concentrated instead on going down proud, buckling into my time and doing it all right.

It was the least I could do; but a prison, any prison, even a reasonably soft one like Chelmsford, soon kicks some of all that out of you. It's designed to, isn't it? I mean, eventually you're supposed to realise you deserved what you got, you always did, you was worth no better. You can't say no to it, can you? It's a violent shock to the system, a short sharp, or long shock. But I don't think that, normally. I was secretly proud of all we'd done together; that's more me really, saying it like that, and pretending all the bad stuff just ain't happened.

Mum came in to visit me every weekend. And we all wrote to each other quite often. Proper letters. I got myself an email address, but then realised no one else had one. Will's letters went on for pages in a handwriting I couldn't read. He wrote anything that came into his head. But I did read them somehow. I answered him, but quickly, because I couldn't be bothered to puzzle it all out. There was no puzzle, not really. It was just what he made up to make the time go. Charley's letters was short, usually about half a page with lots of exclamation marks. She was a fool there. She could have got off with community service, probably, if she'd played her cards right. But I weren't bothered about her anymore. I knew she'd be alright. Charley had a star quality which would see her alright. Once a star always a star. When I thought about Will it preyed on me that he was going to be out soon and I wasn't, he was going to be with Charley, and I weren't.

A few weeks into the sentence Mum said she'd heard something that might interest me. The Hopkins' had all moved out of Jaywick. Went somewhere else, no one knew where. The burnings all stopped after that night, so we done a good thing there. The developers bought their land off them straight away, she said, and bulldozed what was left of their place. They was building something else there, one of those small blocks of flats with views over the sea wall, or maybe it was an old people's home. Everyone said no one would ever buy them, but I expected they would, someone would, even if it was only Tendring Council.

I dreamed I was going to get out of there. I was going back to Jaywick. I was going to live there for the rest of my life. And see what happened. We was in charge now and we'd just have to try and do a better job than the last lot. Bring back the Elsans. Bring back the Bisto Kids. Mum told me they was starting a campaign against people who parked on the pavements, stopping prams from getting past. Get on with it, that's what I wanted. Walk around the car boot sale. Buy things: Freddie and the Dreamers. Ziggy Stardust. Keeping my eyes open for that odd, unrecognisable something or other from some other place. When I got it home it might start glowing and shooting out sparks. It might turn out to be something that could throw a new light on everything.

That's really what I wanted to do. But it was nothing, was it, just a delayed, distorted dream from somewhere or other, just a stupid fantasy about living happily in a place I'd always hated and wanted to leave. Prisons do that stuff to you. Okay, it was only a fantasy, but it kept me running around in circles for a good bad time. Charley always came into it. Will died or something, or he just accepted to be our friend. Charley and Lee was going to stay together for good, forever. I couldn't forget it, it kept me going that did.

I even thought about you sometimes. I wondered what happened to you. I couldn't even remember you, not that well. You seemed like a right pervert when we ran into you that time in the park, but then you always was a bit of a weirdo. That time I thought you looked different somehow, like you didn't want to think about nothing no more, and you didn't remember me even though it was only a couple of months after the end of term. But you remembered Will, from the other class, all his best ideas seemed funny to you. You liked him, didn't you? I expected you liked Charley as well. A lot of people don't like her when it comes right down to it, but some people think she's alright.

Everyday it was teatime again. Out in the canteen we ate our tea. Well, what else? I wrote this for ages and ages and saved it on a black disc, which I carried around with me in my back pocket for safe-keeping, and when it was completely finished I was going to send it to you. It was easy, writing, I found it was, anyway, once I got the smell of Mum's dope out of my lungs. I thought the college would do. They might find you, even if you was a part-time doss-bag. The best teacher we never had. A right laugh. They could always send it on to you, I thought. But what was the point of that? It would most probably be better to get it up on the screen one last time and rub it all out. I'd do that, later. I weren't reading all that much in there, I couldn't concentrate on the words. Anyway, never mind. If it's only a story and it ain't totally true, which it never is (well, is it?) then it's not going to hurt you much to forget about it, which is what I generally do do.

You know why they send us to such shitty schools, don't you? Why people like you have to teach us? Because it don't matter, right. We can't be taught, we can't learn nothing, that's the real reason for it. Not one of them will ever say that though. It's not allowed to be said. Let me say it then. Charley never done no good at school, but she could turn her handwriting into anything she wanted at the drop of a hat. Charley: I could walk around Jaywick as much as I liked but Charley was always waiting for me somewhere.

216

TWENTY

About this time I started to get really really famous. I became this famous boy from Jaywick Sands who was going to be sent back to Holland to stand trial for a murder he hadn't even committed, maybe, and anyway what chance of a fair trial did some Essex cunt have at the hands of a load of tulip-chomping Dutch-uncles? It was in most of the papers day after day, the police never done nothing to stop it.

What could they do? I was over-age now; I had my birthday in Chelmsford nick. 18 years old. What a fucking joke. I still felt about fifteen. I didn't see all the stuff that was written about me. It weren't that sympathetic. As far as I was concerned there wasn't nearly enough of it and that drove me mad, even more madder than I was already, madder than fucking anything. I'd look through the papers at all these stories about some asylum seeker they was or wasn't deporting. No one seemed to give a shit about me being cast into the black hole. It's always the same for us. I know someone out there agrees with me, and I knew it then, which helped me a bit.

The Star said they should send me back to face Dutch justice as soon as possible and throw away the keys, because I was just the sort of person who gives England football fans a bad name in these foreign countries. That didn't help me and there was fuck-all I could do about it. I was gutted. I didn't even like fucking football.

I felt important. I had a lawyer coming in to see me regularly to sort out my defence. Tom Chaser. Whose side was that bastard on? That's all what we talked about first. When he turned up I thought he'd been assigned to me, you know, that I had to talk to him. But you've got a choice apparently. You can choose your lawyer. But somehow I had to choose him or they'd want to know why not. On his side it was different. It was him who'd chosen me, he said, he'd chosen to take on the case because he thought I was innocent, or I could be, and he was there to find out if I was telling the truth. He was hard to follow. He muttered out of the corner of his mouth, explaining things clear and simple, except when he went away again you found you hadn't quite followed him. I don't know. Maybe he fancied a trip to Holland to see how they done things over there. He told me he'd never been in a murder trial before, so this was all a bit of luck for him.

He made it clear to me I had to convince him my story was the truth, and after I'd told it to him again and again, he explained what he thought was its strong and weak points. He started coaching me. I'd been through it all so many times I almost believed it myself. Except I didn't. When Yop came back to me at night it weren't no accident I saw by the canal, it was that look of amused surprise on his face. I was as surprised as he was. Surprised by what he'd done, surprised to be in that situation, surprised by my own reaction. I was looking at it from outside.

Going through it at night was like walking through the same steps, watching myself doing what I'd done, and then, when I went back to the hotel, Charley was never there. I ran through the hotel, opened doors on empty rooms with rumpled beds, or I'd be talking to her and she'd walk out or disappear, and the body in the canal was turning over and over, bobbing up and down in the wash from a glass-top tour boat. Everyone was looking out of its windows, first at Yop, then at me. In these dreams Yop was Yap.

Sometimes we had different conversations on the way down to the canal. I stood slightly apart, listening to them unfolding.

"You are cowboy," he'd say. "You want to come to my place and play Scalextrix? My other friends will play with us."

"Yeah," I'd say, "brilliant. Let's go for it." And I'd really mean what I was saying, but the way never seemed to lead to a house. Whatever routes we took led back down to the canal, and the gun was hard in my pocket, pressing itself into my hand, pulling itself out and aiming quickly at Yop or Yap, who started to put his hands up in that way which was always the same.

I'd told Tom Chaser the same story, that we was going to his house to play with the cars when it had happened: the same as I'd told the pigs. Why didn't the others come? Why was it only you? Why so early in the morning? That was the sticking point, and all I could think of to say was that it had just happened. The others didn't want to come. I thought Charley might spoil it by saying something, but she didn't say nothing, not so far as I knew. Needless to say she stopped writing to me once her sentence bit her. Out of sight, out of mind. Will kept blathering on. He seemed to have met some weird people where he was, people like him, so he thought.

There weren't much point writing to them anyway, since the pigs was obviously going to read every word. The law of the land is their law at the end of the day and once its sentence has been passed on you the law don't seem to exist no more except as it being their total power over you for good. I was totally on my own with it, with them, from then on.

Mum was crying and crying all the time, crying like there was no tomorrow, and when tomorrow or next week came—there she was again, full of new tears: a waterfall flooding past my eyes on all her visits. I wished I had a raft to jump on and float away on them, but I didn't have one. I couldn't run and I couldn't swim to save my life.

"It's not true, is it?" she said. "You didn't kill this Dutch boy, did you? Why don't you just tell them you didn't do it?"

"I did do it, Mum," I said to her. "But it was an accident. A bad accident."

"You were an accident, Lee. You were a bad accident one night when I was pissed."

"Mum, I've got to get out of here somehow. I'm way out of my depth."

"If it was an accident, they'll take that into account."

"It's like they're lining me up for the big chop. If they put me in a prison over there, I'll die, I know I will."

"You've killed me already." She started crying again, she wailed on and on; but whether it was for myself or herself I couldn't tell you, really. Then the hour was up and she left. I watched her go: a small, hunched, snuffling figure, an old lady already, and all because of me. I was on my own again. I always had been. I always would be. Left alone to think about how many times I'd killed my Mum, and the main methods I'd used.

Everything my Dad ever told me came back, but not much of it was relevant to me. Besides, he weren't only my Dad. He was Warren Hopkins' father too. That seemed to make a difference somehow. All of that, all of them, went away from me. It didn't seem to matter, as if I'd ripped them out of my life for good.

I myself was like the gutted amusement arcade of Brooklands, with no machines left inside me—all the old flexes hanging down the walls like whips with nothing to connect to, nothing to light up and make a game start; and the people wasn't real people anymore, just a pile of broken deckchairs that real people used to sit on. They was gone. Done, used up, broken, and waiting to be chucked away, like me.

There was still a lot of waiting to be done. But it was like waiting under a big wave, a big long wait for it to crash down on top of you. Not the kind of wave you bob up over, the other kind that nails you down in the deeps. Nothing could change my situation. There wasn't no way out of it. I was running but I was getting nowhere fast. Am I making myself quite clear?

I weren't looking much forward to going back to Holland. But soon enough there we was, getting into another twin-motored Cessna at Clacton airfield for the long flight over to Utrecht. A couple of screws with me, and Tom Chaser, who had a well-packed bag with him, I noticed. I never had nothing, just my own clothes, which they'd give me back early that morning. We lifted off, wheeled over Clacton and out across the North Sea. It was a clear, sunny day, which give us the impression of flying through endless light. The screws pulled their blinds down. One of them dozed off straight away.

Tom Chaser pulled his blind down but carried on looking in the direction of the window, as if he could see through it into the clouds. He said nothing. He was thinking about something. It was obvious he didn't like me one bit and didn't care if they banged me up for good. I hoped the plane would crash, but I didn't really, did I. I didn't hope nothing not no more.

"Just try and concentrate and answer the questions they ask you to the best of your ability," he said when we was munching through ham sandwiches and drinking our tomato soup. "I'm afraid that's all you can do." And then he said: "Rodriguez is in very serious trouble for bringing that gun into the country. I think you'll find he's said goodbye to his pension."

This thought seemed to interest him more than anything what was going to happen to me.

220

Utrecht airport was a little place on the outskirts. We came in over the town. Perhaps they wanted to show it to us, I thought. I caught sight of it: a big disc of patchy brightness winking under our right wing. At first I didn't recognise none of it. Suddenly I made out the buildings of the University and, tracking in, I made out the spire of the Dom and the dog-leg of the canal, which looked like it had been painted in a lighter colour with a fine brush. Our blinds was up and we gaped out at the small glittering city, which was lit from above in brilliant sunlight. It really was a beautiful place. The pilot said he had clearance to land in fifteen minutes. He climbed up a little bit higher and treated us to another circuit of Utrecht. I tried to take it all in, not wanting to land at all but hang there circling above it forever, like a reflection rolling around the edge of a big tilting plate.

The pilot dropped us down on a corner of the main runway and we made our way to the buildings where we parted company. Tom Chaser went off to find a cab to take him to his hotel room. I climbed up into the back of yet another police wagon.

"See you in the morning, Lee!" he called over to me.

So there I was, on my own. I didn't like being stuck between a pair of Dutch stormtroopers with fucking great big sticks hanging off their belts, not much like. Neither of them even looked straight at me. I settled into my bucket seat and tried to switch off, deciding that, whatever happened, I was going along with it for the ride this time. I was going to stay put on this planet for as long as I could manage. One of the Euro pigs stared right hard across at me. I pulled the seat belt hard hard down across my shoulder and clicked it into place.

I didn't know who was in charge of my life. In the old days it was Mum and Dad. Then it was just ... no-one. But the king of that little town was an ugly little perisher, he always is. His mouth is an open Elsan, his words are a river of shit. I don't know who he is, not really. He is a good liar with a way of looking like he's telling the truth. He is a stealer of your life, a father of your lies. That ugly man is named ...The Fire Man. But I didn't know what to do except to wait for whatever happened next. Charley will come back to me, I thought. She had to, didn't she? It was her I wanted to see more than anyone else in my life. But would she? I didn't know. But I did really. Because if I knew anything I knew that that one would never be coming near me again.

The proper way to do it was with a piece of flex—a length of heavy duty electrical flex, if you could actually get hold of it. Imagine the jolt coming down on that and you was at the end of it, tied up around the top of the bars at the window and a solid set of braising welds held them in a thick metal plate keeping each bar the right distance apart. I couldn't believe how easy it was to get hold of a length. A big fat reel of it in the corner of the yard, where some outside contractors were rewiring the recreation block down from the roof. Cutting it was going to be the main problem. That and getting anywhere near it under the eye of the fucking beady-eyed Dutchmen.

Never mind how I done it. I done it. I went and done the impossible again. I was the boy with the impossible touch. I'd borrowed Haup's penknife, the one he knocked up in the metalwork shop and hid down his trousers. Anyway, anyway. There was a bar of soap out in the bogs which had a razor blade hidden inside it. I got the flex and then I waited till late exercise on Saturday afternoon, just a couple of minutes, more or less, when that Dutch screw was wanking off round the corner. I tied the knot late at night in my cell. I made a good slipknot with thirteen turns, looped it around my neck and launched myself off the radiator. It didn't break my neck though, I just strangled there. It took me a long, long time.

I sat there on the bed watching myself going, going, and then I was finally gone. One last flicker and I sparked out. Hanging, my arms loose. I found it quite difficult to tear myself away, but I knew I had to, I had to in the end. I stood up. I patted my coat pockets down. Yep. I had everything I needed in them, everything I'd ever need where I was going to go to. I slid out under the door: a ghost I walked away slowly, slowly down the long grey corridors of Utrecht prison. Iron bars couldn't hold me, they always bent so easy. Everyone else had gone to sleepy-byes. Goodnight everybody. Goodnight, Mum.